DEVIL IN THE DAYLIGHT

ANNIE ATKIN

RADIANCE

RADIANCE

An Imprint of Roan & Weatherford Publishing Associates, LLC
Bentonville, Arkansas
www.roanweatherford.com

Library of Congress Cataloging-in-Publication Data
Names: Atkin, Annie, author.
Title: Devil in the Daylight/Annie Atkin | Gunpowder and Honeysuckle Book 1
Description: First Edition | Bentonville: Radiance, 2025.
Identifiers: LCCN: 2025947311 | ISBN: 979-8-89299-075-2 (trade paperback) |
ISBN: 979-8-89299-076-9(eBook)
Subjects: BISAC: FICTION/Romance/Western
FICTION/Westerns
FICTION/Romance/Action & Adventure

LC record available at: https://lccn.loc.gov/2025947311

Radiance edition November, 2025

Cover Design by Casey W. Cowan
Interior Design by Natalie Brianne
Editing by Lindsay Flanagan, Danielle Bean & Rachel Santino

For my Mémère

Bluff City, Missouri – September 1882

THEY SAY A MAN WHO STUDIES REVENGE keeps his own wounds green. Guess it's a good thing God saw fit to make me a woman. I don't need to dwell on vengeance to know I'll find it one day, and it'll finally heal the pain I've carried these past five months.

From the wall outside Hoffsteder's General Store, his name glares at me—Ansel Dawes and his gang of ruffians, wanted in connection with the bank robbery this past spring. That poster sends my stomach into spasms, but my eyes find it every time we come to town. It's practically a tradition now.

"You coming, or what?" Cole stands in the dusty street, squinting past the morning sun. My younger brother is the spit of Ma—all big, brown eyes and wavy golden hair. Too bad all that pretty got wasted on a boy, and here I'm stuck looking like Pa.

My thumb and forefinger shove into the corners of my eyes, pinching back tears before they can even think of spilling out. "You need me to hold your hand?" I call, voice gruff enough to hide the waver Pa's memory always puts there.

Cole scowls and takes off for the church. With a quick swat at my cheeks to be sure they're dry, I follow.

My eyes slide over Ansel's name to the poster beside his, just for a breath. A ritual.

As if passing by Hoffsteder's doors without the reminder would bring damnation upon me.

Main Street is lined with reputable businesses—the general store, a tidy hotel, the surgeon's office. At the end of the dusty road just past the bank, the church stands tall, keeping a watchful eye on Bluff City. The jailhouse squats across from the Gazette building, and behind that, all hell is liable to break loose any given night. Cathouses compete for the drunks stumbling out of the Bell and Iron Saloon, those who wouldn't rather take their pick of the ladies offering themselves alongside the beverages within. Drinking, dicing, cards, or whores—whatever a person's vice—the aptly named Defiance Row will provide. Most trips into town end with me there, dragging my older brother away from a game of cards.

Not so today, fortunately.

Today holds its own joys—the one Sunday a month we venture into town as a family to attend church. And today's service just so happens to be followed with a harvest-season picnic. As if it isn't hard enough smiling across a sanctuary at all the nosy old ladies claiming to only care about how our family is faring.

With a deep breath, I cross the threshold into the stale air of the church and take my place beside my mother in our family's pew.

◇━◦━━◦━◇

CHURCH PICNICS IN BLUFF CITY are a special kind of hell. The unrelenting sun sends droplets of sweat rolling down my neck, sticking my braid to my skin. Cole races one of the Mueller boys down the lane, to the main road and back. Meanwhile, my skirts seem to tangle between my legs at the mere thought of running free. I'm left sipping lemonade and stretching my lips at every lady pulled into Ma's orbit.

If Pa were here, he'd think up some surreptitious game to play. We'd count how many men linger after greeting the reverend's pretty new wife from Saint Louis, or how many women cast her scathing looks from beneath their sunbonnets.

But he isn't here. And if one more person simpers an empty platitude at me, I will lose my ever-loving mind.

A gaggle of grandmothers eyes me from the shade of the church. Before they can send an ambassador to exclaim how well I look despite losing my father a mere five months ago, I drain the rest of my lemonade in one gulp and slip around the far side of the building.

Pa's gravestone is near the top of the hill rising beyond the shadow of the steeple, far from the hubbub in front of the church. Even from the grave, Pa's still rescuing me.

I'm not at all surprised to find Della nestled against a nearby tombstone. My best friend's got a cigarette between her lips and a mischievous spark in her eyes as she watches me approach. The sun turns the tops of her tawny shoulders red where they've slipped free of her drooping sleeves.

"Don't worry," she calls, her voice like the finest ash at the bottom of a fire pit. "I'm keeping him company."

My hand trails the top of Pa's stone and what feels like my first true smile of the day lifts my lips. Pa always did like Della—even after our schoolyard days, he claimed I was a shining example of Christ's redeeming love. I think he just appreciated how much it scandalized Ma that I've stayed friends with a *sporting woman*.

"Hey, Pa." I kneel beside his grave. Shadows catch in the hollows of his name, *Henry Bennett*, in the cold dates below it, his entire life represented by a small dash between them. My fingertip covers its entirety. *You had so much life left to live.* Pa had visions of playing the hero, but heroes always die. Hamlet, Odysseus, Jesus Christ himself.

Before thoughts of that day can take hold, I flop to the grass beside Della. She holds out the cigarette.

"Better not," I say. "If I come back to the picnic reeking of tobacco, Ma will have my hide."

One of Della's dark eyebrows flicks up, but she doesn't comment—

just takes a long drag. She's made it clear I don't have to stay beholden to Ma and her expectations of me. One word, and I can join her at the Bell and Iron Saloon. She calls it freedom, and in a way, I suppose she's right—she doesn't have to worry about polite society or becoming trapped by wifely duties and child-rearing. But at the end of the day, her livelihood depends on the whims of men, just like Ma's plans.

Not to mention the fact I'm a far cry from the soft sort of beauty she offers. If Della's a fluffy housecat, I'm a porcupine, all elbows and knees and sharp glances. No way I'd make near as much as she does, and certainly not enough to cover the cost of my family's good graces.

"I think I've got fresh mint leaves," Della says. She blows a stream of smoke downwind, bless her, before turning back to me and pulling a small pouch from the pocket of her dress.

I tug open the drawstring and peer inside—sure enough, there are a few curling green leaves, though "fresh" might be pushing it.

"Ah, hell with it, then." I hold out my hand, and she slips the smoldering cigarette between my fingers. Hers are dainty as a china doll's against mine, tanned and calloused from the fields.

"How *is* the picnic?" Della has never been good at hiding her feelings from me, and her wistful curiosity creeps through her attempt at nonchalance.

Smoke curls into my lungs before I release it. "You're not missing anything special."

Like I said, her brand of freedom is just an adherence to a different set of rules. Guess everyone wants what they can't have. Me, I want independence *and* familial security. Still trying to figure out which one I want more, seeing as how getting both feels near-on impossible. For now, I'm just trading one for the other, back and forth, trying not to get caught in the middle.

"Wonder what that's about?" Della's voice keeps me from getting too introspective. She nods toward the church, where a gaggle of men gather.

Sunlight glints off the chest of the man in the center of the cluster—

Sheriff Kline. Can't say for sure why, but a tingle starts at the base of my neck.

"Only one way to find out." I hand her the cigarette and rise in a rustle of skirts.

"Maggie, wait—" Della doesn't follow. Not that I can blame her preferring to steer clear of a crowd of men.

Sheriff Kline's rough voice takes on words the closer I get. "...gathering a posse to round up an outlaw."

That tingle unfurls across my shoulders.

"Jedidiah Dawson," Sheriff Kline says, holding up the Wanted poster that has seared itself into my brain. My body fills with lightning. "Spotted not far from City of Kansas and overheard to be headed this way."

Under the sketch of a young, stubbled man is the reward. *$2,000 DEAD OR ALIVE*

Personally, I'm not too worried about the cash. Sure, we could use it for the farm, but once the posse splits the pot, a single share won't amount to much. No, I perk up because I know that name, sure as I know my own.

Jedidiah Dawson killed my pa.

2

FIVE MONTHS AGO, I GALLOPED THROUGH TALLGRASS, sighting after the bobbing hat of a fleeing bank robber. Gunshots cracked somewhere behind me. Pa kept steady on my six, his curses reassuring me of his presence. My finger steadied on the trigger.

"Let him go, Mags!" Pa called. "It's not worth it."

I ignored him. Exhaled and squeezed.

Damn outlaw was too fast for my bullet. I blinked away the frustration, took aim again as he turned.

His six-shooter flashed, the report delayed as he emptied his cylinder.

"Mags," Pa gasped behind me. I squeezed off another shot myself, futile though it may have been, then glanced over my shoulder.

My father hit the dirt with a solid thump, his chest a blossom of red. Everything else faded—the gunshots, the shouting, the retreating horses.

I was on my knees beside Pa with no recollection of leaving Huckleberry's saddle. My hands shoved Pa's bandana against the blood leaving his body in spurts. The bullet hole gushed more until the scrap of fabric was sticky and stiffening. Crimson froth bubbled over his lips.

"Hang on, Pa," I said through my tears. Dust rushed in with each ragged breath I took, coating all the way to my lungs. This wasn't supposed to happen. I was meant to protect Pa, see him home safe.

The other horses were long gone, bank robbers and pursuing townsfolk with them, swallowed by the hayfields and trees just past the town limits. I cried for help anyway, not caring that no one heard.

The dirt clouds gradually dissipated. Pa had gone still. *All return to dust.*

I didn't know how long I sat holding Pa.

"Maggie!" Wyatt dropped from his horse and skidded to his knees beside us. "Hank?"

The wind kicked up, and my hair tangled in front of my face as I turned to him. I reached to push my hair back, a flash of rust-red filling my vision. My stomach heaved, its contents spilling onto the ground beside me. I wished it were me lying in the dirt.

No amount of scrubbing would ever remove Pa's blood from my hands.

"No, no, no." Wyatt's hand found my shoulder, his other cradling Pa's head like a newborn babe. Pa's mischievous hazel eyes had dulled, a face creased with laugh lines gone slack. *It wasn't supposed to end like this.*

When I met Wyatt's gaze, the pain in his soft blue eyes shattered the careful numbness I was erecting around myself.

"Maggie," he murmured.

"Don't."

"I'm so sorry," he said anyway. He returned Pa's head to the ground with gentle hands. I was crumbling within myself. Wyatt eased around Pa to wrap both arms around me.

"Don't touch me!" I didn't recognize my own voice as I ripped free from him. He held his hands out, hovering. All my building rage turned toward him. "Where were you?" I shouted. I no longer saw one of my oldest friends, but the young deputy who hadn't been where he was supposed to be. Maybe the bullet in Pa's heart would have found a better target. Maybe Wyatt would have been the one drenched scarlet.

"I'm sorry," was all he said. He shifted, held his left arm closer to his body. Guilt stabbed through me again when I caught sight of fresh blood streaking his tattered sleeve.

Looked like I was the only one walking away unscathed. So why did it feel like *my* chest had been torn open?

Wyatt was talking, planning, but I stopped listening. I was taking every detail of that day and locking it up tighter than a jail cell. Only two things mattered—the bullet in Pa's chest, and who put it there.

"Why would he come back here?" one of the men asks, rescuing me from that horrible memory.

Who cares why? This is my chance to set things right.

"Lord only knows. Law in Jefferson City thinks he could have buried some of the take from the bank robbery. Could be he's coming to collect." A buzz of murmurs at that—shortly after the robbery, folks looked all over for signs of a recent burial. Cole's friends still pretend they're treasure hunting some Sundays. No one's ever turned up so much as a half dime.

"Whatever the reason," Sheriff Kline goes on, cutting through the chatter, "I aim to catch him. I know it's coming on harvest time and manpower is tight, but I could sure use any man who's willing." He rolls up the poster and tucks it in his back pocket. "We'll be gathering at the jailhouse at dawn. Hope to see y'all there."

He mashes his hat back on his head and gestures an arm for his audience to rejoin the picnic. They do in twos and threes, murmuring among themselves. None spares a glance for the girl in the graveyard behind them.

Let them overlook me. It won't stop me from joining them tomorrow. I return to Della and fill her in. "This is my chance," I say. "I'm finally going to set things right."

I'm practically giddy with anticipation. The cigarette kisses my lips again.

"Margaret Bennett!" My older brother's voice makes me choke and cough.

Della plucks what's left of the cigarette from my hand, but the jig's already up. Good thing it's only Jonah. A furtive glance beyond him confirms he's alone.

"Sometimes you sound too much like Pa," I say as soon as I've recovered.

He gives me a roguish grin, like he knew exactly what he was doing, then turns to my friend. "Miss Della, how are you this fine morning?"

"Oh, you and your 'misses.'" She rolls her eyes, but her lips are trying too hard not to smile. We all know she loves how polite he is to her in public. Few people acknowledge her at all. She finishes off the cigarette, then squints up at him. "Speaking of, where's *your* missus?"

That's the other game they play—Jonah reminds her she's a lady, she reminds him to watch his flirting.

Not that she needs to—for all the charm he spreads around, Jonah is besotted with his wife.

"Camila's distracting Ma from the fact Maggie's up and disappeared. Even she is reaching her wit's end, though, so I'm here to rescue my wife by delivering my sister."

"You disloyal bastard," I say, but without any malice. Hell, I'd choose Camila over Jonah, too, most days. She's the sweetest thing that ever happened to this family. I wonder why I can't be as happy about the idea of fitting my life into someone else's.

Jonah tuts. "Swearing on the Lord's day?"

"I'm thoroughly corrupting her," Della says.

I was already corrupted. But not even Della knows the whole of it.

My patience reaches its limit. "You talk to Sheriff Kline?"

Jonah scratches the corner of his mouth with the back of his thumb. "Spoken with a lot of folks today."

"There's a posse—"

"Can we not do this here? It'll only upset Ma and Camila."

His lack of enthusiasm douses mine, just a bit. "As long as I can come too."

"Maggie...." Jonah shares a long-suffering look with Della. I could throttle them both. "Let's talk about it later. Once I've had the chance to discuss it with my wife."

As if Camila's opinion could carry more weight than our father's memory. Still, it's as good as an agreement to have my back with Sheriff Kline, so I'll take what I can get.

"Now, shall we join the others so Ma can stop fretting?" He winks at Della as he offers me his arm. I take it, only because I want to. Anyone else and I'd insist I can make it the short distance to the churchyard on my own two feet.

Of course, once we've rounded the corner and Ma's little table comes into view, I wish I had insisted. Jonah's arm tightens into his body, pinning me close. "Be nice," he murmurs.

"You could have warned me." We're still a few paces away, but Wyatt Murray has already spotted us approaching. He stands and says something to Ma, who twists around.

"There you are!" She frowns at me when we stop in front of her.

"Found her smoking behind the church," Jonah says easily, moving to join Camila on Ma's other side. Not fast enough—I give his foot a hearty stomp.

"You were not." Ma's honey-colored eyes dart around, checking for eavesdroppers.

"I'm sure Jonah's only teasing," Wyatt says. "Miss Maggie wouldn't do something like that."

"Nah," Jonah agrees, "she was visiting Pa."

Ma relaxes and wags her finger at Jonah, so I give Wyatt a conspiratorial grin as I take the empty seat between him and Ma. When he turns his guileless smile on me, though, my lips droop. *Of course.* He can't see anything but some other version of me, perfect and holy as the Bible sitting beside his plate. An urge rises to blow my minty, smoke-laced breath right into his face.

Cole saves me from doing anything rash. Sweaty and out of breath, he skids to a stop beside Jonah and gulps down an entire glass of lemonade. A belch rips from his open mouth.

"Oh, good heavens," Ma gasps. My lips are pressed against a laugh until I catch sight of Jonah doing the same, and we both lose it. Even Camila has to cover her mouth, though she rests one reassuring hand on Ma's arm. Wyatt thumps Cole's back, as if my brother suffers from choking, rather than bad manners.

We've drawn the gazes of the tables nearest us—the grandmothers frowning and the pretty wives recoiling—but I don't care. The sun washes my family bright and golden and, with justice for Pa in my sights, in this shining moment we feel almost whole.

◇━◇━━◇━◇

THAT GILDED WHOLENESS LASTS ONLY until dinnertime this evening.

Ma stands at the head of the table, hands on her ample hips when Jonah and I walk in from our afternoon chores. Her graying hair is pulled into a sharp bun, so tight I swear it's the only reason her face isn't full of frown lines. I wonder if she's somehow heard the news, but she just tells us to wipe our feet and wash up. Camila smiles at us as Jonah and I join Cole at the washbasin beside the back door. Next to Ma, she couldn't be more different. Camila is dark and warm where Ma is all frost and light. Silver and gold, like the heirloom candlesticks on the fireplace mantle. Camila adds a steaming bowl of *arroz rojo* to the table already laden with sliced pork steak and crisp-edged potatoes.

In front of me, Cole flings his wet hands to his sides.

"Come on, Cole." I scrub droplets from my cheek as Jonah smacks the back of his head.

Cole scowls and wipes his hands on his dirty pants on his way to his seat. The fire in the woodstove overheats the small room, adding to the sweat that's been gathering under my braid since the first mention of Jedidiah Dawson. I join my family at the table, crushing the desire to blurt the news.

"Saw Luis is back in town," Jonah tells Camila.

A cowboy from El Paso, her brother would have been at one of the cathouses lining Defiance Row. That Jonah had run into him tells me he was doing his own sinning on the Lord's day—gambling, most likely. Camila gives him a tight smile. "I hope you told him to visit before he leaves again." Her Spanish accent wraps each word into pretty little packages.

Jonah nods, though I bet he did no such thing. To Ma, he says, "Our loan is coming due. I'll bring a payment to the bank Friday and speak with Mister Skinner about a little more time."

That catches my attention. "*You* will?" I look up in time to catch the death glare Jonah shoots at me. When he doesn't walk it back, I press him. "You don't think you'll be busy?"

Jonah leans back in his chair. The oil lamps take over for the waning daylight through the back windows, flicking shadows across Jonah's impassive stare. "Fine, Maggie, *you* can see about the loan."

I haven't been able to step foot in the bank since the day of the robbery, and Jonah knows it. The thought alone makes my gut go watery. "Not me. I'll be long gone by Friday."

"Where are you going?" Ma looks from me to Jonah.

"Not now," he hisses, stabbing his food with vehemence.

For half a second, I mind him. After all, he *is* supposed to be in charge now that Pa's gone. But this is a chance for our entire family to see justice done. It shouldn't be left to Jonah to decide.

The seat at the head of the table feels especially empty right now. I catch myself wanting to appeal to Pa, remembering a hitched breath too late he's the reason we're having this conversation.

This isn't Jonah's secret to keep.

"Jedidiah Dawson was spotted in these parts," I tell the table.

Jonah throws down his fork. "What did I tell you?"

Everyone else has gone still, even fidgety Cole. Camila turns to Jonah with wide eyes, her hands dropping beneath the table. I don't need to look to know she's touching the small swell of her stomach.

"How do you know?" Ma's voice shakes.

"Sheriff said so," I say half a second late. My eyes are still on Camila, my next words hesitant. "He's gathering a posse."

"And you will go?" Camila reaches out, curling her small fingers around Jonah's forearm. When he doesn't answer, she leans closer and murmurs to him in Spanish. I only catch *peligroso* and *por favor*.

A promise he'll be fine rises to my lips, but that little reminder of their unborn child gives me pause before I goad Jonah further. Try as I might to deny it, outlaw hunting is a dangerous sport. I know too well the pain of losing a father, and I got almost eighteen years with mine.

The conversation has continued without me.

"What brought him back to Bluff City?" Ma asks. Her fingers fuss the yellowed lace at her throat.

"If Maggie's going, I want to go." Cole's voice cracks over the last word, making him blush, but he keeps a determined gaze on Jonah.

"You need to mind the farm," I tell him.

"Why can't you? Leave outlaw hunting to the men."

He puffs his scrawny chest and grins at Jonah, but our brother has his head tilted toward his wife. Camila still pours rapid Spanish into his ear, too soft for the rest of us to eavesdrop.

I flick a chunk of potato at Cole. "Thirteen years old, and you think you're a man now?"

His face falls. "Practically fourteen! And more man than you'll ever be."

"I don't need to be a man—"

"Enough." Ma's hand smacks against the table. She so rarely has an outburst that it shuts us all up. "This is a chance to see justice done for your father. Would you really leave that responsibility in someone else's hands?"

Surprisingly, it's Camila who speaks up first. "Vengeance belongs to the Lord." Her voice is small, but firm.

"An eye for an eye," I mutter before I can stop myself. She throws me a look of betrayal, and I cringe. But hell, Jonah need not go. I'm the expendable one here, and justice is my responsibility.

Jonah closes his hand around Camila's. The hope in her eyes when she looks at him makes the rice curdle in my gut.

"Ma's right," he says without looking at his wife. "I'm going with

Kline's posse. I'm the head of this family. It's my duty to bring Pa's killer to justice."

Ma eases back with a satisfied smile. Camila tugs her fist free of Jonah's hold.

"Maggie will see to taking care of the farm," he continues.

"Like hell I will. I'm going with you." This is it. That same certainty from earlier tingles in my fingertips. A chance for adventure, a duty to my family. Between avenging Pa and making sure Jonah makes it back to his own budding family, there's nothing more important that could keep me home.

"Margaret—"

"Don't 'Margaret' me. I'm not your wife or your daughter, so you can't make me stay."

Jonah drives the point of his finger into the table. "But I am in charge, and as long as you live under this roof—"

"The roof *Pa* built. I'll honor him however I see fit, and right now, that's hunting down the man who took him from us."

"The trail is no place for a woman—"

"Oh, horseshit—"

"Maggie," Ma starts, but I'm not close to finished.

"I've ridden a leg of a cattle drive, for Pete's sake. I can handle a few days sleeping rough. I'm stronger than Cole, faster than you on a horse, and I shoot better than the both of you."

"You see?" Camila says, gesturing open-palmed at me. "Let her go."

I smile at her unexpected support, even though I know she only hopes Jonah will stay home.

"You are not stronger than me," Cole mutters, but we both know it's the truth.

"Ma?" That Jonah is appealing to her tells me I've exhausted him almost to the point of surrender.

Ma takes a moment to look around at all of us. "Your father would be proud of each of you." Her gaze settles on me, her wild horse of a daughter. Camila is so much more the lady Ma hoped for in a daughter, but I'm blood, and she's long given up hope of my being satisfied sitting home sewing clothes or tending children.

She turns to Jonah. "You know she'll go, on her own if not with you. Look after your sister, Jonah. Cole will take care of Camila and me." She smiles at our younger brother with just enough warmth to swell his chest again. "But see to it you bring that man back alive. I *will* see him swing for his crimes."

I nod. It's the closure our family needs—a life for a life, a debt paid in blood. We'll all sleep better once Jedidiah Dawson hangs.

TWO DAYS LATER AND I'LL BE DAMNED if some of the glamor
isn't wearing off already. Birdsong fills the clearing where our posse has
made camp, the chirps and twitters too lighthearted for the manhunt
to come. The fog that clings to the oak branches and settles in my lungs
feels far more fitting—adding an ominous chill to the early fall warmth
of the morning.

I settle on a log, dew-damp, and hold my hands to the growing fire.
One of the men has already started the coffee, filling the air with its
rich, nutty aroma. The sizzle of salt pork follows. While I wait with the
others for breakfast, my hand finds the Wanted poster in my pocket.

I know fate brought me here, that if I hadn't been there when
Sheriff Kline held it up and called for a posse, I might not be here now.
I unfold that same poster, the creases growing more worn with each
passing day. Righteous anger burns my veins, almost enough to distract
from my aching muscles. Still, I reach a hand over my shoulder to press
a knot, and a sigh slips out.

"Having second thoughts?" Jonah squats beside me, as if a full day in
the saddle and a night on the hard ground means nothing to his hind-

quarters. Across the campfire, Wyatt offers a sympathetic grimace. The latter, I ignore.

My brother is not so easy to dissuade. "Not a one," I say. I'd never give Jonah—or any of the other men here—the satisfaction. I've already heard enough of their muttering about *women knowing their place.*

"It's not too late to head home, you know," Sheriff Kline says, looming over me. "You've proven you can sleep rough. No one would think any less of you."

"Just mock me as soon as my dust settles," I mutter. The posse's opinion of me isn't what's driving me onward. I couldn't save Pa, but I can see his killer dead.

A few horses nicker in the shadows between the trees, as if to agree with my assessment. Sheriff Kline crosses his arms.

My neck tightens as I peer up at him, and I tug at the hem of my sleeves. "I'm not here to prove myself to you or anyone else. My only goal is to see Jedidiah Dawson brought to justice."

"Listen." Wyatt joins us, dropping onto the log beside me. Across the fire, more of the posse are turning toward us, and what is quickly becoming a confrontation. "I'm heading back to Bluff City myself. I'll see you home safe."

"Why are you going back?" I ask, momentarily distracted from their efforts to persuade me to join him.

Wyatt shrugs. "Can't leave a town without its sheriff *and* deputy for too long, can we?"

Considering that's part of what got us into this situation—a quiet Sunday ripe for a bank robbery—he makes a good point. But then....

"Why come along at all in that case?"

"Well, I...." Wyatt's earnest eyes dart to the sheriff and my stomach clenches.

Sheriff Kline sighs and rubs the back of his neck. "We've humored you this far, but a woman on the trail is a liability. Let Wyatt take you home, Maggie."

I turn to Jonah, conspicuously silent. "Did you have a part in this too?"

His gaze is hard on the sheriff, his voice as tight as his jawline when he responds, "No, I did not."

Something in my chest eases, knowing he at least hasn't betrayed me in the interest of deciding what's best for me.

"Now, Jonah—" Sheriff's voice is all fatherly and patronizing. My brother is having none of it.

"You said you need all the men you could get."

"*Men*, Jonah."

"You send her home, I'm leaving too. If Wyatt's truly heading back, that's three less people you've got. We both know she'll just go right back to looking for Dawson, and I'd rather it be with me than on her own."

What little boost of sibling loyalty I felt withers with that caveat, but I know enough to keep my mouth shut.

"Ah, hell," someone says from the direction of the horses. Jonah's brother-in-law, Luis, gives me a nod when our eyes meet. "I'll go with them too."

Sheriff Kline throws up his hands. "Fine, she can stay, but on your heads be it."

"But...." Wyatt gapes after him as he stomps to the other side of the camp. When he looks back at me, I raise an eyebrow, the desire to gloat warring with the urge to deck him for trying to undermine me. His mouth opens and closes a couple times before he finds his voice, smaller than normal. "We just want to see you safe, is all."

"Wyatt." I reach out and adjust the shining, nickel-plated deputy sheriff star on his chest, making him blush. "Your skin is no more bulletproof than my own." I pat him twice over the heart and turn away. "Now if you *gentlemen* are done deciding my future, I need to see to my horse." I get up with every intention of trading their sorry company for that of Huckleberry but can't resist one last rejoinder. "And it shouldn't take a woman to point out your pork is burning."

One of the Mueller brothers scrambles to rescue the pan from the flames as I turn my back on the campfire.

Jonah follows me to Huck's side. He watches as I brush her, then hands me the saddle pad before he finally spits out what's on his mind. "Go easy on Wyatt. He can't help that he's sweet on you."

"He doesn't even know me if he thinks I'd be content to sit at home and let the *men* do *man's work*."

"That's not fair, and you know it." His lips press together and his fingers tap against his thigh, but he's the one who brought it up. "He just feels protective of you. Especially after what happened to Pa."

My lungs twist at the memory—grit sticking in my tears, Pa's blood in the dirt, Wyatt crouching beside us. I tug at Huck's harness to give my trembling fingers something to do.

Jonah runs a hand through his light hair then settles his hat more firmly on his head. "You can't blame the man for wanting to keep anything like that from happening to you again."

"If he thinks I'm too weak—"

"That ain't it, and you know it. He can love your fire and still want to protect you." Jonah grins and leans closer. "And he ain't the only one, Mags." He tugs the tail of my braid. "Still, I know how important this is to you."

But he doesn't, not really. He sees retribution for Pa's death, sure enough, but he doesn't suffer the nightmares that plague me most nights. He didn't scrub Pa's blood from his hands. My hand finds Pa's watch in my pocket—my last piece of him. *I'll make you proud, Pa, if it's the last thing I do.*

Problem is, I'm a liar. I can twist a half-truth faster than Ma can darn a sock.

But I will do whatever is in my power to see the reprobate responsible for Pa's death brought to justice.

And that's the God's honest truth.

◆◇━━◇◆

THIS EVENING, AFTER THE MEAGER meal has been eaten and the supplies cleaned and stored again, Jonah folds his tall form next to my bedroll.

"Boys are starting a faro game," he says, his tone a touch too casual.

I'm not one for cards myself, so my neck tingles with anticipation. Whatever he wants, it can't be good. "Say, you got Pa's pocket watch on you by chance?"

"I fail to see what the latter has to do with the former." Despite my words, my hands tremble with the urge to throttle him. That bastard thinks to use our heirloom as collateral in a throwaway game.

Jonah, for his part, drops all pretenses. "It's not like we've got extra cash lying around," he says. "It helps sweeten the pot."

I don't like the way that sounds, like this isn't the first time he's bet the watch. "Next time, save some of your winnings to gamble when your friends come to Bluff City."

He leans his shoulder into mine, close enough for the breeze to carry the scent of stale tobacco clinging to his shirt. "It ain't gambling if I know I'll win."

"*Isn't*. Shit, you're as bad as some know-nothing cowpoke."

"*You* have a dirty mouth, young lady." Jonah's dark eyes crinkle at the edges as he grins.

"*You* can't guarantee a win every time," I fire back.

"Not every time, no, but only 'cause that would be suspicious."

When I raise an eyebrow at him, he winks.

"Jonah Bennett. You cheat?"

"Keep your voice down," he says, though it's unnecessary. Our whispers are lost to the crackle of campfire and the grunts and laughter of the men across the way. "It's only cheating if I get caught. And before you start lecturing, Pa taught me that."

A smug challenge lights in his eyes, but I believe it. Pa was a good man—a *great* man—but his scruples could be a bit shifty. Ma blames the war. Pa never talked about it, so I guess we'll never know for sure.

"I like to think he's laughing every time I bet his pocket watch on a stacked hand," Jonah adds.

"Neither of you will be laughing if you're caught."

"So I won't get caught."

"Answer's still no, you mule. Find something else worth betting and leave me—and Pa—out of it."

Jonah scowls, but when I refuse to relent under his glower, he finally gives up. Not that I'd say it aloud, but I wouldn't mind him staying put and avoiding the game altogether. He's already made it clear I'm a nuisance. No sense nagging him like a needy wife.

Of course, that doesn't stop me from glaring at him as the cowboys deal him in. I swear, if he does something stupid and gets caught out in a gunfight, I'll kill him myself.

My eyes grow heavy, but I can't look away from their game. As if by watching, I can keep my brother safe, even from himself. If only it were that simple....

◇━━◦━━◦━━◇

STRONG HANDS COAX ME AWAKE, a whimper I thought was a scream still caught in my throat.

"Maggie?"

Pa? I press my face into my bedroll before any sobs escape.

"You were dreaming again." It's Jonah crouching over me, not Pa. His touch is just as gentle as he rests his hand on my hair. "The robbery?"

I don't need to answer. It's the only specter that haunts me in the night. I focus on my breathing instead—lungfuls of wool, damp earth, campfire smoke. Once I've gotten myself under control, I sit up.

"I'm all right," I say.

Jonah nods, eyes on the sleeping campsite. His jaw is tense and eyes dark when he turns back to me. "Did Pa ever say why he took you along that day?"

My entire body goes taut as one of Ma's threads just before she snips it. The nightmare lingers, crackling gunfire and rivers of blood. And the money, all that gold, swept away by the current.

It bleeds into a very real memory.

"I don't have your money, but I'll get it." Pa's voice leaked around the corner of the general store. Calm enough, but with a note of a plea that kept me from interrupting. I pressed into the rough boards just out of sight, listening.

"You think I'm stupid? You're trying to rob Peter to pay Paul, friend, but I'm both. You won't get another cent from me, not from my bank, not from my own pocket."

Then came a snuffling sound, almost as if—

"Are you crying?" Skinner snorted. "You're pathetic. Tell you what, Hank, I'll cancel all your debts, but it'll cost you something dearer than money."

As if I were standing right beside him, I knew in my bones my father would agree, no matter what god-awful price Skinner might concoct. I had to save him, save all of us. I took two steps backward and called his name. As if I didn't know exactly where he stood, making deals with the devil.

Footsteps shuffled. We met at the corner of the building. When I glanced around it, Skinner had gone.

Pa kept me a little closer after that. Not that I minded, not that anyone else noticed. Ma always said I was the apple of Pa's eye, after all. I felt those eyes on me every time we went to town, watchful, waiting. Scared. Whether he was afraid of what he'd almost done or what he might yet do, I'll never know.

Now it's Jonah watching me, gaze steady in the sputtering firelight. How much does he know? Part of me wants to confide in my brother like I used to, swapping half-secrets about schoolyard crushes and contraband candy stashes. A bigger part can't bring myself to sift through the dirt for the right tarnished truths. If the wrong ones are dug up— well, I'm not ready to besmirch Pa's memory out loud.

Jonah does anyway. "I know you know about the gambling."

Slicing to the core, that's my brother. Don't much matter if it's the right core, long as he hits seeds.

"We just needed more supplies for the cattle drive," I hedge. A rush of wind stirs the leaves overhead and sends a shiver through my arms.

"Don't play dumb. It's never looked good on you. Pa liked his cards, no matter how often it got him in hot water."

"He was done with all that."

Jonah smirks. "So you *did* know. For how long? Why'd he really have to go back to town that day?"

It's the same question he asked after the funeral. *"Why'd he have to go back?"* At the time, I thought it was rhetorical. We all wanted our own answers to the same *why* questions.

"There was a game, wasn't there? Some big fish he just had to catch?" When I don't answer, Jonah nods. He's always been good at telling his own stories. "What I can't figure is why you? He could've used me there." His voice softens. "I should have been there."

I look up at the catch in his voice. All this time, my brother's been carrying a weight similar to mine—the guilt of the living.

"Maybe he didn't want you falling into the same dark pit he was trying to claw out of." Maybe he'd spotted a darkness in me.

"Well, he sure didn't succeed there."

Anger flares. "You don't have to join their games. You could choose not to—choose *us*, just like Pa was trying."

"He didn't choose shit. Let me guess, he told you one more game, one big win, and he'd be done?"

Close enough. Jonah eyes me, reading my thoughts. He looks so much like Pa in this moment, my heart hurts.

"He told Ma the same thing half a dozen times," Jonah says, breaking the spell. "The only way to truly stop him would have been to cut off all his fingers."

"Bullet in the chest seemed to work just fine." I gag on the words as soon as they reach my tongue and spit them like bile. Those secret, bitter darts are better aimed at my brother. "You're unbelievable. Talking about Pa like he was some degenerate all while tossing down money that's not yours into the same Godforsaken pot."

"There you go gettin' on that high horse again. Before you ride off, know this—Pa's debts didn't die with him, and every game I play, every hand I stack, every pot I win, it's all that's standing between us and retribution for Pa's sins. So go ahead and judge me like you do everyone else. Next time you can suffer through your nightmares by your damn self."

He shoves to his feet and drags his bedroll closer to the others. It's better this way. On my own, I can't fail anyone else the way I did Pa.

IN THE MORNING, I THROW my stuff together and saddle Huckleberry without so much as a returned "good morning" for my brother as
he passes. He slaps his hat against his leg, loosening a cloud of dust, and
walks off, muttering to himself. We don't speak for the rest of the day,
but come evening, when the cowboys invite Jonah to join their card
game, he settles to the ground beside me instead.

Without a word, he offers me the slim novel he's carried in his saddlebag—*The Adventures of Tom Sawyer.* The spine is rubbed raw, the
pages dirt-smeared and ragged. We Bennett children have loved this
book well over the past few years.

I remember the day Pa brought it home. At seventeen, Jonah insisted
he was too old for kids' stories, but Cole and I devoured it. We'd have
long fireside conversations about whitewashed fences and blood oaths,
musing about the taste of candles and debating the rules of ownership
over found gold known to be stolen. It wasn't long before Jonah had to
find out what the fuss was all about. Here we are, four years later, still
passing it around like a peace offering.

I don't speak and neither does Jonah, but our silence has become
that of a sibling ceasefire.

TWO OF OUR POSSE ARE trackers, and they lead us through the
state following any trail they deem promising. Pa took me hunting
plenty, but I never learned the patience for tracking prey—I only like
the part where we catch it. I'd rather eat my hat than admit it, but I'm
bored stiff. Long days in the saddle and nights on the unyielding ground
aren't helping matters.

Our fourth night in, luck and lightning strike. Luis brings the news
through a cloud of fog. *"Lo encontramos."*

Rain sheets down, forcing us to huddle under a copse of trees. We're
shivering together, horses and posse alike.

Luis, who'd gone scouting ahead, jerks his chin, sending rainwater rolling off the brim of his hat onto my shoulder. "*El bandido* is not far."

Sheriff Kline appears on my other side and confirms it. "Dawson's camp is through yonder trees. Maggie, stay with the horses. The rest of us'll surround him, close in on him nice and slow, and hopefully, this'll all be over before daybreak."

I nod. Sheriff and Luis are already moving through the woods with the others, but Jonah hangs back long enough to blow a fog-laden sigh.

"Just do as you're told, for once."

"I didn't say anything!" Truth be told, I'm happy to watch the horses. They're tethered together, so it's an easy job, and this way, I won't be tempted to shoot Dawson outright. After all, they won't hang a dead man, and Ma's waiting to watch him swing.

"Well." Jonah hesitates. "Good."

Time crawls by. I'm starting to realize that "over yonder" isn't the best explanation. Are they circling his camp just beyond my line of sight, or is it a half-mile slog through the storm? God willing, the first. My fingers drift to the watch in my pocket. The last time I was left watching the minute hand with my heart in my throat—I shove it away and tuck my hands under my arms. I strain to hear signs of a scuffle, but the rain ripping through the leaves drowns out everything else. The horses shift and snort, as restless as me.

Huckleberry lifts her head, ears alert. Someone's here.

Jedidiah Dawson. I know it in my bones, though I can hardly see anything more than shifting shadows, even with the occasional burst of lightning. My frozen fingers work my revolver free from its holster. It'd be awful dumb to try shooting at anything that moves, considering the horses, but I feel better having the weapon at hand.

I'd feel even better with a higher vantage, so I swing into Huck's saddle. Just in time too—sounds like the bandit has managed to break a horse away from our pack. My revolver chills my hand as I raise it overhead, intending a warning shot to alert the others. The black powder's gotten too wet. Nothing happens.

"Over here!" I holler as I kick Huckleberry into a gallop, praying someone hears me over the storm.

We race through the trees. Branches claw at my hat and dried leaves scratch across my cheek. Huck leaps a fallen log. Wet-shrouded night clings between each tree trunk, rendering visibility practically nonexistent. It's more a sense, a gut feeling, keeping me moving, waiting for the next snatch of lightning to confirm I'm still on his tail.

The landscape shifts from woods to rain-soaked grassland. I hunch over Huckleberry, my gaze pinned on Dawson's fleeing horse. Without the tree cover, it's easier to follow the dark shape as it slides down and charges up hills. Thunder rends the air in two. I feel the crackles in my teeth. Heavy breaths eat up the night—seconds turning to minutes, stretching longer. Still, we fly, following each of their zigs with a zag of our own. If the posse is behind me, they're lost to the raging wind that hurls raindrops like baseballs. There's a sinking in my gut, sucking like the mud beneath Huck's hooves, warning me I'm on my own—one that gets deeper the longer I chase Dawson.

Memories of the last time I raced after this outlaw threaten, but this time, I swear the outcome will be different.

My fingers are numb around the reins, the bite of the storm sinking past my waterproof slicker, but Dawson is just ahead. I peel one hand free, reaching for my revolver, only to remember the wet powder's rendered it useless.

"Come on, Huck!" She must feel my desperation, picking up her pace to match the drumming in my chest.

We're close enough that mud from the other horse's hooves splatters across my face with each pounding gallop. If I stretch my fingers, they might brush the horse's flicking tail.

Lightning sends a blinding flash across the sky. Dawson swerves down another gentle bank. We skid behind him, pushing to make up the ground. The landscape evens out into a field, and I refuse to let another chance slip away.

My rope is slick with rain, but I'm a rancher by blood. I've lassoed lumbering beasts in similar conditions. I say a prayer and let the rope fly. God must be on my side because it snags around Dawson's shoulders, the loop cinching tight and pulling him sideways. He manages to hold on to the reins, but his horse slows. Huck shoots past half a pace before I tug the reins. When I pull level with Dawson, he's already scrabbling one-handed at the lasso. I take the tiny advantage I still have and launch myself at him. We tumble down to the mud. Without our weight driving them, the horses come to a stop.

My hat flies off—the leather cord pulling tight around my throat—and now the rain is so thick in my eyelashes I can hardly see, even with the occasional lightning flash. We're reduced to elbows and knees, mud scrabbling, slick leather, and hard bone. I've managed to pin him when another bolt flickers light across our faces. In that split second, his eyes go wide.

"You're a girl?" he asks into the darkness. The revelation must have stunned him because he freezes beneath me. I've gotten into enough scrapes with my brothers to know the best response. I slam my forehead into the general direction of his face. Whatever I connect with is hard enough to fill the blackness behind my eyelids with sunflowers.

It takes me a disorienting second to realize he's gone slack. I blink the fuzziness and rain from my eyes and set about tying him up, winding an extra saddle string around his wrists, then securing his bound hands with the lasso. My hands search his bulky slicker for weapons, pulling a small knife from his front pocket and the Colt Peacemaker holstered at his hip. The revolver is coated with mud. I raise it anyway and squeeze the trigger. Nothing. It's as useless as my own. My numb fingers come up to my lips. It takes me a few tries, but finally, a whistle pierces the storm, leaving the taste of mud and desperation across my lips. Lord only knows if it'll do any good. Nothing but the pounding rain answers, rising in a spray from the ground.

I'm alone. With Jedidiah Dawson.

Well, shit.

4

DAWSON IS AS TALL AS THE PAPERS claim, but leaner than my memory of *that day*. It would seem life on the run hasn't been keeping him well-fed. Even still, getting his limp, bound form up onto one of the horses is too big a feat for the moment, so I lie back in the mud and catch my breath. The rain rinses my face, stinging my cheek where the skin must have split under a well-placed fistful of knuckles.

My forehead throbs with an ache I feel clear to the back of my skull, and now that the struggle is over, I'm noticing how much it hurts in my ribs each time I breathe. After a few fortifying breaths, I press my fingers across my midsection, checking for anything out of place, half expecting my bones to be shattered.

All seems as it should be—though there's a bruise forming across my breastbone—and even if the bastard had broken a rib or two, it would be worth it for the looks on the posse's faces when I return with their quarry, single-handedly subdued. We're too far from where we started to hope Jonah and the rest will happen upon us. It's up to me to return this varmint to the posse.

This thought is enough to get me to my feet. I soothe the horses and find another length of rope snubbed to the saddle horn of the horse Dawson stole.

I might be stronger than Cole, but it still takes me a while to get Dawson hoisted over the horse's back. In the end, I loop the rope around his chest and use both Huck and the saddled horse as leverage to pull him up and over. Once he's settled and firmly tied to the horse, I climb back into Huck's saddle, ready to turn for home.

While lying in the mud, I'd reasoned it would be easy to retrace my steps, rejoin the posse, and return home the hero.

Sitting on Huck, squinting through the rain, I realize I have no idea which way is east. The trees we started in are long gone. What's more, the rain has left a mess of tracks through the mud, but nothing distinctive. The storm blots out the stars.

With a deep breath, I choose the direction that looks the most trodden and pray I'm right.

<hr>

NOTHING AROUND ME LOOKS FAMILIAR after at least an hour of riding, but I'm trying not to panic. Of course things look different—it was pouring rain, night-dark, and I was focused on catching Dawson when we rode through here.

My slicker is heavy with mud and rainwater, my waist overalls chafing my thighs with each slight movement in the saddle. I've got an extra union suit in my bag—damp, probably, but clean at least—but no idea how to go about changing now I've got Dawson to worry about, so I suffer through the stiff discomfort. The rain tapers off to a drizzle as the sky lightens toward morning. I keep telling myself I just need the sun to break through and I'll be able to judge where we're going. Until then, I'll keep hoping and praying we're closing the distance to the posse.

My gaze drifts to Dawson's back, slung over the stolen horse. He's been silent since he woke a while ago and realized he's bound tight, whether plotting or resigned to his fate doesn't much matter to me. A drop of pride hits my chest and ripples outward. None of them believed me capable, and now look. Outlaw apprehended, and not a shot fired. A smirk presses against the healing split over my cheekbone. My finger traces the freshly scabbed line, the skin around it warm and swollen. It makes me smile wide enough to hurt.

The drizzle kicks back up into a full-on rain, as if even the weather is cheering me on. Images fill my mind—headlining the *Bluff City Gazette*, a ceremony to award me Dawson's full reward. Maybe I'll even inspire a dime novel.

"Can we stop?" Dawson's voice filters over the top of the horse. "My ribs ache, and I could really use a piss."

My hand rubs across my own ribs. "So piss. No one's stopping you."

"Just my dignity," he mutters.

Now that he's said it, the need strikes me too. For once, I wish I was wearing a skirt—I could just squat and be done with it. Trousers make things a bit more complicated. I shove a hunk of soggy jerky into my mouth and try to ignore the discomfort in my lower gut.

A scraggly trio of oak trees at the top of a nearby hill catches my eye. "If you try anything," I say, as I veer toward them, "I'll shoot you."

Not that it's been dry enough to reload with fresh bullets. I wonder if Dawson realizes it. He doesn't say anything. Maybe he's smart enough not to push his luck.

I tie our horses to the trees, then leave Dawson slung over the horse as I relieve myself behind the widest oak. Its low, spreading branches provide a decent amount of privacy. I doubt he can see much from that angle, anyway, especially with the rain sheeting down, but honestly, I don't even care anymore. It's all I can do not to yell, "Hallelujah!"

Once I'm good and finished, I unwind the rope tying Dawson to the horse. He flops to the wet earth with a sound somewhere between a groan and a sigh. While he's down, I tie the other end of his rope to Huckleberry, so he can't go far. He blinks up at me through the rain and a shiner darkening his right eye. My lips twitch with another urge to smirk at last night's handiwork, never mind he gave as good as he got.

"Looks like you can manage from here," I say. I start looking through his saddlebag, taking stock of what all we've got. From the corner of my eye, I keep track of his movements.

He rolls to his knees, then staggers to his feet, his bound hands pulling him off balance. "Don't suppose there's any chance you'll untie me so I can do my business?"

I snort as he fumbles his fingers around his belt. He's grown a beard since his likeness was captured, a full, light brown scruff that clings to each passing raindrop. It might hide his face a bit, but it doesn't disguise his youth. Probably no more than me or Jonah's age and known throughout the West for thieving and murder.

And here he is, struggling to get his pants down.

He glances up and catches me looking. An amused grin turns him stupidly handsome, and I think about punching his other eye. "Could you at least undo my buckle?"

Heat rushes into my numb cheeks, so I scowl. "No."

"Guess I'll just piss myself then."

"Already said that's an option."

"You'll have to deal with the stink."

My breath clouds as I huff. "The rain'll take care of that, and besides, I've smelled worse than you."

I'm thinking of a reeking herd of cattle, but he grins as if I've complimented him. There's a metallic *snick* and that smirk widens. "Got it!"

He turns to the tree as his waist overalls loosen, and I go back to my search through the saddlebag. Among the bits of foodstuffs, tobacco, and a flask about three-quarters full of—gentle sniff—whiskey, there's a small sack of about three dollars in coin.

I wonder whose horse this is—who'll be shivering without his bedroll tonight? I can only assume one of the cowboys who joined us, since I don't know the horse. Her mane is the same shade of chestnut brown as the rest of her, with tall white boots on three of her legs that make her stand out.

"What's your name, stranger?" I murmur, as if the horse might answer back.

Boots squelch in the mud. "You mind doing me back up?" Dawson fiddles with the belt buckle again.

"You can manage. And if not, at least we'll avoid this pleasant conversation next time nature calls."

While he relieved himself, I tied our horses together. I could have used the rope to bind him to the saddle again, but since he's awake, I'd rather let him do the work of getting onto the horse on his own.

It takes him a couple tries with his bound hands and the slick leather surface, but he manages to get astride newly dubbed Stranger, and I swing into Huckleberry's saddle.

We don't get very far before he starts with the questions.

"You gonna tell me what brought you out here?" And a few steps later, "I never heard of a woman bounty hunter before."

I almost tell him I'm not a bounty hunter but decide to keep ignoring him. Hell, it could play to my advantage if he thinks I'm that dangerous. And while he may not exactly be coming willingly, telling him about Pa might send him into a frenzy I don't want to deal with.

"That was some mighty fine lariat work, by the way."

Maybe he thinks compliments will get me to respond. I've half a mind to warn him nothing he says will change my mind about bringing him in, so he can stop trying to form some sort of bond with me. But that in itself would be engaging, something I have no desire to do.

He sighs. "Most people don't like the rain, but I never minded it."

Me too. When I glance at him against my will, he's got his face tilted toward the sky.

The storm lifts a deep, earthy scent into the air, and the slow wind makes the tallgrass shiver. Inside my slicker, though, I'm cozy.

"There's just something peaceful about it," he continues, "even when it's violent."

"Then be quiet and enjoy the peace," I snap. *And let me do the same.*

Not long after, the rain lets up but leaves behind a swath of low, gray clouds threatening to drench us again. Mud sucks at the horses' hooves, the squelching loud in the empty space between us. We only make it a little ways before he breaks the silence yet again.

"Why didn't you kill me and be done with it?" Dawson's tone is too tentative for me to make out whether it's fear or gratitude halting his words.

I glance at him, eyebrow raised.

His gaze moves from me to the horizon, no emotion on his bruised face. "I know my reward is dead or alive. Woulda been a lot easier on you to kill me while I was knocked out."

I face forward too. He doesn't need to know my reasons, that it will be more satisfying to watch a noose closing around his neck than to put a bullet in his unconscious body. That I promised Ma she'd see him drop.

"I didn't want to deal with the stink," I say.

◇━○━━○━◇

WE'VE WANDERED ACROSS MUDDY PRAIRIE most of the day, but now that the sky is darkening, I know we need to find shelter. My insides squirm as I wonder how I'll go about securing Dawson overnight. It's one thing to tie him to my horse while we travel, but what if he overpowers me as soon as we stop? How can I be sure he won't manage to get away once I've fallen asleep?

When I spot a stretch of white oaks, I lead us toward them. Part of me wants to press on until full dark, but I know trying to maneuver Dawson without the benefit of seeing what I'm doing would be detrimental.

"Stopping already?" he asks.

Instead of answering, I wrap his rope around my arm and untie it from Huckleberry. He's fast, though, already swinging out of the saddle, trying to pull himself free. Still on Huck, I've got the small advantage of height, which I use to my benefit to pull him right back, as if he's some stone-headed bull.

He stumbles a step forward. Close enough I'm able to kick him in the gut, winding him. While he's recovering, Huck and I get his rope up and over a tree branch, then twice again before I tie it off and dismount.

Dawson secured—at least for the time being—I set about making camp and try to ignore his wheezing. He tugs at the rope, testing the strength of my knots, maybe hoping to fray it along the ridged, gray bark. I tell myself he's wasting his time, but the fear that he'll break free squats in the back of my mind the entire time I'm heating beans and rehydrated jerky over a small fire. At best, he'll make off with my supplies. I don't even want to think of what else he might do to me before that.

"You hungry?" I ask when the beans start bubbling.

"Little hard to eat." He no longer sounds charming or friendly as he wiggles his fingers at me over his head. They're pale against the deepening twilight, his whole frame just out of reach of the fire's light.

I rummage in my saddlebag for the last hunk of pemmican. The small, greasy brick crumbles at the edges as I break off a chunk, powdered venison and berries sticking to my fingers.

"Oh, you gonna fee—"

I shove it in his mouth, making him cough, then return to my meal. He glares at me while he chews.

"Thirsty?"

After a thick swallow, he says, "You gonna dump it on me?"

"That would be a waste of water." I give the canteen from his horse a shake. It's more than half full, but if I'm right about our current direction, it'll likely be another day before we reach the Missouri River. I'm not familiar enough with these parts to know if we'll happen upon a decent water source before then. "You gonna hold still when I come over there again?"

"Guess you'll have to come over here to find out."

I got lucky with the pemmican, I know that. He could've kicked me, head-butted me, wrapped his legs around my ankles. Now that he's had time to formulate a plan of attack, I'm not getting within striking distance before I've reloaded my Colt with fresh cartridges.

I take my time doing so, watching Dawson as each bullet fits into the chamber with a comforting *snick*. It's enough to make him behave, tilting his head back and opening his mouth for me to pour in a few gulps of water.

As I'm cleaning up before bed, my plate slips from between my fingers, clattering against the tin saucepan, which gives me an idea. Between the two saddlebags, I've got two tin cups, plus the saucepan, which I tie all together. Holding the looped hide strips, I give the bundle a shake.

Dawson looks over with a scowl. "There a reason you're making a racket?"

I step around the tree behind him and grab the other end of the rope, then secure my noisemaker to it. He shifts, trying to see what I'm up to, and the tin items clang together.

"Now I'll be able to hear if you try to escape." A burst of pride swells my chest as Dawson gives the rope another experimental tug. The woods fill with clunks.

"That won't get annoying," he mutters.

"Just hold still," I say sweetly. "Night."

◆━●○━━○━●━◆

MY PLAN WORKED—DAWSON IS STILL here when the sky lightens from black to cloudy gray—and then again, it didn't. Every time I nodded off, that bastard shook his rope, the tinny smash bringing me back awake. Now I glare at him through puffy eyes.

"Morning," he says evenly. "May I be untied now?"

I console myself with the fact he's got smudges under his bloodshot eyes. The swelling around his right eye has diminished some, but the bruise is a gorgeous blackberry color. The sight's enough to make me smirk, until the movement tugs at the scab across my cheek.

The drip and pop of falling acorns matches the sounds of my joints as I take my time stretching. My body aches in all the various places Dawson's knuckles found purchase yesterday, and lying all night on the root-littered forest floor didn't help. He's got to be feeling even more stiff after spending the night tied to a tree. At least there's that.

God willing, I'll track down the posse today. If not, I'll have to come up with a better plan before nightfall. For now, I'm too tired to think about much beyond getting back on the road. Dawson seems exhausted too—he doesn't fight me at all when I free him from the tree, and I'm able to tie his lead rope to Huckleberry without incident.

"Let's try to pick up the pace from yesterday," I say as we plod through the death-bitten foliage. "Hopefully, we make it back to Bluff City in less than three days."

Dawson snorts. "You didn't strike me as the optimistic sort."

"The Pony Express could make the trip in less than a day."

"This ain't the Pony Express, sweetheart."

"*Isn't*," I say automatically. I shake my head and mutter, "My brothers always—" before catching myself. I don't owe him any explanations, much less personal details.

I can feel Dawson's gaze crawling across the back of my neck like some furry insect, but I refuse to look at him. Instead, I swat the mosquito buzzing near my ear. A sharp slap splatters brown and red across my fingers.

The vast grayness lingers through our midday break, but the sun finally splits the late afternoon cloud cover. We follow it back onto the open plains. Shadows stretch behind us, and the warmth finally dries my damp clothes.

"You heard of Leadville?" Dawson asks in a crawling drawl. "It's in Colorado. They got silver in their mountains. I'm hoping to find me some, buy a bit of land, live a quiet life."

I catch myself before snorting.

"Could share it with you."

This time, I do snort. He must have an awfully high opinion of himself if he thinks he can charm me into daydreaming about a future with my father's killer.

"No, listen." He leans over the pommel, handsome face earnest. "You turn me in at the next town and get a payout, sure, but how far will that get you? Eventually, the money will run out, and then what? I'm offering a trade. You help me get to Colorado, and I'll pay you back with half the silver I mine for the rest of my life."

There are so many things wrong with that offer, it takes me a minute to decide where to start.

"Even if I *did* trust an outlaw to keep his word—which I don't—and supposing you managed to find any silver—which you won't—I have absolutely no desire to go to Colorado."

"Dodge City, then?"

"The only place I'm going is home to Bluff City, and the only silver you'll see is the treasure in Heaven before the pearly gates close in your face."

Dawson blinks at me, then glances over his shoulder. He settles back in his saddle, blessedly quiet. Probably formulating another ridiculous offer, but I'll shut that one down just as firmly. My legs and back ache, and my throat is parched. All I want is a crisp cup of lemonade, a hot bath, and a good long sleep under Ma's patchwork quilt. And the only way Dawson can give me that is by shutting up and following along.

He clears his throat, ruining my peace. "Say, you got a name?"

"Yup."

He nudges his horse to draw alongside mine again. "You gonna tell me?"

"Nope."

"Gonna be a long journey if I don't even know what to call you."

"You could try not talking."

"Suit yourself, Miss Lady."

I cringe. *Lady* was Pa's pet name for Ma, murmured in the few tender moments between them. "Don't call me *that*."

"Tell me what I should call you then, sweetheart."

My teeth grind. "Maggie."

"That wasn't so hard, was it?" He smiles wide enough to dimple his left cheek. "You can call me JD."

I could tell him I don't plan on talking to him at all, but that would rather defeat the point. A hawk circles overhead. I follow its calculated laps with my gaze, tracking Dawson in my peripheral.

He tilts his head in a halfhearted shrug. "Or don't. Still nice to know each other's names. First step to becoming friends."

I pull Huckleberry up short and give Dawson my full, glaring attention. "We will never be friends."

He just looks back, solemn enough despite an odd warmth in his brown eyes. Overhead, the hawk screeches, claiming his territory.

I cluck Huckleberry forward and pretend I didn't just notice Dawson's eyes at all. The rope between us tugs taut before Stranger follows.

"Shame," Dawson says. "If we were friends, I might point out we're headed the wrong direction."

I stiffen but bite back my retort. He's trying to rankle me, after all.

"You hear me?"

"I know where I'm going."

Dawson makes a low humming sound in his throat. "Well, that's me put in my place."

We're both silent, the click and chirp of insects filling the twilight between us.

5

A SECOND NIGHT OF CAMPING GOES SMOOTHER than the first, but only because we're both too tired for any antics. If Dawson had attempted to escape, I likely would have slept through it no matter the racket he'd have caused. Fortunately, he's sleeping propped against his tree when I wake.

Dawson wakes with a snort that sends a squirrel racing through the branches overhead, chittering a reprimand. He watches, wolflike, as I eat a tin of fruit. He's solid enough to survive without breakfast—if he slumps over from hunger, I'll give him something to carry him through until Bluff City, but I'm not sharing any more of my dwindling rations with him until necessary.

When I'm done, his predatory gaze turns more puppy. "Nothing for me?"

I consider giving him the empty tin—he could lick the juice clinging to the sides—but the sharp edges could quickly turn into a weapon. I toss it deeper into the woods and set about packing up.

Dawson takes his time standing, stretching and twisting before following me to the horses.

"Come on," I say. "Another couple days' hard riding and we'll be back." I've accepted my hope of rejoining the posse is a naive one. My best chance for justice, especially before dying of exposure, is to find my own way back to Bluff City directly.

I suppose I can understand why he isn't feeling the same urgency I am. It doesn't stop me from voicing my annoyance when he lingers beside Stranger, staring through the gaps in the vibrant leaves at the climbing sun.

"Let's go, Dawson." I nudge Huckleberry forward, and Stranger, tied behind us again, takes a step.

He sighs and hoists himself into the saddle before his horse can move farther away. "Told you, it's JD."

"And I told you," I say over my shoulder, "I don't care."

He doesn't respond, but there's an aura of inexplicable smugness around him. It hangs heavy in the autumn air between us as we ride. Growing up with two brothers taught me better than to mention it, though, so I let him stew in whatever thoughts are so pleasing to him and turn my focus to home.

Has Jonah returned? Ma will be worried sick. No, Jonah wouldn't go home without me. I'd have expected to cross paths with the posse by now, but if we're chasing each other, we'll both end up going in circles. I stifle a groan, thinking how our posse likely *has* turned into a search party. That'll put a damper on the celebration when I show up with Dawson in tow. Even now, Jonah is probably muttering to himself how he *knew* he should have left me home.

I glance up to try to judge the time and estimate the remaining distance. My heart drops like a stone in a pond, sending ripples of unease to my extremities. We are definitely heading west, something I should have paid more attention to yesterday. Goldarned Dawson, distracting me.... But what if he'd been telling the truth?

The issue that only just occurred to me—one that's starting to settle into my skin like a day-old sunburn—is that I have no idea what is the right direction. Our posse was headed west when we came upon Dawson's camp, but once he got free, he could have gone north or south or kept heading east.

Even if Dawson did go east, Bluff City is days farther in that direction than we could have gone during our chase. Which means west is decidedly the wrong direction now that Bluff City is the destination. My grip tightens on the reins, slowing Huckleberry.

We're coming up on a milepost half obscured by tall Missouri prairie grasses and goldenrods. Further proof of my mistake since there should be nothing but homesteads between here and Bluff City if we were pointed the right way. Unless we're farther south, closer to Jeff City than I realized....

"Odd," Dawson says, though his tone is anything but surprised.

The air squeezes from my chest as I urge Huck over to the carved wooden sign. My heart pounds between my ears.

WARRENSBURG – 2

CITY OF KANSAS – 60

Two days' ride from Kansas City is absolutely the wrong direction. Which puts us about a day shy of a week from Bluff City, clear on the other side of the state.

I pull Huckleberry to a stop and stare at the etched letters. As if a swarm of gnats has engulfed my head, all I hear is a whiny buzzing. Beside me, Dawson stretches his bound arms over his head, twisting to and fro, completely at ease.

The bastard.

"Funny thing," he starts, but I don't need him to explain it. I had an excuse at first, but with the sun leading us, I should have recognized we were headed west—and that of all the directions, west was the only *wrong* possibility—as soon as it appeared.

"Shut up."

"See, the sun rises in the east—"

"Yes, thank you." Ma's in my ear, countless reprimands never quite sticking. *"You don't pay attention...."*

My head is shaking before my mind catches up. None of this can be happening. We're a full two days farther from home than yesterday, and we don't have enough supplies to make the trip back.

"Suppose the good news is you're a lot closer to collecting your reward than you thought," Dawson says.

Hell if I'm letting some nothing-town like *Warrensburg* string up our outlaw.

The relentless sun heats my already burning face. Sweat rolls down my spine and clings to the back of my shirt. "You committed your crimes in Bluff City, and that's where you'll hang."

"How poetic."

I scrub my face with my hands, then prop them behind my head, thinking. Maybe I could ask the Warrensburg sheriff to transport Dawson to Bluff City. Doubt he'd spare the manpower or give up the notoriety without a hefty chunk of the reward money, though, and if Jonah's insinuations about Pa's debts are true, we need every penny we can get.

No matter what, I'll need to resupply. "Let's give the horses a break." And hopefully I can come up with a plan.

While Dawson drifts to the far side of Huckleberry to relieve himself, tugging the rope as tight as it'll go, I take another inventory of our meager belongings. I group them into piles and pace around them, strategizing.

Suppose I could trade Dawson's revolver, but there's no way I'm continuing this trip without the protection the extra Colt offers. The tobacco and whiskey might come in handy as trade items with other travelers but won't amount to much at a general store. The coins jangle as I count them again—several two-bit pieces and a silver dollar, totaling $2.75. It could be enough for the barest of essentials if I'm smart about rationing the rest of the way home.

Pa's pocket watch is warm in my hand, smooth under my thumb as I think. It's really the only item of worth, but can I part with my only piece of Pa? Jonah's voice fills my head, calling me a hypocrite for even considering it.

"Any luck?" Dawson says, coming up behind me.

I sigh. Pa would trade his watch to feed me. I know it without question. Sentimentality is no reason to risk the weakness hunger and exposure will certainly bring—especially not in the company of a known murderer, traveling through unknown parts. I bring the smooth surface to my lips, then tuck it in my pocket and turn.

Jedidiah Dawson is holding a banknote between the first two fingers of his right hand. When I don't move, he waves it at me. "Go on, buy yourself something pretty."

"Where did that come from?"

He cocks his head. "I am a bank robber."

"And what, you stuffed your pockets with the cash?" I'd patted those pockets down while he was unconscious, but other than ridding him of weapons, I didn't really think about what else he might be carrying in that bulky slicker.

"Some, sure. Hid the rest, 'course." He holds the greenback out again. "You gonna take it?"

My fingertips close over the edge of the bill, the number five emblazoned in the corners, and I meet his gaze. "Why?"

One shoulder lifts in an easy shrug. "Not like I can stroll into a town papered with my face and buy myself vittles. But I gotta eat, same as you, if you want to see me hanged as bad as you claim."

I tug the money free, my eyes never leaving his.

"'Sides, the way I see it, I'll need to be well stocked to make it all the way to Colorado. You're saving me the trouble of scrounging for food once I make my escape."

I make a mental note to buy more bullets and a few bandages in case I end up needing to wound him. "We'll see about that."

◆──◇──◇──◆

WARRENSBURG IS A RAILROAD TOWN, and the rails cut through a forest on their way to the depot. I don't want to get too close—like Dawson said, his face is too well-known, despite the scraggly beard— but I also need to be able to find him again. A sturdy, towering sycamore tree provides a good option. Its red-seared golden leaves stand out against the buttery foliage of its neighboring elms, but it's relatively well hidden from view of any passersby following the train tracks.

Considering the money he's given me, I'm foolish enough to believe Dawson'll let me tie him up easily. I manage to get his lead rope over a tree branch, but before I can tie it off, he sinks his knee into my gut. The rope burns my hands as I stagger backward, clinging to it. He comes at me again. Quick as I can, I wind the rope around my arm and sink back. My body weight snaps his arms up overhead. I pull harder until I'm on the ground and his feet barely touch. He's struggling, too, but without any sort of leverage. My foot shoots out for good measure, clipping him between the legs. He gasps, and the fight leaves him.

Once he's fully secure, still breathing hard, I put my face right next to his. "Quit trifling with me, or I *will* shoot you."

His breath wavers, almost like he's laughing at me. My fingers itch to put a bullet between his eyes. I walk away before I can give in to the urge. I take Stranger with me, partially to carry supplies but mostly to keep Dawson from making off if he somehow manages to escape.

My hair came loose during the scuffle. I scrape it back into a tight, low tail secured with a strip of leather rather than waste time braiding it. Ma's in my head, tutting over my appearance, making me want to scrub my face clean and tuck my shirt in nicely. As usual, I ignore her nagging voice. The more travel weary I appear, the less attention I'm sure to garner. Besides, with my face covered in bruises, keeping my hat low and head down is the only option.

As Huck and I cover the mile or so to the town limits, I turn my thoughts toward planning. The general store is my obvious destination, but I debate wiring a message to Bluff City first in case Ma's worried sick. Might not be a bad idea to alert them to our location—better than dragging Dawson across the state on my own.

Then again, I'm not too keen to linger in one place too long, especially not one so close to civilization. That's just inviting trouble, even if I do manage to keep Dawson tied up the whole time.

Ultimately, I decide against the telegram—if Ma doesn't yet know

I've been separated from Jonah, a telegram would only cause her grief. Besides, the money is better spent on supplies.

The dusty road becomes a ramshackle thoroughfare lined with saloons and hotels. There's a whitewashed cathouse across from a crumbling wooden church, and a smithy belching smoke at the end of the strip. Outside the general store, I pause to look over the Wanted posters. Sure enough, Dawson's smirking mug is papered alongside a half dozen others listing various crimes and rewards. Rather than vindication, the sight of him staring back fills me with dread. He's pretty well hidden in the woods outside of town, but seeing his Wanted poster here makes that distance feel a lot closer.

There's a woman—Belle Starr—up here, too, mixed in with all the men's posters. A $750 reward, wanted for horse theft, rustling, and harboring outlaws. In her picture, she's wearing a dark dress that would make my ma sigh with envy, but she holds a pistol, bright against all that dark fabric. I linger over her poster, wondering how many horses she had to rustle to become as "notorious" as her poster claims. In a fit of pure fancy, I picture my own face there, wishing I knew the sort of confidence to be both feminine and deadly, unheard of yet infamous.

I duck into the dark store, determined to finish quick as I can and get back to my own notorious outlaw. A fine-dressed man and a portly woman stand at the counter. They pause their gossiping with the shopkeeper to eye me, looking to add a traveling stranger to their roster of stories, no doubt. My boots echo on the hardwood floor, and their quiet conversation resumes.

Like Hoffsteder's back home, the shelves are crammed with all sorts of odds and ends. Normally I'd like to linger, looking over all the wares. That this is a town halfway across the state only makes that desire stronger. The scent of old wooden crates and sharp licorice sends a pang of homesickness through me. But I've got a job to do and an ornery outlaw to get back to, so I move between the tables and assorted crates with purpose, collecting supplies.

At the front, that couple is still jawing with the shopkeeper.

"...paper said he'd be caught in no time, between the Westport posse and Bluff City's."

My town's name perks my ears. The old man behind the counter leans forward, eyes dancing between the other two. I can tell he relishes the attention. "Gerald at the *Daily* told me hisself the Bluff City posse is hung up around Booneville. He heard it from his cousin in Columbia—cousin works for the *Missouri Statesman*, you know—that not only did Dawson slip through the posse's fingers, but he took one of their number with him."

Heat flushes my neck, crawling toward my hairline.

The woman gasps, her fat fingers fluttering in some approximation of daintiness. At her side, the man asks, "Dead, or *taken* taken?"

"Disappeared!" The shopkeeper throws up his hands.

My feet shift, and a board creaks. Every one of us freezes, then three pairs of eyes turn to blink at me. My lips shove into something like a smile.

The woman snags her man's arm and tugs him to the side. "Go on ahead. We're just visiting."

I force my smile wider. "Thank you, kindly," I murmur.

I lay everything out on the counter—a roll of bandages, two boxes of ammunition, as much coffee and dried food as I can afford. Over my shoulder, I feel the couple eyeing my stash, making assumptions, exchanging raised eyebrows.

"You're not from around here, are ya, son?" the shopkeeper says as he tallies my purchase. "Traveling alone?" His bushy, drawn-together eyebrows rest on the tops of his spectacles as he looks me up and down.

I swallow a smirk. It's not his fault, not really—who'd expect a woman to be this dirty, sporting a rainbow of bruises on her face and traveling without a chaperone? Lord Almighty, the very idea! I could give him what for, but it's easier letting them believe me a man. I lower my voice to complete the effect. "Just passing through to Westport." I only hesitate a moment to think of a town near City of Kansas.

The shopkeeper tuts. "Well, keep your eyes peeled. There's dangerous men in these parts."

Don't I know it. I offer him a nod as I pay for my goods with Dawson's stolen cash.

On my way out, I pass two men examining the Wanted board. One wears a cracked tin star, identifying himself as the town sheriff. My chest seizes as if I've been caught stealing.

"See?" The threadbare one points excitedly at a poster. "I'm telling you that were Jedidiah Dawson I seen!"

My stomach turns to stone. Blood pounds in my ears. My steps don't falter, though.

"All right, calm down. Where is he now?" The sheriff sounds skeptical, but who knows how deep his patience runs?

I do my best to keep my movements nonchalant as I tie everything to the horses before climbing into Huck's saddle. Inside, every drop of blood is chomping to leave.

"Shoulda kilt him and brung him in m'self," the first man mutters. "Left Carl watchin' over him, but he's a good-for-nothin' simpleton, and I just *knew* it were him."

The sheriff opens his mouth beneath a bristly handlebar mustache but pauses and glances at me. I blink as the other turns too. *Ah, hellfire.* Another smile pastes across my face.

"Afternoon, gentlemen." With a nod, I cluck for Huckleberry to circle around. I keep our pace plodding—Stranger walking behind us—but I feel their eyes between my shoulder blades long after I've cleared the town limits.

When it finally feels far enough, I glance back. No sign of pursuit—yet. I encourage Huck faster, praying I can get Dawson untied and back in the saddle before they come looking.

6

VOICES FILTER THROUGH THE WOODS BEFORE I reach the red-tipped sycamore where I left my outlaw. *Shit and damnation.*

"...please," Dawson is saying, "before they come back."

"How do I know they ain't got good reason tyin' you up?" A man's voice, his words a slow crawl. My revolver whispers free of its holster.

"I swear it." Dawson's voice is all silk and slippery as a serpent. "There's been a misunderstand—"

"I think Leroy's right. You a dead man walkin'." A rangy-looking man stands across from Dawson when they come into view. I slide off my horse as he's pulling his revolver.

"Drop it." I level my Colt at him.

His body goes taut, weapon still aimed at my outlaw. "This here's Jedidiah Dawson." He spares a quick glance for me. "Guessin' you already know that, seein' as how he's tied up. Be easier to bring him in once he's dead."

Dawson's gaze flits from the man to me, assessing.

I step closer, drop my voice lower, my eyes on the newcomer. "Can't let you do that."

He looks at me again, a leer showing off the gaps between his yellowed teeth. "Might I could split the reward with you." His eyes dart along my frame, my wounds. He'll sooner take me out too.

"He's my fugitive, and the reward's mine too. I'll ask you one more time, drop your weapon and go."

Instead, he thumbs down the hammer, his grin still turned in my direction. I don't think past that.

A crack sends birds flying into the air, and he drops. I'm frozen, my eyes stuck on the blood oozing from the hole between the man's eyes. Dawson lets out a low whistle.

I turn my back to him as I holster my gun with shaking hands and try to breathe. It's not like I haven't killed before. I've put down plenty of sick animals in a similar way. Hell, I've even shot at men a time or two, present company included. Just never seen one of my bullets hit.

Guess now I know I can shoot to kill. I just don't know how to feel about that.

Sunlight streams between the trees, forest noises slowly resuming. Life moves on—for us, at least.

There's a certain sort of power, heady as it is gut-churning, to recognize I can control such a thing as a man's next breath.

Dawson clears his throat. "Well, damn."

"Still think I won't shoot you?" I turn. A newfound confidence squares my shoulders.

He spreads his hands, still bound overhead, in a gesture of surrender. He doesn't say any more as I free him from the tree with jerky movements, but when I rejoin him in front of it, his eyes are a wary sort of soft. My stomach clenches.

"Thanks for that," he says. "You done the right thing."

"'Course I did. He'd have killed me after you." *Practically self-defense.*

Dawson's still watching me like he's worried I'll start crying or scream or shoot him after all. All three sound appealing. None seem appropriate.

"We should get going," I say, tying his rope to Huckleberry again.

"We're too close to town. Sheriff's already been alerted, and besides, someone might've heard the shot."

Dawson nods. "Grab his horse. You could get a lot for it in these parts." He kneels beside the dead man, bound hands patting at his pockets.

I yank Dawson's rope, sending him sprawling, and grab the man's gun before Dawson can reach for it. A slow grin stretches his lips as I tuck the weapon into my saddlebag.

"Can't sell the horse here," I say. "Someone might recognize it."

"Now you're thinking like an outlaw." Dawson staggers to his feet.

I coax the dead man's horse over while Dawson climbs onto Stranger, and we hightail it away from Warrensburg.

Once we've put enough miles between us and the corpse for my insides to unclench, I slow down to give the horses a rest. Dawson rides up alongside me, close enough for our legs to brush every few steps. I throw an elbow, clipping his bicep, and he falls back a half pace.

"You know," he says, undaunted, "that's twice now you've passed up the chance to kill me. Can't blame a guy for thinking you like having me around."

"I'd prefer to bring you in alive, but if there's no other option, I'm the only one who gets to kill you. Sure as shit not letting some back-woods bounty hunter do the honors."

"So, just you or the hangman."

"Keep talking, and I might convince him to let me give you the drop."

Dawson reaches up to the edge of his brim. "Ma'am."

<hr />

DAWSON HAS REMAINED UNCHARACTERISTICALLY QUIET since our encounter with the would-be bounty hunter. We've left the forest for the peaceful openness of grassland, and his silence feels like a boon. Maybe he's finally taking my threats seriously. He's fumbling with his hands in his lap when I look over at him—trying to alleviate the chafing on his wrists? It's a minor punishment, but it's satisfying. I hope every tiny movement brings him an echoing pain.

Wildflowers brush at my feet—light blue lobelias and purple cone-flowers, lacy pink milkweed, white puffs of wild carrot. It's almost as if God Himself were a suitor, offering me a bouquet along with the gift of Dawson's deliverance.

"Believe it or not," Dawson says, breaking into my happy musings, "I've enjoyed our time together these past couple days. So don't take this personally."

Quick as a salmon in spring, he cuts through the rope that ties him to me. He's kicked into a gallop before my mind catches up, and I spur Huckleberry—and the extra horse—after him. Hooves pound the grass. Our two guns bounce against me, and my knee bangs into the hard metal of the third in my bag, and I realize—he must have taken a blade off the dead man.

I pull my six-shooter and fire, but he's too far ahead. The extra horse isn't helping me gain ground. Dawson swerves toward tree cover, into the forest, where I'll surely lose him for good. With a *H'yah*, I follow.

When he entered, he was still headed east, but with the trees block-ing my view, he could easily circle around and be halfway to Colorado before I find my way through the oaks and pines. Hopefully, the draw of his hidden treasure is enough to keep him headed back toward home.

I just hope the Warrensburg sheriff hasn't ventured this far and doesn't find him first. God willing, my brother's still out there with the posse looking for him. For us.

It's not the victory I envisioned, but it'll do, so long as Dawson is caught. Otherwise, the chafing, damp clothes, the hunger, the man I killed—it's all for nothing.

I pull Huckleberry up short and try to listen over the sounds of our heavy breathing. Hoofbeats crunch leaves, but the sounds could be coming from anywhere.

Damn his blood.

Doesn't matter how I spur Huck on now. She's spent, and Dawson's good as gone.

I NEED TO MAKE CAMP for the night. The horses need the rest, and with the way my itching eyes keep blurring, we could be riding in circles at this point. I keep hoping we'll stumble across Dawson by some miracle, and it feels like stopping is accepting it's truly over.

There's also the matter of fear. Even tied up, Dawson provided a small comfort with his presence. It couldn't have been easy to sleep tied to a tree, so he was a lookout by default. I check my revolver and determine to sleep as near the horses as I can—hopefully, they'll alert me to any danger before it arrives.

When I find a good, flat spot to squeeze us between a few syca-mores, it's like my body remembers all the other functions it'd been ignoring during my search. It's all I can do to loosen the horses' cinches before stumbling off a little way to relieve myself. As I finish, I notice we've stopped near a creek. With a guilty glance over my shoulder—I really should unsaddle and rub Huckleberry down fully—I close the short distance and drop to my knees.

The water is cool, carrying the fresh, rocky taste of spring. It's been at least a week since I've had a decent bath, splashing water on my face and sweatiest parts notwithstanding. I'm not dumb enough to strip down to nothing alone in the middle of unknown woods, but after I've drunk my fill, I do indulge myself in a good long scrub under my dust-grimed clothes. Nowhere near clean but refreshed enough to return to assessing my predicament with a clearer head.

My fingers rake through damp hair, pulling it back into a braid. The stream bubbles happily over stones, and the creak and sigh of the night trees coaxes me to relax. Then, from deeper in the woods beyond the creek, comes a jangle of harnesses and the low-pitched hum of human voices.

What are the odds…?

I know it's improbable—nearly impossible—but the idea that it could be Jonah prompts me to investigate. I slip across the creek and through the trees, following the sounds of a small group making camp.

As I draw closer, the voices separate and develop characteristics. There's a rough, drawling one that could be Sheriff Kline. Someone makes a retort, sharp but smooth-toned, like Luis. My heartbeat kicks up, relief tempered by a surprising dash of dread. I'm not looking forward to their questions, their condescension. *Leave it to a woman to lose an outlaw as fast as she caught him.*

Still, I'm ready for this ordeal to be over. It's this thought that carries me closer with less caution than I should use. I barely have time to register the three men gathered around a campfire are *not* my posse before three weapons are aimed at my head.

I throw up my hands.

"You lost, chickadee?" The rough-voiced one lowers his pistol—only slightly. He's stocky, with a grizzled beard and long gray hair matted to his head.

My voice sticks when I try to speak, and I have to clear my throat twice. "Pardon the intrusion. I was just looking for my brother."

The truth feels stupid on my tongue, but hopefully, the idea that I have a brother nearby will keep these ruffians from trying anything.

"Foolish man to let a woman out of his sight in these woods." His gaze catches on my forehead, my cheek. I can only hope the remnants of my fight with Dawson dissuade this man from trying his luck with me.

Across the campfire, the other two men are younger but just as mangy-looking as their leader. The taller one has short-cropped, thinning hair and eyes that appear black in the firelight. There's a twisting scar along the other's jaw. They exchange dark looks and darker chuckles. I take a step back, the crack of a broken twig ringing in my ears.

"Hold on now," Rough Voice raises his pistol again. "We can keep you company until your 'brother' comes looking for you."

"I should probably just head back the way I came...."

He cocks the gun. "Wasn't really asking."

My eyes dart between the three of them, gauging distance. I'm far enough that at least one of them might miss if I turn and run, but close enough that one's bound to hit me. Then again, a bullet might be preferred to what else they have in mind for me. My tongue darts out to wet my lips as I decide my next move.

My left foot eases back, trying to increase the space between us. Something solid and warm and very large presses against my back. Meaty hands close around my upper arms.

"Hiram invited you to join us," a fourth man says, his voice rumbling through my back to shake my bones. He shoves me into the ring of light around the campfire.

"What's your name, chickadee?" Rough Voice—Hiram, I presume—asks.

"Chickadee is fine." Hell if I'm telling them anything about me.

"Not the sociable one, is she?" Hiram looks at the others with a sinister grin, runs his tongue along his tobacco-stained teeth as he assesses me. "Maybe you'd prefer I take you somewhere a little more private?"

He grabs my arm and rips me from my captor. The other two still have their guns trained on me, but lazily, like they'd rather enjoy watching us struggle. And struggle, I do, wrenching and clawing, but Hiram's grip is strong. He tows me from the camp.

I scream for help—futile though it may be—and Hiram slams me into a tree.

"Do that again, and I'll put a bullet in your throat," he says. "Not that there's anyone around to hear."

I whimper because I know he's right. *Where are you, Jonah?* My head throbs where it connected with the tree, but that's the least of my concerns.

Think, Margaret.

My mind clears enough to remember the revolvers half hidden by the fold of my shirt. Hiram presses against me, his hand at my throat. I slam my forehead into his nose. It isn't as effective as when I subdued Dawson, but Hiram pulls back enough that I'm able to get my knee up into his tender region.

He gasps, "Bitch."

Praise the Lord he was too stupid to think of disarming me. I pull the Colt from my belt and aim it at him. We're far enough from the others that they may not have heard our scuffle, but a gunshot would certainly bring them running, and I don't know that I have the speed to shoot them all. I flip the gun around and bring the butt of it into Hiram's temple as he's starting to recover. He crumples. Before any of them come to investigate our sudden silence, I turn and run.

Right into a fifth man. His hand smothers my scream, his other arm snaking around me to pull me deeper into the woods. I wriggle and squirm, but his hold is like a shackle. All our movement does is make his hand over my mouth slip enough that I'm able to sink my teeth into one of his fingers.

"Ah, shit, Maggie!" He shakes out his hand as I freeze.

"Dawson?"

"Don't stop now." He tugs me forward. "I'm trying to help you—"

"HEY!" The shout comes from behind us, followed by the report of a gun. Dawson shoves me to the ground out of the way, pulling the revolver from my fingers as he turns.

He aims and fires in the time it takes me to suck in a breath. One of the men falls. The others return fire. Dawson drops the second with a single shot, two more to take out the big one who pushed me into the camp. He ducks behind a tree beside me. "How many were there?"

I'm still struggling to catch my breath, so I hold up a finger. "One more," I gasp out.

The woods are quiet, though.

I crane my neck to peek over the brush that provides us cover. "Maybe he got scared off?"

"Could be." Dawson sighs.

"Should we let him go?"

"And leave him stewing in a desire for revenge? Don't know about you, but I won't sleep easy knowing he's in these same woods." He stands and peers out from our cover. A bullet splinters the tree a few feet from Dawson. He shoots back. A garbled cry reaches us.

Slowly, we make our way back toward the camp, toward the bloodied bodies. The snarl and twist of half-naked branches let through just enough moonlight to make out the one still moving. Hiram clutches at a hole in his stomach.

"He's the one who had you on his own?" Dawson asks. When I nod, he offers me the weapon. "Do the honors?"

I shake my head, my eyes on Hiram. "Leave him."

"He's already dying. Go on and end it."

"Please…." Hiram coughs.

"He deserves to suffer," I say.

Dawson cocks an eyebrow at me. With a flick of his wrist, he flips the gun and shoots Hiram between the eyes. "Not a lot of mercy in you, huh?"

I cross my arms. *Wilt thou condemn him that is most just?* "I prefer justice."

He looks me up and down. "No surprise there." Then the bastard tips his hat. "Well, I'll be off, then."

"No," I say, following him through the trees. "The only place you're going is back to Bluff City with me."

"How do you figure that?" he asks over his shoulder.

"I won't let you get away again."

He spins and levels the revolver at me. "Yes, you will. You can repay me for saving you from those bandits by letting me go. Think of it as justice."

I scoff. "I'd already gotten away. I didn't need your help."

"Guess we'll never know now. All the same, let's say it's a debt you owe." He cocks the gun. "And I'm collecting now."

Looking down the barrel of my own revolver might have made me hesitate before tonight, but I'm exhausted and in no mood for this back and forth. "You're not gonna shoot me."

I lunge before he can retort—or fire. My foot lands wrong on a rock, rolling with a pop. My fingers brush down his arm, but my momentum carries me down the incline, tumbling through brush and briars to land sprawled on my back halfway between Dawson and the creek where I'd bathed in what feels like a lifetime ago.

My leg spasms with pain, and my chest feels heavy with each breath.

I lay here, my face hot enough to warm the cool night air by several degrees, listening to Dawson's footsteps come closer. He stops over me, blotting out the few stars I could see between the night-dark leaves.

"Still here?" I sit up and run my hand along my ankle, checking for cracks. It's already swollen fatter than Ma's balls of yarn.

"Is it broken?" he asks. I can't help but notice my revolver is now tucked in his holster.

"I don't think so." Hurts like it, though.

He crosses his arms and looks out across the creek. I want to tell him to go away. I'm terrified he'll leave me alone here. Finally, he turns back to me.

"Can you walk?" Dawson holds out his hand, which I grudgingly take. It's warm and sturdy in a way that makes me feel too vulnerable. Calloused fingers close around mine, softly scraping in a way that sends tingles to my elbow. I fight the instinct to rip my hand free.

He hoists me to my good foot, and I try giving my injured one an experimental roll. Nearly bite through my lower lip doing it, but I swallow the groan. Putting pressure on it is an entirely different story. As soon as I shift weight to my right foot, the ankle buckles.

Dawson is there to steady me, a comfort and annoyance all at once. "All right, then."

The balance shifts to full annoyance when he bends and sweeps me into his arms. We're nearly the same height, but—lean as he is—he's got maybe fifty pounds on me. Crammed against his chest, that difference strikes me as a lot bigger, and I don't much care for feeling this small. "Put me down!"

"So you can topple over again?" He starts walking.

"Where are you taking me?"

In lieu of answering, he sets me—none too gently—on a flat rock beside the creek. "Soaking it should help the swelling some."

"I know that." I rip off my boot and sock with petulant movements. He crouches beside me, watching the water tumble along the creek bed.

The cold water does feel heavenly, numbing the pain and cooling some of my humiliation. I lie back and let my eyes slide closed. Somewhere in the trees, a whippoorwill calls out its name. My skin prickles, heavy under a gaze, but when I open my eyes and glance at Dawson, he's looking in the opposite direction.

"All right, here's the deal," he says. "I'm headed back toward Bluff City myself, so why don't I see you home safe, and in return, you'll let me go, no hard feelings."

I blink at him, wondering if I'm dreaming. "Why help me?"

One side of his mouth crooks up, teeth flashing in the moonlight. "Always been a sucker for a damsel in distress."

"I am not in distress." Though I might become distressed if left to my own devices—not that I'd admit it to him.

"Not much of a picture-perfect damsel, either, but beggars can't be choosy."

My eyes narrow, but I bite back my retort, intrigued by his proposal beyond my better judgment. "Why go back there?"

"I've got my reasons." When I hold his gaze, he says, "Three thousand of them. I'll give you half. Not quite the reward amount, but that plus the fact that I'll have helped you twice should be enough to call us square."

I snort. "Are you forgetting I saved you from that man outside Warrensburg?"

"If I recall, you were more concerned with your own well-being once I was dead."

I brush that away. "You think fifteen hundred dollars is enough to erase what you did?"

"Of course not. I think rescuing you—"

"Debatable."

"—from a band of delinquents, then tending your injured limb and escorting you home, should come close to redeeming myself."

"What does it matter what I think of you?"

He tilts his head. "You're awful determined to see me hang. My first guess was you're with the bank, but no banker's daughter should rope and ride like you. Farmer, maybe, which leads me to believe your money was among the take. Figure you'll find a way to track me down, injured or no, and I'd just like to start new somewhere. The money should sweeten the deal."

I almost tell him just why his execution matters to me, but good sense prevails. Admitting how personal this is will only scare him off, and I *could* use him on the trip home. Having him go willingly is a lot easier than tying him up again. Maybe I can even figure out a way to get him to reveal where he hid the money—then we'll get *all* the cash and the satisfaction of watching him hang.

So I say, "Deal."

DAWSON HELPS ME BACK TO WHERE I'VE left the horses. Huckleberry nickers as soon as we come into view. Normally, the sound is
welcoming, but tonight, I hear a reprimand.

"Can I get my gun back?" I say as Dawson pats her side.

"Nope."

"It's not even loaded."

He looks at me, steady-faced. "You sure about that?"

I mentally tally the shots and nod.

He pulls it and aims it at me again. "Willing to stake your life on it?"

"You're bluffing."

After a moment, he holsters it with a flourish and turns back to the
horses. "Until I get back my gun—fully loaded—I'll hold on to this one.
After all, an outlaw is only as good as his bluff."

"I'll keep that in mind."

He sets my saddle down near my feet. "You'll want to prop your bad
ankle up." He slaps the seat. I do as he says, and he resumes untacking
the horses, checking their legs and hooves.

"Let's get you something to drink," he says to Huck. With a glance my way, he leads her down to the creek. My insides tingle the entire time he's gone. Surely he wouldn't have waited until *after* he'd removed the saddle and supplies to run off?

I try to calm my heartbeat, resting my head back against my rolled slicker, but find myself counting breaths until I finally hear them moving through the woods again. When they come into view, Dawson's leading two horses. I sit up, reaching for my revolver before I remember he's got it. My left hand fumbles for the other gun in my saddlebags.

Before I can draw it, Dawson's already tugging the saddle from Stranger's back and setting it beside me. "Figured we'd want the supplies you left with Sal. Not that there was much in the way of food."

In all the furor, I'd forgotten half of my purchases from Warrensburg were tucked into Stranger's saddlebags. "Sal?"

Dawson grins at me. "Decided to name her Salvation since that's where she'll carry me."

"I've been calling her Stranger." Not that it matters much, but it feels like he's stolen the horse all over again by giving her a name.

"Well, she's mine now, and I prefer Salvation."

"Damnation might have been a better choice."

As if she knows we're talking about her, the mare gives an impatient grunt. Dawson runs his hand along her chestnut neck. "Can't call her 'Damn' in polite company, can I? Now about that food...."

The hard ground sends a chill down my legs. "Were you on your way to steal my supplies when you found me?"

"I was wondering at the odds I'd find you again, then I heard you scream."

My head throbs at the reminder. "Too bad you came across me before finding the unattended horses."

He gives me a funny look, his dark eyes narrowed. "I wouldn't ignore a scream like that."

He sounds so offended I almost laugh. "So you really were trying to rescue me? Why?"

"Look, I may not have many qualms about taking something that doesn't belong to me, but that shouldn't apply to women."

"So you're some sort of gentleman outlaw?"

He gives me a courtly bow. "Ma'am."

He goes to water the extra horse, and I start sifting through the supplies tied to Stranger's—Sal's—saddle. With the gap between the trees, stars twinkle like shattered glass, chasing away the deepest shadows. Dawson had enough coffee to keep him wide awake the entire week, as well as the bandages and flask of whiskey. At least I had the foresight to store all the ammunition on my own horse. The bounty hunter's bag holds little more than greasy pemmican dust and powdered tobacco bits, but from the filmy rubble, I pull a scuffed compass. Sure coulda used that two days ago, but I'm grateful for it now all the same.

When Dawson returns, he settles to the ground on the other side of Sal's saddle and lifts the flap nearest him. He holds out the flask to me. "This'll help take the edge off the pain."

I take a swig, breathing through the burn as the whiskey ignites my chest.

He settles back against a tree trunk, and I turn my gaze to the stars. After a few moments, a gentle clicking brings my attention back to Dawson. In the muted starlight, the barrel of my revolver glints.

"What are you doing?"

He looks over at me then pushes another bullet into the chamber. "Reloading."

A chill wraps around my chest, and I push myself to my elbows, my left hand drifting back toward the revolver now at my hip, hidden from Dawson's view. "Where'd you get the bullets?"

He sucks in his bottom lip. "Found 'em."

He gives the chamber a spin and snaps it closed. My eyes drift to the saddle under my foot.

"Look, Maggie, if this is gonna work, we're gonna have to trust each other."

He's unhinged if he thinks I'll trust the word of a thieving murderer like him. And he's awfully naive if he thinks he can trust me either.

"Trust takes time," I say.

"Sure enough. But what I'm talking about is the simple faith that we'll look out for each other, at least as far as the Bluff City line."

"And when we get there?"

He lifts one shoulder. "Well, that's a decent amount of time from now. We'll have to see. For now, I think we've proven we won't kill each other. And I'm more help to you armed."

He waves my revolver before tucking it back into his holster.

I settle back to the ground. "Don't go through my stuff again."

"No need. You don't have anything of interest beyond the bullets I already took."

Did he take them all? My fingers strain to check through my things, but I won't give him the satisfaction. "I'm no good to you unarmed either."

He grins. "You'll get more bullets if you need them."

I'm not sure I like this turn of events, but I'm too exhausted to argue anymore tonight. Besides, he's right—his shooting back there proves he'll be an asset on the road home. I shove worries over what we'll do when we get there to the back of my mind.

⋄━◦━◦━◦━◦⋄

DAWSON IS SILENTLY SADDLING THE horses when I wake.

I sit up. "Son of a two-bit trollop—"

He turns, eyes wide, before I can get the whole insult out, much less my revolver from its holster. He lunges at me—I register raised hands before one crushes my mouth, the other clamped behind my skull. My insides cool from rage to terror, matching the fear showing off the whites of his eyes. A gentle *shh* hisses between his teeth as he shakes his head.

Then comes the slow twig-snap of a deliberate boot. Someone is creeping through the woods toward us.

More than one someone, judging by the silence of the animals and the careful crunching of dead foliage. My lungs tighten at the thought of being discovered—then I remember I'm not the one on the run.

Dawson's hand falls from the back of my head first, coming to rest one finger against his lips before he releases my mouth too. *As if I'm scatterbrained and reckless.* I'll take the devil I know to some stranger who can't even sneak up on a person properly.

As Dawson finishes readying the horses, I shove my boots on. The excitement made me forget my foot, but now a sharp pain stabs up my shin bone all the way to my stomach. My teeth close around my cheek to keep from crying out. Then Dawson's at my side again, his hands none too gentle as he hoists me to my feet and helps me onto Huck. The bounty hunter's horse is tied behind his, all our supplies already stashed haphazardly between the three of them.

As Dawson's circling to Sal, a man's voice calls out from behind us, "This is Sheriff Wilkerson of Warrensburg, Missouri. We've got you surrounded. Dismount and remove your weapons so we may talk peaceably."

The urge to comply with a voice of authority wrestles with my instinct to flee. Would the sheriff believe my innocence? I look to Dawson—he's frozen, his hands on the saddle, his gaze probing the trees ahead of us.

Sheriff Wilkerson doesn't give us long to consider. "Dismount, or we will be forced to fire upon you."

Over the top of Sal's back, Dawson's eyes flit to mine. I wonder what he makes of my indecision—I wonder what to make of *his*.

"I will give you to the count of three," Wilkerson says. My fingers tighten around Huck's reins. He only gets past *one* before Dawson springs into his saddle and we're kicking our steeds as fast as they'll go through the trees.

Gunfire chases us. Bullets rip through bark and spray dirt. Only behind us, though.

Got you surrounded. Ha. That Wilkerson is a damned liar.

Heat flashes across my cheek, sobering me. Splinters burst from the tree I've just ducked. Liar he might be, but the lead he's sending our way is as honest as the grave.

We dodge trees and bullets with no sense or direction beyond safety. My heart pumps enough lightning through my veins that my ankle's forgotten how to ache. Dawson's got the extra horse slowing him down, but I'm not worried. The sheriff and his men must have dismounted to sneak up on us, so we've got the jump on them. I've just pulled fully ahead when a wet *snick* is followed by a short cry.

I turn to find Dawson holding the side of his jaw, blood rolling through his fingers.

My breath catches. My hands must have tightened around the reins because Huck slows.

"Bastard shot me!" Dawson says, staring at his bloody hand. His neck is coated crimson, but the fact that he's talking makes me think he'll be all right.

"Keep moving," I call, "or the next might finish you."

Hoofbeats are pounding after us now, eating up whatever advantage we had. Ahead, the trees thin. The sun winks at us from the ground. *Odd—oh!*

"River!" I shout over my shoulder. Not sure crossing it will make much difference—it's not like they've got hounds chasing our scent—but I like the idea of the physical boundary all the same.

Breaking out onto the bank reveals it's more a wide creek than river. Enough to make Huck stutter-step, enough to maybe slow our pursuers, but not for long.

Dawson follows as I guide Huck straight for the bank. Frigid water sloshes up over my boots and sprays across my face. I get a few drops in my mouth, tasting like rocks and freedom. I glance back to check on Dawson.

Sal stands on the riverbank, riderless. Dawson's hat bobs beyond her rump. The thick smack of skin on flesh reaches me over the wet slog we're making, and the extra horse charges back into the trees.

Dawson doesn't waste time watching—he's back in the saddle and halfway to me when there's an excited shout behind us.

I wait for him under cover of the trees on the far bank. Now that I've stopped moving, everything is crashing inside—my heart and lungs and the blood to my bad ankle. Dawson's chest heaves as he slides from Sal's back beside us.

"What are you doing?" I ask.

He gestures me down and staggers behind a thick-trunked walnut tree. I crouch beside him, avoiding the rounded fruit rotting in the yellow leaves at its base. A blackberry thicket beside it provides a good cover as we peek back the way we came.

"Hopefully they take the bait," he whispers, then takes a ragged breath. "If not, we can pick 'em off as they cross the river."

I glance at him. His gaze is on the water, the woods beyond it, waiting. Shooting that bounty hunter was one thing, the men last night as well, but I can't in good conscience plug lawmen full of lead.

Can I?

One of Pa's favorite phrases comes to mind. *You gotta do what you gotta do.* He'd repeat it when Cole complained about the early milkings or when I'd refuse to eat my vegetables. I'm not so certain he'd spout it for this situation, but then, he was nothing if not practical. *You or them, Mags.*

Huck's reins bite into my left hand, my revolver sits heavy in my right. My ankle screams, and my legs shake as my muscles tighten. No one breaks out onto the bank. The distant sound of hooves pounding the earth has faded.

I ease to my backside, relieving some of the pressure on my bad foot. It doesn't do much to stop the jagged pain wrenching my entire leg. Dawson glances at me but returns to watching the river without a word. Sunlight catches in the water droplets speckling his beard. With some of the blood rinsed away, I can see the bullet missed his neck entirely. It tattered his left earlobe and cut a pink gouge through the top of his beard. *Lucky bastard.*

And lucky me—I don't fancy the idea of dragging a corpse all the way to Bluff City.

After what feels like hours—but is likely only one—Dawson eases back from his perch. His shoulders drop, from relief or exhaustion, I couldn't say. "I think we're in the clear."

"We should keep moving in case they come back after finding the horse."

"Nah," he says, holstering his weapon, "we're safe enough here. They'll assume we kept on, and there weren't but a few of them. They're not likely to chase two people of uncertain identities farther outside their jurisdiction."

I catch myself before asking how he'd know such a thing. "I suppose this *is* your area of expertise."

"I did avoid capture for quite a while." He grins, then scowls when the movement tugs at his mangled ear. "The good guys are always predictable."

"Are you—don't touch it," I say. His fingers tentatively graze the wound anyway, and he hisses. "You saying I'm not one of the good guys?"

His gaze runs the length of me, sprawled out next to him. River water sticks my shirt to my stomach and my hair has pulled free from its braid. I resist the urge to curl into a ball. "Well," he says, "you're sure as hell not a guy. Jury's still out on whether you're good."

I bristle. His opinion shouldn't matter—*doesn't* matter—and yet, a small part of me shares it. After all, I've done bad things too.

"YOU KNOW WHERE WE ARE?" I ASK, chewing on a piece of day-old bread.

Dawson scratches a thumb across his back and squints at the creek as he pops pieces of dried apple into his mouth. Sunlight tugs shadows from the trees, reaching dark fingers away from us across the shining brown water. He pulls out the compass—when did he stash it with his belongings?—and tilts it away from the creek, deeper into the woodlands. "We're still headed in the right direction."

I guess that's all that really matters. "You're still bleeding," I point out. His ear drips, slow but steady crimson, onto his shoulder. Dawson digs through our supplies for the bandages. He fumbles with them in silence—I wonder if he's hoping for me to help.

My impatience breaks first. "Oh, give it here." As I help him clean and bandage his ragged earlobe, it occurs to me I'm mopping up the blood of the man who spilled Pa's—*no.* A good yank on the knot of the bandage also squelches the threatening pain.

Then—finally—we hit the trail. By my reckoning, we're about six days from Bluff City if we push our horses hard. Dawson doesn't seem to have any issue with the pace I set. I'm sure he's just as anxious to put distance between us and our ghosts.

Only about an hour more into the ride, though, and my ankle decides it's done cooperating. It's swollen to near thrice its normal size, and each plodding step sends a jarring ache all the way up to my knee. My face feels fixed in a permanent grimace, no matter how I try to ignore the pain.

"Maggie?"

My teeth are gritted too tightly to answer, so I grunt.

"We should take a break."

Loosening my jaw is a new kind of ache. "Hasn't been long enough."

"We won't make it much farther, neither."

"Distract me. Tell me a story." The ache is so bad, for a second, I've forgotten it isn't Jonah beside me. Heat rushes to my cheeks. "Never mi—"

"Oh, I've got stories."

I bite back another groan, already sorry for asking.

"You want to hear about the bank robbery?"

"No," I say, too fast. Just the thought of that day makes my ankle feel like the least of my agony.

"No crime?" He pats his horse's neck. "That's fine, let me tell you about all the things I *haven't* done."

I roll my eyes, but he presses on, undeterred.

"Lots of stories out there about me just ain't true. *Aren't,*" he corrects himself with a sly grin for me. "I've never robbed any trains."

My eyes cut to him, and he nods.

"It's true. Now, I *did* ride with the Blue Devil Gang, and *they* did commit a train robbery or two, but that was before my time with them."

The trail we follow dips over a gentle ridge. My ankle throbs.

"People say they *saw* you," I say.

"That's my own damn fault, sure enough. I'm the first of the Blue Devils to have their likeness captured alongside their name, so I got stuck with all the crimes. I was a fool kid when I started, eager to prove myself, get my name up there on the posters. Hardly ever covered my face." He shrugs. "It worked, I guess."

"Congratulations," I say, my voice flat.

"It ain't—isn't—something I'm proud of, mind. Sure did come back to bite me in the butt, now half the country's out looking for me."

My shoulder blades itch, but I resist the urge to glance behind me. "Think they haven't heard of you in Colorado?"

"I'm hoping they're a more forgiving folk. I can't be the only one running from trouble in them mountains."

"You sound awful confident you'll get there."

He nudges up the brim of his hat and raises an eyebrow. "*You* sound like you're not planning to uphold our deal."

Damn. I bat my eyelashes before they can widen at being caught out. "Just considering all my options."

Casually—so nonchalantly I almost miss the threat in the action—Dawson rests his hand on the butt of his gun. "Then you'll forgive me if I do the same."

It strikes me that I'm bantering with a murderer, as if a few exchanged words will protect me should he decide to turn that weapon on me. My pulse kicks up at the thought—the pain crawling up my leg isn't helping. The throbbing has become an insistent stabbing that feels like a knife to the gut with each jostling step. I grit my teeth, but a sound escapes.

"That's enough," Dawson says. "You look near-on faint, and what good will that do?"

"Least I won't have to listen to you jabber," I mutter.

"My jabbering is better than your groaning, now come on." He leads the horses down a gentle incline. After a good half hour of elevating my foot—and a couple hearty gulps of whiskey—we set off again.

This continues, with our stops growing longer and more frequent until we finally call it a night. A second day passes much the same, our pace plodding across fields of wildflowers and tall grasses drying in the autumn sun. My ankle is near beyond help, fat and violet.

"You sure it's not broken?" Dawson peers down at me the next time we stop, throwing a long shadow across the prairie. He drops to his haunches and reaches for my shin. I could give him hell for taking liberties, but his fingers are methodical, prodding along the bone.

"Well?" I ask.

He gently lifts my leg and carefully moves my foot, his other hand feeling the ankle joint. I grimace and suck in a breath.

"I don't think so," he says.

"Do you even know what you're doing?"

Dawson settles my foot back to the ground. "A bit. My uncle's a sawbones."

"Your uncle?" It's hard picturing him with a family, a history beyond the one tied to mine.

"He about raised me. Took me and Ma in after my pa died."

Knowing he's also lost his father sends a twinge through my heart. A beat later, I remember he's the reason I lost mine.

"It's hard, losing a father." I'm not sure why I say it. I certainly don't intend to console him. Maybe I want to see the hurt those words can bring, prove he's suffering the same pain he's inflicted on me.

Dawson's gaze shifts away from me, and he tugs at his beard. "Wouldn't know," he says, voice breezy. "He died at Antietam. Same day I was born, come to find out. Put a damper on celebrations all my life, but I never knew him to miss him."

Lucky you. The thought catches me around the throat, fills my stomach with guilt-laced vinegar. I wouldn't trade my good memories of Pa, not even if it meant taking away the ache of missing him. Not even to loosen the weight of his death on my shoulders.

◇━◦━━◦━◇

WE ENTER ANOTHER WOODED STRETCH, slowing our already glacial pace to account for the underbrush. When Dawson suggests another break, I shake my head.

"At this rate, it'll be winter before we reach Bluff City." I doubt we're much less than five days away—at best. My first four days with the posse flew by compared to the same number spent with Dawson.

"Look," he says, "the river's there. Let's make camp, and we can follow it all the way to Bluff City starting tomorrow."

Sure enough, the trees thin out ahead. "It's not even close to sundown."

"It will be soon enough."

"How do you know it's the right river?" After all, the Missouri forks and twists all over the state. Considering my posse crossed near Rocheport a full day before we found Dawson, chances are we're nearing an offshoot.

Dawson blows a heavy breath through pursed lips. "All due respect, Miss Lady, I been traveling this fine country a lot longer than you."

My eyes narrow, but I let him have that one. I've learned from my brothers that when a man thinks he knows right, it's best to just let him keep thinking it until I've got the evidence to prove otherwise.

"Give me a bit more whiskey," I say instead, "and I can push on another hour." I've been leaning on it something fierce today.

He shakes the flask. "Nearly out." He hands it to me anyway. The burn no longer makes me grimace—and the warmth in my bones isn't as numbing. All it seems to do is make my tongue feel heavy and my eyesight wobble if I turn my head too fast.

We break through the trees onto the bank. This river is narrow and a deeper blue-green than I've ever seen the brown waters of the Missouri.

"Well, shit," Dawson says. He peers up and down the length, across then behind us. I wait for him to reorient himself, enjoying the moment now that I'm the one who's right.

"Figured out where we are yet?" I raise my voice over the whiskey-fuzz in my ears.

He picks at the beige-stained bandage covering his ear and squints at the river.

"See," I say, "Missouri is full of rivers, not just the one—"

"Yup," he says loudly. A muscle jumps in his cheek as I bite my own to keep from laughing outright. "Must be the Osage."

"*Must* be."

He darts a glare at me. "Least we're still headed in the right direction."

That wipes the smirk off my face.

"Well, come on. Might as well cross it before making camp."

"You want to cross it now?" Following the river was one thing, but crossing at dusk? Shadows already crowd the oaks overhanging the far bank. What's more, I'm wearing the whiskey tight enough to sour my stomach and trip up my thoughts. I almost point out I'm in no condition to wade into moving water, but if Dawson hasn't noticed, I won't be the one to tell him.

"I'd rather not follow this particular river to its confluence," he says, his voice tight, "seeing as how that would put us rather close to Jefferson City and the state penitentiary."

My lungs seize like I've been running too long, but I'm not the wanted criminal here. Still, he's got a good point. If I want justice served back home, we can't risk him being discovered near the capital.

The sky is still a faded gray-blue, but a half-moon already hangs, limp and pale, overhead. "We could wait until morning to cross, though," I say.

"We go now, we won't be riding soaked."

"Just shivering all night."

"So we build a fire. It'll give us time to dry out without losing daylight. Don't know 'bout you, but I'd rather not deal with saddle sores on top of my busted ear."

Considering I'm dealing with an injury of my own, I rather think Dawson's becoming a mite crotchety. Then again, I've never suffered through a bullet wound, however minimal his appears.

Beneath him, Sal stamps her white-booted foot.

I don't need her impatience too. "You're suddenly so pressed for time?"

He groans. "You're suddenly not? All day, every day, it's 'let's go, let's go,' and now you hesitate? Sorry I was wrong about which river this is. Only way to make up that time is to keep going." He lifts his hat and shoves a hand through his hair, cursing when his fingers hit bandage. "Besides, you already drank the last of the whiskey, so it's now or never."

"Is that what this is about? The whiskey?"

He swings off his horse. "It's not that deep, and we're losing light. Stay on your horse if you want, I'll lead them both across."

Reds and oranges reach along the horizon like a warning. A silty, river scent mixes with the dead foliage at our backs. Dawson tugs at Huck's reins. My fingers tighten around them, the leather biting my palms.

"You don't need to lead me like I'm some fancy lady." I slide from the saddle and suck in a hissing breath when my ankle takes some of my weight.

A flash of contrition lights in Dawson's eyes as he reaches for my elbow. "I'm sor—"

I jerk away—thank the Lord I'm still holding on to Huck, or I might have toppled myself. "No, you're right, time and whiskey's wasting. It'll only be worse tomorrow." I wave a hand at the river. "Lead on."

The river comes up to my waist. It's cold enough to numb my legs and shock my mind clear. Despite the pain in my toes, the chill does bring some relief to my ankle, at least.

As orderly as my thoughts have become, my limbs only feel more leaden. Huck moves at a clipped pace, ready to be out and dry again, and I struggle to match my plodding steps to her confident ones across the slick-stoned riverbed. We're nearing the opposite bank when my foot slides on a moss-slimed rock and lodges under a submerged log.

"Blast it all." I wobble, and Huck's reins slip from my fingers. "Wait!" I try to whistle. Nothing but a dry hiss gets past my chapped lips and sandpaper tongue. *Damned whiskey.* Huckleberry continues to shore, but I'm stuck. Without anything to brace myself against, the gentle pull of the current makes my already impaired balance precarious.

"What are you doing?" Dawson calls.

"My foot's caught." I submerge my arm to my shoulder, but the water's too deep. I can't reach my ankle without going fully under. I straighten and give my leg another tug, gritting my teeth against the wrenching in my already-injured joint. When that doesn't work, I fill my lungs, count to three, then drop below the surface.

My leg sinks deeper through the jagged bark, the angle all wrong to work free on my own. I break the surface, gasping.

I'm working up the nerve to swallow my pride and ask for help when I glance at the bank. Dawson stands there, horses in hand, and even in the encroaching darkness, his thoughts are plain on his face.

He's got both horses. All our remaining supplies and weapons. And no real allegiance to me.

"JD?" I hate how scared I sound. It's like hearing the fear in my own voice is all it takes for me to feel it, washing over me colder than the river water. My molars clatter together. If he turns and leaves, I'll die out here. Even once I make it free of the river, how far can I get on foot, injured, with no protection, no food or water?

His name seems to have stirred him from his thoughts. He drops the reins and charges back into the river.

"I got you," he says, reaching for me.

I grab his arm and pull—it's just the leverage I needed. My foot rips free, and we stumble, splashing our way to dry land. Damp, cold earth never smelled so inviting. We lie on the bank and suck in air. Dawson starts to laugh.

The sound kills the relief, slowly thawing my limbs. "I told you crossing at dusk was a bad idea."

His laughter peters out. "You're just mad I saved you, yet again. That's three times now, by my count."

"Your counting's flawed."

"How so?"

I push back a damp strand of dark hair stuck to my cheek and hold up one finger. "I rescued myself from those miscreants." A second finger. "Just now, all I needed was something to grab onto—a tree or rock would have done the job just fine." I pause at three, thinking over our limited time together. "I don't even know what you're claiming for the third."

"Why, I helped you back to camp the first time you hurt your ankle."

He turns onto his good ear, facing me. Moonlight washes him silver, catches on the golden hairs in his beard. "You get injured a lot?"

Despite the cool night chilling my wet clothes, heat flourishes in my cheeks. "Not usually."

"That's a relief. Was starting to think you're dead weight."

My jaw clenches tight enough to give myself a headache.

"And don't think I didn't notice you calling me JD." His elbow drives into my upper arm. I blink at the gathering stars, missing my chance to shove him back before he climbs to his feet. "Let's get a fire going before my extremities fall off."

I lie here a moment longer, mulling over his words despite myself. Why *would* he save me—and on more than one occasion? Can a killer also be a hero?

A small voice buzzes at the back of my mind, tiny as a gnat and nearly as elusive. *Pa was.*

I swat it. All Pa's killing took place during the war. Wasn't anything cold-blooded about it.

That damn gnat again. Neither was Dawson's shot.

He's whistling to himself somewhere behind me. I try to comfort myself with thoughts of his upcoming trial and inevitable hanging but give up and join him beside a just-struck flame.

9

OUR ESCAPADE LAST NIGHT HAS MOTTLED MY entire foot
plum and charcoal, the bruise crawling up my calf when I remove
my sock in the morning to check. JD watches me across the campfire
embers with bleary eyes. He didn't get much sleep, if his shuffle-and-
huff sounds were any indication. The rich scent of heating coffee wraps
around us.

"Some cold river stones might help," he offers. He sways as he stands,
then disappears through the trees, returning with an armful of rocks.

Now that he's called me on it, I figure might as well continue refer-
ring to him as JD. For all his smugness, I suppose he's earned it—not
that I'd give him the satisfaction of thinking I agree, but he *has* proved
himself beneficial often enough. I might as well call him what he wants.
Least, that's what I tell myself, ignoring that pesky, too-honest voice
warning me we're becoming close.

The frigid stone against my bruise does calm the worst of the ache.
Compared to the chill, JD's hand feels hot on my skin. When I glance
up to thank him, I'm eye level with the dingy cotton covering his bullet
wound.

"When's the last time you changed that bandage?" I lift my hand, but he moves out of reach. Doesn't much matter—the rancid stench assaults my nostrils. "I think your ear's infected."

"It's healing, that's all."

"Let me see it."

"It's fine." He huffs but shifts his way back to my side. The bandage over his shot-off earlobe is crusted yellow-brown, the wound beneath oozing enough to make me gag. JD hisses when the air hits the ragged flesh.

"It's gonna be worse when I clean it," I warn. "Didn't you say your uncle's a doctor?"

JD scowls. "It's not like I hung on his every word. You bandage a wound, it heals, the end."

I shake my head. When he was twelve, Cole got a splinter lodged deep in his palm. Didn't even realize it was a problem till the hand swelled, all red and hot. The surgeon lanced the wound to drain out the pus, then cleansed it with hot water and smeared some sort of salve all over the place, which seemed to do the trick. If only I'd paid more attention, I might know what to do here beyond heating some water.

"Well, we'll get it cleaned properly and hope that helps."

"You worry too much."

He's probably right—in fact, I should be wishing him ill. Dying a slow, agonizing death from a gunshot wound to the earlobe seems a just punishment for my father's killer. Perhaps this is as God intended.

Instead, I find myself stirring up the fire when I should be smothering it. I hate how high the sun has gotten without an inch of ground gained, but neither of us are fit to travel.

Sitting side by side in the grass suddenly feels too intimate once I'm turned to have a better vantage. My good leg is tucked beneath me, leaving a respectable gap between us, but every so often, his back brushes my knee. Heat crawls up my thigh. There's no denying JD's attractive, despite what he's done, and the pain he's surely feeling lends a certain vulnerability to his dark eyes. Inspecting his ear makes it too easy for my gaze to drift, following the bearded line of his jaw to his lips.

My brain knows better, but my body is responding—lungs tightening, heart quickening—no matter the *who* or *why* of the current situation.

My hands tremble when I dip a bandana into the pot of boiled water. Short, quick jabs at the shining, stinking wound hide the worst of my tremor. JD grunts and leans away.

"Hold still." I reach for him again. His back is pressed firmly against my knee now.

"It hurts." He bats away my swipe.

"It's gonna hurt. It's *infected*, numbskull."

He dodges my next attempt, so I take a fistful of his hair to hold him in place. His fingers dig into the dirt between my knees, and his jaw clenches so tight it's a sharp line beneath his beard. He hisses and moans, but I manage to get his ear cleaned and a new bandage applied.

When I'm done, he pulls away with a scowl. "Real gentle touch you've got."

"You picked the wrong line of work if nurturing's what you're after."

He grimaces, but when his gaze shifts past me, he stills. *The posse?* My heart pounds as I turn to find a woman not three paces away, staring down at us with her hands on her hips. Three squirrels hang by their tails from a belt at her waist.

"You're not gonna get very far with that ankle," she says by way of greeting.

I want to ask where she's come from, but I'm too stunned to form words. JD is the first to recover, naturally. "Well, howdy, ma'am."

"Don't 'ma'am' me, son, I'm not that old." Her long, reddish-brown braid is streaked heavily with gray, wisps of it curling around a tanned, lined face, making me think she *is* that old—old enough, at least. "It's rare to get folks wandering these parts. Y'all lost?"

"Passing through," JD says. I want to point out we're not wandering *anywhere*, given our current state. "I'm JD, and this here's Maggie." He stands and holds out his hand to the stranger while I shake my head. Giving our real names like some kind of goose, what is he thinking?

"Jane," she says simply, grasping his hand firmly enough that he blinks. She nods to me. "Welp, might as well help get you fixed up so you can be gettin' on your way."

"Just like that?" It's the first I've spoken, and maybe I should have tempered my tone into something approximating gratitude, but I can't help the suspicion pooling out.

"Don't go calling me a Good Samaritan, now." Jane barks a laugh. "I like my privacy, is all, and like I said, you won't get gone with a busted foot, so it would behoove me to help you rather than leave you to the wildlife. I got some old remedies that should help." She glances at our packs. "And if you've got some coffee you can spare, I'd accept that trade."

JD shakes his head, but I speak before he can claim all the coffee for himself. "Deal." This time, I'm the one sticking out my hand for a firm shake.

Despite her gruff appearance, as Jane makes her way to my side, a warm, comforting feeling steals over me—like when Ma would coo over a skinned knee or scraped elbow. Like everything will soon be put to rights. She kneels beside me and reaches toward my ankle. There's a question in her eyes now, so I nod. She takes my bad foot between her hands, running her fingers over it similar to the way JD did earlier. She sucks in a breath, her tuts more reprimand than any lecture Ma might give.

"You've made a rightful mess of this, haven't you?"

She isn't looking for an answer, which is handy because she doesn't seem to catch the glower I direct at the top of her head. From the satchel at her side, Jane pulls out a cloth-wrapped bundle and a glass vessel the size of a whiskey bottle. It's full of clear, slightly cloudy liquid and long, thin strands of bark. She unwraps the cloth to reveal large, wilted cabbage leaves. "You're lucky I grabbed my healing kit on my way out to check the traps. Always handy to have, but sometimes I don't bother with it."

Jane lays the cabbage leaves on a rock to warm beneath the sun, then dabs the cloth with the tincture. With soft, quick strokes, she spreads the solution over my entire bruise.

JD stands, but Jane puts a halt to whatever he's thinking of doing.

"You can stay right there while I work," she says. "I'm not fool enough to let you go skulking out of sight only to attack me from behind as I fix up your lady." Her cool gaze clicks from JD to me and back again. "Rest assured, you'd have one hell of a fight on your hands if you try anything."

JD raises his hands. "Was just going to get your coffee beans together."

"It'll wait." Jane nods to the ground beside me. "Go on, sit there. You can brew me up some coffee to drink if you're needing to feel useful."

I bite at the corners of my lips to keep from grinning at how she handles JD. He squats obediently to my right, stirring up the fire and moving the pot with the remains of this morning's coffee back to the heat.

Jane wraps the sun-warmed cabbage around my ankle, then secures it with a bandage and nods. "That should do for now. You'll want to change the leaves in the morning." She puts the remaining leaves back in the cloth and passes it to me before accepting the mug of coffee JD offers.

"Thank you," I say.

She takes a long drink, then lets out a satisfied breath. "It's been a minute since I've had real coffee."

"Don't tell me you bother with chicory root," JD says, commiseration in his voice and a grimace around his mouth.

"Beats trekking to a town unless absolutely necessary," Jane shoots back. Her attention turns to enjoying her coffee, both hands wrapped around the tin mug, breathing in the steam.

A breeze stirs the leaves overhead, shaking the tiny, black fruit of farkleberry trees. Cole's favorite—not for the berries, which are dry and mealy, but the name sends him into such giggles that Jonah and I made it a habit of pointing out whenever we come across them. Even now, the thought makes me smile. Guess Jane's not the only one nostalgic for comforts of the past.

We sit in something akin to amicable silence as she finishes her cup.

"And how 'bout you?" she says with a jerk of the chin toward JD. "Could patch that ear up if you got anything else to trade."

"We've got some fine burley tobacco," I offer. Once again, why I'm helping him, God only knows.

JD darts a glare my direction. "Was hoping we could trade that for more whiskey at some point," he mutters.

Jane rummages in her kit. "Would brandy do? Got a bottle of apple brandy somewhere... ha!" She holds up a small bottle of rich, amber liquid. "Your tobacco for my brandy and a poultice for your ear?"

"Done." JD reaches for the bottle, but she pulls it into her chest. "Let's see the tobacco."

JD glances at me before scowling at her. "Am I allowed to get up now?"

"Just keep it slow, hands where I can see them."

JD eases toward the horses, hands outstretched at his sides. Slowly, he lifts the flap of Sal's saddlebag, one hand still up in surrender, then produces the pouch of tobacco. Once he's rejoined us, Jane sets about packing a poultice of purple coneflower roots and black walnut leaf tea. She presses it against JD's swollen, mangled earlobe, and he doesn't flinch at her touch. In fact, I do believe I hear him let out a sigh. Why that bothers me, I can't say.

As the day wears on, Jane keeps finding reasons not to leave. She helps JD tend the horses, goes with him to refill our canteens with fresh water, rolls a cigarette with her newly acquired tobacco.

The sun is well past its apex by this time. Jane squints up through the foliage, then sighs out a stream of smoke. "Suppose the rest of my traps will keep until tomorrow. Might as well eat together before I leave you, seeing as how it'll be dark soon." She grins. "Makes it harder for you to follow me home."

"You could take us at our word," I say. JD nudges me hard with his elbow.

"Squirrel and beans sounds mighty good," he says, eyeing her belt.

Jane narrows her eyes, but all she says is, "Get that fire stirred up."

For all her brusqueness, I do believe she's enjoying our company.

"Here, this might help the pain some." She passes me what's left of her smoke, then starts skinning one of the squirrels.

A gentle buzzing fills my ears as I finish off the cigarette, and it feels like a layer of film is spreading just beneath my skin, like pond scum in the summer.

"How long have you lived out here?" JD asks Jane.

"Wouldn't you like to know?"

"Just making conversation."

Jane puckers her lips. "Going on seventeen years now, by my reckoning."

"How'd you come to be stuck so far in the woods? Husband move you out here?" I ask. That would be just like a man, uprooting his wife only to leave her all alone. A shiver runs across my shoulders as I recognize Ma's voice in that thought.

Jane snorts. "No husband. Never seen the need. In fact, that's how come I'm out here. Only way to ensure my privacy and peace of mind."

Her words stir something inside me. Here's living proof that independence is indeed an option. "Don't you get lonely?" The question slips from me before I can reconsider.

Jane eyes me a moment across the fire. Her gaze drifts to JD, to where our shoulders brush every now and then. I shift to increase the space between us. A cool draft rushes to fill it.

"Truth be told, it is nice to have someone to talk to now and then," she finally says, confirming my suspicions over why she's lingered so long. "As for more intimate companionship, that's never appealed to me."

My face warms with the insinuation that JD and I have any sort of intimate relationship, and I'm thankful for the heat of the flames before me. Then her words fully sink in—however appealing the thought of carving out my own life on my own terms might be, I'd certainly miss companionship of all variety. It doesn't seem fair to have to be one or the other.

She's taken a small pipe and satchel from her kit. Carefully, she packs the pipe with dried herbs from the satchel and lights it, taking a deep puff. The spicy scent is reminiscent of the tobacco taste coating my mouth, mixed with a muskier odor. She's passed it to JD, who holds it out to me as he blows a stream of smoke over his shoulder.

"It's *kinnikinnick*," JD says, as if I have any idea what that is. "Indian tobacco, mixed with other herbs. Sage, hemp flower. It'll help."

I only ever sneak smokes with Della, and the salt-spice fumes curling around us now make me miss her with a stabbing ache. In all my fantasies of adventure, she's always been right there beside me.

The pipe makes its way around our circle twice more before I start to notice the night has gone fuzzy around the edges. Beside me, JD lets out a low chuckle.

"Why, Miss Jane, I do believe you are trying to impair our sensibilities," he says in that way of his, accusing and amused all at once. "Could be you're the one looking to take advantage of us."

That makes her cackle. "Thought did cross my mind. But seeing as how you could come after me in the morning, my only recourse would be to slit your throats before making off with your things, and truth be told, I like you too damn much."

"Plus, you ain't seen the way this one fights." He nods at me. I scowl and mutter, "*Haven't.*"

"Nor you, me," Jane shoots back.

Twilight blurs the shadows between the trees, gives her a phantom glow in the firelight. JD uncorks the brandy and tilts the bottle toward Jane in a toast. "To mutually ensured destruction, then."

After his swig, he passes Jane the bottle, who sends it back around to me. I take a tentative sip. Fresh, fruity flavor bursts across my tongue.

"Well," Jane says with a slap to her thighs, "guess I'll be gettin' on, then."

"Sure you'll be all right making your way on your own?" JD asks. Both Jane and I glare at him so fast he raises his hands. "Just meant you're welcome to stay, share our fire tonight."

Jane contemplates the fire, like she's weighing whether it's worth sleeping beside. Part of me hopes she'll join us, worries her leaving will pop the little bubble floating around us. A grin tugs at her lips even as she shakes her head. "Nah. Delightful as the pair of you are, I've had my fill of company. Thanks all the same."

We say our farewells, and she disappears between the trees as silently as she arrived. We're quiet, too, both of us watching the woods. After a few breaths, I realize I don't know what I'm looking at or why. I shake my head to clear it, but it only feels foggier.

"What a strange woman," JD murmurs.

"I envy her freedom." I almost don't realize I've spoken aloud, then JD snorts.

"Becoming a hermit ain't really freedom." Before I can correct him, he leans closer. "*Ain't.*" He laughs and tugs the brandy from my loose grip. "Why do you hate that so much?"

I don't even know why, truth be told. I start laughing too. "Ma spent so much time correcting us, it stuck, I guess." I pause, summoning a high-pitched, exaggerated twang. "'You *ain't* gonna get a husband if you keep talkin' like you *ain't* got a lick o' sense.'" A long sigh leaves me. "Sometimes I think she hated Pa for taking us from Baltimore and all the culture and education back East."

"Well, she should be real proud, considering how quick you are to correct everyone. I'm sure it'll do wonders to land you the perfect husband."

I snort so vehemently my nose tingles all the way up to my eyes.

"There's that sophistication," JD adds, laughing. I join him, fits of giggles that spark tears in my eyes. "So, Baltimore, eh? Was born in Annapolis myself."

"Like hell you were." *What are the odds?*

He cuts me a narrow-eyed glance, lips twisted down. "Upset you're not the only 'cultured' one here?"

"I hardly think birthplace accounts for all of one's sophistication."

He just smirks.

JD and I are on our backs now, staring at the stars and passing the bottle of brandy back and forth. Between that and the hemp-flower smoke still lingering over us in a haze, my foot feels much better. And not just my foot—my entire body has relaxed on the leaf-strewn ground.

JD props his arm behind his head. "You telling me you don't have a man waiting for you in Bluff City?"

I forget what we were talking about, but I shake my head. "I've had offers, sure. A couple widowers needing mothers for their children—one of whom was over twice my age, by the way. There are only so many young women in Bluff City, after all." Sidney Ritter's proposal flashes in my mind. "The idea of sliding into a ready-made family never appealed to me, funny enough."

"A shortage of women can't be the only reason."

"Are you going to try to tell me *I'm pretty*?" I ask, batting my eyelashes. I've heard enough cowboy talk to know I'm not a man's ideal of beauty—at least not enough to be *only* pretty. Della's always been the one with the hourglass curves and creamy skin.

"Pretty's for paintings. Dresses. A fresh-caught trout. You're no fish, Margaret."

I can't tell if that's a backward compliment or insult. "Thank you?"

He takes a noisy gulp from the bottle and sighs into the night. The stars blur, halos the exact blue-shade of Wyatt Murray's eyes. The thought of him surprises me, and it's not unpleasant, which surprises me even more.

"Suppose there is one fella," I say. "He's my age at least and has all his teeth."

JD laughs and holds out the bottle. "What more could you ask for?"

"Plus, he's real kind to my ma, and my brothers like him."

"What's the problem?"

I blink at him, the bottle still raised between us. My fingers close around the warmed glass neck. "There is no problem."

"Sounds like there's a 'but' coming."

JD's right. There's always been some unspeakable "but" in the back of my mind where Wyatt's concerned. I take a sip, considering, then pass him the bottle back. Jane comes back to mind. "Sometimes, I think the only way to be happy is to leave home for good. I don't want to be stuck somewhere."

I've never spoken that out loud. I'm not sure why I do now, only that it's a truth I need to share with someone. I don't know what I expect him to say. *So leave,* or *Wouldn't marriage do that for you?* And I'll have to explain how disappointed Ma is that I'm not some china doll for her to play with then hand over to the first man to ask. That I won't be satisfied tending to children or cooking meals while my man is out, riding around the farm with the wind in his face.

JD's quiet instead. Bats screech into the night, searching for a home. The brandy-warmth retreats from my fingertips, curls tighter into my chest.

"It's why I did," he finally says softly. "It was more complicated than that, but it's the same old story. Girl I loved chose the son of the local doctor instead, so I didn't see much cause in sticking around. Left town seeking adventure, and boy did it find me." He spreads his hands overhead, indicating our current predicament as his adventure, no doubt.

"Thought your uncle was a doctor?"

"Yup."

"The *local* doctor?"

He makes a sound of assent in the back of his throat.

"Did your cousin know how you felt?"

"Welp, considering she broke off our engagement to marry him, I'd say they both had an inkling."

His voice stays casual enough, but I can't imagine shouldering the weight of such a betrayal. Just the thought makes me want to break something, yet here he is, cool as a spring morning. Something shifts in my chest—let's call it pity, even if it feels a touch more like sympathy.

I roll to face him. "JD... I'm sorry."

"Ah." He shrugs, but his eyes on the stars have gone distant. "She made the right choice. I imagine she feels a surge of self-righteousness every time she passes my Wanted poster." After a couple blinks, he takes a long swig from the bottle. "So, where would you go if you left for good?"

I settle back, thoughts drifting from Wyatt to Della. How we'd page through *Colton's General Atlas,* the battered book left behind after her tryst with a railroad baron. Our fingers tracing mountain ranges and rivers.

"Montana Territory." It's the most recent location I'd settled on, though my destination changes with each turn of the yellowed pages.

"You like the cold?"

"Better than the heat." Della already has a whole wardrobe of fur-lined cloaks and stockings designed in her head.

"You might do all right there, then. Me, I'm headed straight for Colorado—"

"I know," I say, but he keeps talking anyway.

"—get a bit of land to share with a nice local girl, raise a few kids together."

"That sounds nice." It's funny, JD's idea of paradise doesn't sound quite as suffocating as the prospect Ma keeps pushing at me. It actually *does* sound nice when put so simply.

We're quiet for a bit, just watching the stars twinkle overhead. I hear JD turn to me, but I don't pull my gaze from the sky.

"He should give you the stars, whoever you choose. Don't settle for someone just 'cause they got all their chompers."

I think of what Jonah said, our second day on the trail—it feels like ages ago now. How Wyatt responded to my calls for help. Maybe my brother was right—in my darkest moment, I cried out, and Wyatt found me. He's always shown up when needed.

A smile spreads across my lips. "I think Wyatt could do that, if I let him. At least, I know he'd try." The thought leaves me feeling settled, like an important piece has shifted into place. I roll to face JD again and find him grinning back. The fire has died down some, but there's still enough glow to catch on his teeth, turn his gaze to honey.

"Hey," he says, "anyone ever told you you got flecks of gold in your eyes?"

"My pa always said 'there's gold in them ponds.'" My voice hitches, and my heart crumbles. I turn back to the blurring sky. Blame the drink or the smoke, but I can't hold back the crushing wave of loss. It crashes over me, presses me into the ground, threatens to drown me.

JD shifts, but I'm too busy trying to breathe to pay him much mind. Inside, I scramble for my anger—my hatred for JD or my fury over my own impotence. All that greets me is sorrow.

This is wrong. We've grown too close in these shared confessions. If I break in front of him, I'll never be able to regain any semblance of control.

His hand settles over mine, and what little fight I was picking disappears. In this moment, in the tiny, warm space caught between our fingers, I'm not alone. Nothing else matters. I turn onto my ear, full of words but aching for silence. He's still watching me, his gaze gone pensive.

Then something unexpected happens.

I kiss Jedidiah Dawson.

It takes a moment for either of us to realize what's happening. *Wait, this isn't the way to avoid the pain*—as soon as my senses kick in, JD's hand is cupping my face, pulling me closer even as that tiny voice tells me I should be pulling away. He's here, and he's listening, and I know there's a reason this shouldn't be happening, but for the life of me I don't want to remember what it is.

His lips are warm and a little salty, his breath sweet with brandy. My fingers, careful of his bandage, find his hair, raking across the back of his head as his other arm comes around my back.

My first kiss was Wyatt Murray, behind the schoolhouse, on a black-dog dare. We were eleven. Since then, I've locked lips with a handful of ranch hands and cowboys. Maybe I was acting out, secretly proving Ma wrong, proving I'm desirable. That nonsense stopped last spring, and I can't say I've missed the hurried tongues or fumbling hands.

This is nothing like any of those kisses. This is everything. It's poetry and music and sunbursts I feel down to my toes.

It's pure magic. And it's with Jedidiah Dawson.

10

I WAKE NESTLED AGAINST JD, my head throbbing. My mouth feels coated in river sand. I shove free of his arms and sit up, only to have the throb turn to a shooting pain behind my eyes.

"Morning." JD sits up with a groan. "Remind me never to drink a stranger's homemade brandy again."

All I'm able to get out is a breath of a laugh past my churning stomach. I glance at him, and the moment our eyes meet, I remember. My already warm face heats further at the memory of last night.

His eyes widen, and he mutters an oath. I turn away before he can say anything to complete my humiliation. I can hear him roll to his knees and stagger into the woods. My hands cover my face.

What is wrong *with me? How could I be so stupid?* There was right, and there was wrong, and now I've gone and muddied the two. I should be angry—furious even. Instead, I'm wrapped in a cloud of confusion, as if I no longer know my own mind. A more honest person than I might admit, there's a new curiosity fogging the air. I've gotten good at hiding truths, though, and this seems the exact sort of thought to stuff out of sight.

Lord alive, but I wish Della were here. She'd know precisely how to handle this sort of situation. I have no idea how I'm going to spend another week traveling with JD. He seemed as taken aback by the memory of last night as I am, but what if he now expects that sort of thing to continue? He might even think he can try for more than kissing. *God Almighty, tell me that's all we did.* That we're both fully clothed is reassuring, but the brandy has scrambled my brain, and a good portion of last night's memories are as forgotten as the dregs within the bottle.

My stomach lurches, and bile charges up my throat. I vomit into the molding leaves beside me, thankful that at least my headache seems to be easing with each heave.

Something hits my shoulder.

"Here." JD stands over me, holding out a canteen. I take it without a word and swish cold river water between my teeth. "How's your ankle?"

So we're pretending nothing happened? Forget the shared vulnerability and the fact that JD took advantage of the situation. Or maybe I did—who's counting? Either way, was it really *nothing*?

Not that it *can* be anything else. Not with him. So fine, I can live with pretending last night never occurred. In fact, I've never been more grateful for anything in my life. Now I don't have to explain myself or suffer through his perspective.

I take a deep breath to clear my head.

"Doesn't hurt as much today." In fact, with my head and stomach aching the way they do, I haven't noticed my ankle at all. I lean forward and pull off my boot and sock. Jane wrapped it loosely with one of the bandages I'd bought back in Warrensburg, which I slowly unwind. The swelling has gone down, and the bruising is tinging toward green.

"God bless that Jane." I give the foot an experimental roll, and though I won't be winning any footraces any time soon, the joint moves without stabbing me with eye-crossing pain.

"We'll still take it easy today."

"We've lost two days already."

JD tilts his head. "You want to end up like yesterday all over again?"

I know he means my ankle, but my mind goes to his lips on mine, his hands in my hair. As if any affection from him is worth dwelling on.

"We'll just take a break every hour or so," he says quickly, turning to stir up the fire.

We share a pot of beans and the last of the bread for a silent breakfast. The food helps settle my stomach, at least enough to make the idea of riding horseback bearable. Then JD packs up the camp, insisting I sit and elevate my foot for as long as possible before we set out. My eyes keep getting drawn to him moving around the site. His shoulders stretching his shirt as he lifts the saddle onto Huckleberry. His hands tightening the bridle. His grin as he whispers to the horse.

He's a thief and a murderer. He shot Pa.

You know that's not the whole story. My body flushes frozen. It's been nearly six months since I've dissected the details of Pa's death. One night of kisses isn't enough to make me revisit that day. I *refuse.*

"Should about do it." JD pats Sal along her neck and peers down at me. "Need help getting up?"

"Don't touch me."

He recoils as if I've swung for him, as I'd hoped. This is all his fault, after all. He might have accused Jane of trying to impair our thinking, but that's exactly what he did. Talked me into feeling vulnerable and then *kissed* me as if it were as natural as breathing.

I ease myself to my feet, careful not to put my full weight on my bad foot too quickly. The ankle can hold some weight. Thank the Lord too. It means I'm able to get myself in the saddle without any assistance. JD hovers anyway but looks just as reluctant to reach out and steady me as I am to ask for help.

With no real outlet, my rage burns down to embers as we travel. I'd love nothing more than to push Huck as fast as she'll go, let the wind rip away the fury the way it would on long rides after Pa's funeral. We've got too many miles stretching between here and home, and my thoughts are just ordered enough to recognize the waste a full-fledged gallop would be. Instead, I'm stewing in my own vitriol. A vengeful sun heats my shoulders through my shirt, pooling sweat beneath my arms. Horseflies whine, raising itching welts wherever they manage to land long enough to bite.

What's somehow worse is this awkwardness that's settled between JD and me. Neither of us has been able to think of anything to break the tense silence—in my defense, I'm rarely the chatty one.

JD seems to be thinking along the same lines. He heaves in a lungful of air. "About last night...."

"What of it?" I snap. Nothing for it but to come out swinging.

He huffs a humorless laugh. "Well, I was going to apologize—"

"Thank you." A curt nod punctuates my words, and I click Huck faster.

"Hold on, now. Let's not forget who kissed who." His lips twist, a mockery of a smile, and all I'm thinking about is how they felt against mine.

Blame the blazing Missouri sun for the heat flooding my face. "I'd prefer not to think on it at all. Last night's not a memory worth holding on to." Cicadas snicker in the grasses, mocking me and the rejection I felt only hours ago, thinking he felt the same. Still, he needs to know it was a mistake I do not intend on repeating. Or maybe *I* need the reminder. "I *do* recall which of us continued, though."

His voice hardens. "I like to think we share equal responsibility there."

"I'm sure you would."

JD tilts his head back, blinking at me. "You didn't pull away." His voice has lost its cocky edge. Damn my bleeding heart, I can't outright lie and say he forced himself on me.

Hell if I'll admit to enjoying myself, though. "Why would I ever be interested in the likes of you?"

A grin spreads across his face like the tail feathers of a preening peacock. "Most women are. I'm charming as all get-out and handsome to boot. I know you've noticed."

The implication that of the two of us, I'm *not* the one worth looking twice at rears up between us. It shouldn't sting, especially not from the lips of an outlaw.

Damned if it does. One more fault dredged up from the mess of last night.

"Go to hell," I spit because it's all I can think of to end this conversation.

"Halfway there already," he murmurs, but falls blessedly silent after. If only I could quiet the voice in my head as easily. No, she rattles on and on. *You must have straw for brains, thinking for even a second he wanted you. You were just a warm body on a lonely night. Still, here you are, wallowing at the rejection as if you care what Jedidiah Dawson thinks of you. Kissing him was bad enough—what would Pa think, dishonoring his memory twice over?*

A blessed breeze unsticks the loose hairs from my neck. Nothing can unstick the thoughts tumbling around my mind.

The air feels as heavy as the tension still thrumming between us as we ride. By the time we stop for lunch, it would seem JD has reached his breaking point.

"We have to fix this." He gestures between us, as if I don't know exactly what he means.

My heart pounds with something sickeningly like hope. There shouldn't *be* anything to fix, and here I am, wishing we were back on friendlier terms. *Friends?* I snort. "Why? I'm finally getting that peace and quiet I've been asking for."

JD smacks his hat against his leg, dislodging a cloud of dust. "You've got to admit it's been easier traveling the last couple days before all this...." He waves his hat over his head. Like that's enough to encompass a night of kissing, a morning of tension. "Nonsense," he finally murmurs.

Nonsense. Heat builds in my chest, my cheeks, despite a chillness in the breeze. "And just what do you suggest?"

He turns to me and puts his hands on my shoulders. "Margaret, I'm going to kiss you."

I pull back. "What? Absolutely not." It's enough trying to untangle my feelings over last night. No way I'm adding to the confusion by indulging him *or* myself. This has gotten too far out of hand as it is.

"It's the only way."

My mouth hangs open, but no words fall out. More kissing is the last thing I need and the last thing he deserves. Better I shoot him in the leg, remind us both what our exact relationship should be. The sun hides behind a cloud, a small reprieve.

"Look, last night is all wrapped up in this mystical brandy haze. But in reality, you despise me, and I don't much like you either." He doesn't sound convinced on either of our behalf, but I cling to the assertion. We *don't* like each other. "If I kiss you now, it'll prove it wasn't anything special, and we can stop thinking about it."

"Who says I'm still thinking about it?"

"Fine, *I* can stop thinking about it."

I blink at him. For all he nearly insulted me earlier, could he have actually enjoyed himself?

Shut that thought down right there. My heart has no business flitting around like some nectar-drunk honeybee, not over a murdering thief. *Might as well piss on Pa's grave, you selfish bitch.*

His lips twist with a scowl. "You know you're thinking about it too."

"Fine. Let's get this over with." If only to shut him up once and for all.

I hold as still as a corpse as he leans in. His beard scrapes my chin—reeking of sweat, stale alcohol, and last night's squirrel supper—and I grimace. Chapped lips peel at my own. Almost as soon as it starts, it's over, both of us pulling back.

"Well, that was revolting," I say.

"You're no peach yourself." JD spits off to the side as if to prove his point.

"Thanks for that." Despite myself, relief spins out to my fingertips until I'm nearly dizzy with it. I almost want to laugh. To think I'd been worried, even for a second, that *desire* had joined the other, more murderous feelings I have toward JD. I'll just go ahead and lock those thoughts up in the jail cell with all the other things I prefer not to dwell on.

"Least we're back to normal." He adjusts his hat. A gentle rain starts up. Loose, heavy drops speckle the earth and us with it. "I can get back to dreaming about my Colorado lady, and you can run home to your beau."

This reminder of Wyatt, of the things I said about him, extinguishes my growing elation. Like kissing JD, the thought of a life with Wyatt is far less magical in the light of day.

◇━●━◦━━◦━●━◇

THE SILENCE BETWEEN US REMAINS as the afternoon stretches, but at least that heaviness is gone. Now, I'm the only one dragging my thoughts down—wishing I could recapture that *rightness* I felt thinking about Wyatt last night. A future with him seems hollow, though, and somehow less appealing than the one Sidney Ritter offered me two months ago. At first, I'd hated Sid for what seemed like spitting on all his late wife had given up for him....

He'd cornered me in the general store, back by the rolls of barbed wire.

"I know your family's hurtin' for cash," he said with hardly any preamble.

Heat licked up my neck. Thank the good Lord we were tucked far from the front windows—the dimness hid my humiliation. "Where'd you hear that?"

His head tilted. The gaslight overhead caught on his face, making his burnt-gold skin fairly glow, and washed the green from his pale eyes. He grinned, but it didn't lessen the predatory intensity of his gaze. My bones felt ready to flee, with or without the rest of me.

"Jonah's my best friend," he finally said.

Blasted Jonah and his fat mouth.

"Also, Bluff City's a small town. People talk."

One of the benefits of living outside the town limits—or so I thought. Murmuring voices drifted from the front of the store. More folks gossiping?

"Look," Sidney went on, voice low, "I can cover your debts."

"Why would you do that?"

He just stared at me again. Even with the new lines on his face from recent hard times, Sidney's not half bad-looking. Probably the most attractive of the wife-seeking men in town. Too bad that's all Sidney had going for him—well, that and his sinful amount of money.

And now he was making me wait for a simple answer to a straight-forward question. My right eyebrow arched.

His hands opened in an apathetic sort of shrug. "Got them kids needing a ma."

The urge to slap him rose up, strong enough I almost lost all sense and followed through. "Are you trying to buy my hand?"

"If that's what it takes."

"Maybe you spend too much time with whores to realize most women can't be bought."

"Maybe you're too young to know most women can be." He stepped back—I hadn't even noticed us both leaning in. "Whores've just figured out how to make a business of it."

"Oh, they're making it a business? Seems to me you're the one who benefits most." He owns the Bell and Iron, after all.

"Hey, I give those women refuge from a world that's turned its back on them. They got to earn their keep, sure, but it's up to them how they do it."

I snorted. "So if Della only wanted to dance and sing, she could?"

"That's all plenty of them do." Sidney's voice went from bemused to downright defensive. "They make more on their backs, but I don't put them there."

"Well, aren't you the saint."

His jaw clenched tight, but it didn't stop him from speaking. "You want a say in how I do business, you got to marry me first."

I'd rather marry a slug. "Fortunately our spring wheat looks to be a decent crop this year, so you can take your oh-so generous and romantic proposal and—"

"Oh, you wanted *romance?*" A strange look crossed his face—like a smug grimace. "Afraid I'm plumb out of that. All I can offer is enough money to maybe make someone overlook the whole saloon business."

Damned if I didn't see the moment Sarah's memory took a hold of him. In a single flicker of gaslight, he was stripped bare and bleeding. He turned away, staring at a crate full of pickled eggs, but he couldn't hide the shine in his reddening eyes.

It had been a whole dramatic saga—the banker's daughter cutting ties with her family to be with Sid. If anyone had cause to hate ol' Skinner more than my family, it was Sidney. Leaving aside his occupation, that he's the bastard-born son of a German immigrant and Black woman was unforgivable to Sarah's lily-white folks. Then Sarah died after giving birth to their little boy, and she'd barely been in the ground a week before Sidney came to me, seemingly trying to replace her.

Now, though, I saw how much pain he still carried. Might've seen it sooner if I wasn't judging him so harshly.

"If I loved you, it wouldn't matter," I said because it felt like I should say something.

Sidney raised an eyebrow and choked out a laugh. In that moment, I got a glimpse of the carefree Sid who stole Sarah's heart. "That so?"

"I don't know. I've never been in love. But it seems to make things not matter so much." Makes everyone act foolish and forget their principles, more like. Part of me longed to know what that might feel like.

Sidney let out a bitter sigh. When I looked back at him, he shoved his hands over his dark, tightly curled hair. "Look, I can't give you romance, but I can spare you the broken heart that comes with falling in love."

Pa was suddenly there, filling my mind. I wondered what he'd say. The wheat harvest would barely cover our debts now, sure, but what would happen the next time a tool broke or a harvest was scant? Sidney was offering me security of both home and heart, even if it came with a heavy price. If I truly wanted to take care of my family, it was not a bad deal.

But then I thought of Ma, of the way her eyes would follow Pa around the little house. Her one-sided conversations with him over supper. Pa was a doting father, but that love cooled when turned toward Ma. He tried to love her in little ways—flowers on the table now and then—but his everyday affection was used up on us kids.

"Loneliness is its own broken heart," I said. Marriage seemed trapping enough. I'd have to be crazy to want it, so I guess I was hoping love would be the trick to driving me crazy.

"True enough," Sidney agreed. "Well, think on it anyway. There ain't an abundance of unmarried women in Bluff City, so I might have to ask Widow Maude—"

I couldn't help it, I laughed. Old Maude ran the telegraph office and was about sixty years old. We both checked over Sid's shoulder, but the store was nearly empty.

Sidney's responding grin was more relaxed. He took a long, slow inhale. "That's all I came over to say, so... I'll leave you to it." He gave me a parting nod, and I was left staring at the prickly rolls of barbed wire.

I shake myself from the memory. The only future that's worth dwelling on is the one that sees Pa's killer brought to justice.

◈━◦━━◦━◈

WE'VE STOPPED FOR THE NIGHT where open prairie meets towering oak woods, wildflowers black against the gray tallgrass under a sky dripping stars. Embers glow inside a thin dirt circle, JD a shadowed figure beyond it. A coyote howls, far enough away to be little more than a lonely echo.

"You awake?" I murmur, a tentative question against my own loneliness. As soon as they leave my lips, I want to pull the words back.

"Mm?" The sound is more sleep-grunt than response, and it doesn't matter, anyway. A conversation would just intrude on this feeling growing in my chest that we're somehow both infinitesimal and infinite.

My gaze traces patterns between the stars until my eyelids grow heavy.

Screams in my ears turn to birdcalls as I rip free of my nightmare—lungs heaving, sweat prickling my spine, blanket twisted around my legs. I glance at JD as I scrub a quick hand over my damp cheeks. He's sleeping fast, chest rising and falling in slow rhythm. *Thank heavens.* This isn't my first morning waking up tearstained and rumpled, but each time, I've recovered before he could notice.

I'm stirring up the fire when I spot it looping over his leg—copperhead. Slowly, I pull and cock my revolver. JD stirs, the snake stills.

"Don't move," I say.

His eyes fly open, his hand twitching toward his holster.

"DON'T!"

The copperhead is inches from his fingers.

"Shit," he breathes.

My swallow sounds loud in the silence as I ease my gun forward.

"If you miss...."

"Trust me." My finger squeezes the trigger, and the snake explodes. Before I can even ask if JD's all right, he's up and leaping away through the grass, brushing at his body and spewing curses.

I limp to what's left of the copperhead. Looks like I hit it near center—its head's still intact, snapping at nothing with its final breaths, while the remains of its tail curls and flops a full pace away.

"You about done?" I call.

"Is it dead?" JD pants and wipes at the back of his neck. "Fuckin' hate snakes."

I pinch it just behind the jaw—careful to avoid the venom-filled fangs—and hold up the head. "Did I scare you?" I ask in a nasally voice.

JD swears again. "Don't *touch* it."

I turn it like a puppet to face me. "I think he's kinda cute."

"I'm serious—" he stumbles backward when I turn the head his direction "—damnation, stop! Put it down, Margaret."

"All right, relax." I toss it toward my bedroll. No way I'm letting go of this upper hand so easily. "Good news is we're having snake for breakfast."

JD squats at the edge of our campsite, as white as freshly laundered long johns. "You're a loon."

"You're yella." I've already started prepping the tail to cook. It isn't long before the pop and hiss of roasting meat fills the silence.

After breakfast, I lie in the grass, my ankle propped up, while JD breaks down our camp.

"Any more snakes come exploring, I'm leaving you," he warns.

I ignore him, and he stalks off, muttering to himself. A breeze drifts across my face, bringing with it the scent of doused coals and drying grass. It's too peaceful a moment for the turmoil inside, getting harder to ignore. I can't quit thinking about that snake, how the bolt of fear wasn't for myself, how a protective instinct shouldered it out of the way, so I was reaching for my gun without a second thought. How relief lit through my veins when JD jumped up, perfectly fine.

It's just 'cause he belongs at the end of a noose, not swelling and rotting into the earth. Like with his infected ear or the law trying to bring him in on their terms, I reach for the ready excuse.

It's getting harder to pretend it's the truth, though.

The sun warms my eyelids. I want to let it melt away the rage, but then what? I'll have nothing. No justice for Pa. No vengeance for my family. And worse, nowhere else to put all the sorrow and guilt that still cling to the memory of that day.

Better to hold tight to an assured atonement—however false—than let the likes of Jedidiah Dawson upset everything.

Harnesses jingle as JD saddles the horses, murmuring all the time in a baritone too low for me to make out the words. It joins the music of a chirping squirrel rustling the leaves overhead.

"You 'bout ready?"

I squint one eye open to find JD standing over me. A quick glance around tells me I must have dozed off—the entire camp is packed, save for the bedroll I'm still lying on. We're just waiting on me.

"What is it you say to them?" I ask as we set off. "The horses. You're always talking to them."

"Everything. Horses don't judge the way people do, so I just say whatever's on my mind."

"You think I'll judge you?"

The smallest smile crooks his lips, like only he knows the punch line to a joke he hasn't told. "You most of all."

I don't know what stings more—that smirk or the confidence of his words or the fact he's probably right.

OUR PACE INCREASES OVER THE NEXT FEW days—although still not near as fast as we could go with fresh horses and full health. We descend from the Ozark Plateau, the tallgrasses depositing ticks for us to pull from the horses each time we stop.

Herbert, as I've named my snake head, has spooked JD twice since his untimely death. The first time, I settled him on JD's bedroll as we made camp that night. I'd never heard a man scream before that. Now, thanks to JD's quick-draw reflexes, Herbert is missing about an inch more of his neck, and JD has a bullet hole in his blanket. Fool.

This morning, I got him good again. He asked if I had the dried beef, and when I handed him the snake head instead, he jumped about a horse-height, fell over the back of the log we were sharing, and cursed me to the depths of hell. He still hasn't returned.

I set Herbert on the ground beside me as I cast around for a long stick. We've had our fun, Herbert and I, but I'm not sure I can top that scare, and he's getting a tad rank, so it's time to dispose of him.

Behind me, JD yelps.

"Wha—" I barely have time to dodge JD's kick that sends Herbert into the dying fire.

"That better not have been for me again," he says, voice hard and threatening.

"I'd *planned* to bury him in the coals, else you'd come back and see his little snake eyes watching you from the flames."

I'm not sure he believes me—he stalks off to saddle Sal without another word.

Now, a full two hours and a handful of miles later, he still hasn't spoken to me.

Ordinarily, I'd appreciate the silence, but as the prairie sprawls, I've got to admit—grudgingly and only to myself—how welcome his chatter is to pass the miles. I've even tried starting the conversation four times. Despite my good humor, I'm a little concerned I've broken him.

"You know you have to talk to me sometime," I try again, riding up on his left side.

He suddenly seems very interested in the landscape to our right.

"Have you ever been this quiet for this long? I'm pretty sure you'll choke on all those words wishing to be set free."

A muscle twitches in his cheek, just above the line of his beard.

"Come on, JD. It wasn't even *alive*."

He whips to face me with wide eyes. "You ever intentionally put a live snake anywhere near me, and I will shoot you in the face."

He looks so serious it's all I can do not to laugh.

"Promise." I draw an *X* over my heart. "So I guess this means you don't want to hear about all the times my brothers put snakes down my dress or in my boots or *one time* in my apron pocket. Ma found that one, and she was *not* pleased."

JD has gone milk-pale beneath the brim of his hat. "No wonder you're off your gourd."

<hr />

AS THE TRAIL CONTINUES, WE pass the time sharing more stories. JD tells me about his travels through Indian Territory, and I tell him about Cole's obsession with dime novels.

"Drives Ma crazy, that he's fascinated by outlaws and gunfights. I think he was more upset about the death of Jesse James than our own pa." My breath catches as I realize what I've said—and to whom. It's as if the past few days of surface-level chitchat have been wiped away to reveal that painful gravesite between us.

News came of the outlaw's shooting mere days after Pa bled out, after all. Cole had collected every news article he could find, asking Miss Hazel at the *Bluff City Gazette* to send for papers from Saint Louis, City of Kansas, Jefferson City, Saint Joe's. As if he wanted to build a shrine to a criminal when his own father was dead and gone at the hands of one.

I burned all the articles when I found them. Maybe I shouldn't have, but I hated the way they stacked up next to the single scrap of news ink mentioning Pa's demise that Ma keeps tucked inside the family Bible. Cole refused to speak to me for three whole days, until Jonah stepped in.

JD's voice cuts into my memories. "Bet he'd be envious of you now."

I cast him a sidelong look. "I'll be sure to tell him how distinctly *un*glamorous a real outlaw is."

He lifts a hand to his chest as if I've wounded him. It only makes me think of Pa again.

"Doubt he'd ever even heard of you," I say, "before the bank robbery."

"Ah, the robbery. The source of all my strife. You still haven't heard my side of things."

Nor do I want to.

"Everyone thinks they know, all the papers, the gossip mill, the dime store novels. Thing is, that was my first—my *only*—bank robbery." He shifts his shoulders, a loose grin on his lips, warning I'm in for one of his long-winded oratories. "There I was on the outskirts of Bluff City, scratching at the back of my neck under the itching bandana knot, sun pushing shadows from the trees, waiting on Heinous Hank and his boy to join us."

My shoulders stiffen, my throat clogging with my own memories of that day—a persistent wind threatening to steal my hat, an ominous tangle in my gut. Pa's voice, quiet but insistent, coaxing me the last mile to town after a full morning of riding.

JD doesn't appear to notice my change in demeanor. He smirks. "Apparently, he was an old war buddy of Ansel's. Never got the details, but he must have been something terrible to earn that nickname."

"I hardly think anyone could survive a war without compromising some morals," I snap.

"Well, look at you." JD leans back, an amused tilt to his lips. "Little Miss Right-and-Wrong finding some compassion for those stuck in the in-between."

My teeth grind together. "There's a difference between doing what needs done to survive and wreaking havoc for the thrill of it."

That shuts him up, but only for the space of a couple plodding steps. When next he speaks, his voice has gone hard. "I wanted out. That kind of money can help a man disappear. I don't take thrills in causing others harm, but I'll do what I can to benefit myself."

"So you admit you're selfish?"

"Aren't we all? You gonna let me tell my story or what?"

I gesture for him to continue with an open palm.

"So Heinous showed up, introduced his son as Mayhem." JD's voice melts a little, flows back into the easy, rolling tone he uses for storytelling. I'm trying not to watch him too closely even as I wait for the story to progress, looking for signs he recognizes me from that day. "Me, I like a good nickname, when it fits, and that boy"—he shakes his head— "he sure was scrawny, but the way he eyed the rest of us through the slit between his bandana and brim made me almost reconsider sticking around, just long enough to really see him in action. He was young, too, which woulda been a relief. I was tired of being the 'kid' of the gang."

The longer he takes to get to the meat of the story, the faster my heart kicks. "Are you going anywhere with this, or do you want to talk about this boy all day?"

He cuts me a bemused look. "Hold your horses, I'm just setting the stage. So Ansel lays out the plan—him and Jasper take the front, let everyone know what's going down. Rufus stayed outside, keeping eyes for the law. Me and Heinous were tasked with collecting the money, and the kid was left in charge of the horses.

"The job went better than expected. We knew the sheriff was visiting family a town over, and that the deputy was just a kid, lunching with his mama at a homestead outside Bluff City. Only a few people were in the bank that morning, and Ansel and Jasper kept everyone in line long enough for Heinous and me to fill our bags with cash. It wasn't until we'd started for the door that one old man decided to play the hero. He rose up from the floor, drawing all our attention and Ansel's gunfire."

My mouth opens to stop him, but the words catch briefly in my throat, gone dust dry.

JD's face pinches, almost like he regrets the turn of events. "Then the bank filled with bullets and black powder haze. Heinous took charge, tossed me his sack of money since I was closer to the horses, and pulled his revolver so fast, even I was jealous—"

"I don't want to hear any more," I say. For all I thought I was ready to hear what happened *inside* the bank, to know how JD saw things, my stomach is tied in knots over the next part.

Ansel may have started the shooting at the bank, but it was JD, fleeing with the money, who hit Pa. I don't care that he wanted out, or that he claims to have no killer instinct. All that matters—all that keeps eating at me—is where Pa ended and who put him there.

JD's chin dips and his shoulders slump. He scratches the back of his neck, but I can't tell if it's disappointment or relief he's trying to cover. Maybe he doesn't want to relive that final moment any more than I do. "Guess you know how it ends, anyway, seeing as you hunted me down."

It ends with my father, dead from a bullet to the chest.

JD's version only confirms that he has no idea—he wouldn't have brought it up if he knew I'd been there that day, or just why I've been so invested in hunting him down. The urge to tell him rises, but I swallow it like bile. There's still a noose awaiting him in Bluff City, and he doesn't need any more chances to plead his case. Not even if I could use the reminder myself.

Pa wasn't the villain of JD's story, I tell myself over and over. Finally I'm able to breathe past the lump that has clogged my throat.

"I didn't know the part where you managed to hide all the money," I say. "Where was that, by the way?"

He casts me a sidelong smirk then clucks to his horse.

<hr />

WE REACH THE MISSOURI RIVER the following day, laying low beneath the cover of elm and oak trees as we assess the situation. There's no hope of crossing it the way we did the Osage—the Missouri is at least three times as wide, and Lord only knows its depth. Scouting downriver, I spot a small ferry station. If it can even be called that. It's nothing but a rickety little raft pushed from bank to bank by a stooped old man.

"I say we wait until nightfall and steal the ferry," I say after relaying my discovery back to JD. "Can't be that hard to steer it across, and it's better than finding a bridge closer to a town."

"What, and deprive the man of his livelihood?"

I cross my arms and ignore the needling guilt. "Surprised you care."

He runs an assessing gaze over me, then turns back to feeding the horses. "Surprised you don't."

"We've got to get across somehow. The state penitentiary can't be that far upriver. You really want to risk being spotted in these parts?"

"All the more reason to avoid larceny, don't you think?"

A frustrated groan stirs in my throat, but I swallow it. "What other option is there?"

"Could always try paying him off."

"With what money?"

JD glances at me over his shoulder, but I speak before he can.

"I know, you robbed a bank."

He grins.

"Doesn't explain where you keep pulling it from."

JD scratches his chest and looks downriver.

"Fine," I say, "don't tell me. I'll just search you when you fall asleep."

He steps toward me, closer than is proper. "Man might get the wrong idea if your fingers start wandering in the dark...."

"Forget it." I shove past him so he won't catch me blushing.

I keep a closer eye on him than I have in days, but still, as dusk creeps in and we pick our way through the trees to the ferry station, he hasn't revealed his loot. I'm almost certain I would have noticed if there'd been a roll of money in his pockets when I searched him that first night, but then, I was disoriented from the fight and my only focus had been relieving him of weapons.

The raft comes into view first, tethered to a post on the riverbank. A wrinkled hound sleeps beside the door to a crumbling shack not far off. From within, a warm glow spills through every crack to chase away the encroaching twilight. JD jerks his chin, a silent indication for me to rouse the ferry master.

The dog lifts his head as I approach, his tail thumping the wall hard enough to shake the door.

"All right, Turnip, I'm a-comin'," a tired voice calls. "Get yer behind on in here—"

The door swings wide, bathing me and old Turnip golden. The old man I noted earlier blinks up at me with watery eyes.

"Evening, sir," I say quickly. "I'd like to enlist your services to cross the Missouri this evening."

He waves a gnarled hand. "First ferry leaves at eight tomorrow morning." He shoos Turnip inside and makes to close the door. I catch it with an open palm.

"I'll pay good money to go now."

His lips pucker and wiggle, as if he's literally chewing on my offer. "How much?"

"I—" *Well, damn.* I have no idea how much money JD has, or what might constitute a fair offer. "What'll it take?"

All vestiges of exhaustion leave his countenance as he decides his price. I know I've misstepped, giving him such power, but my heart's pounding too hard for me to think up a way to regain control.

"Three dollars," JD says behind me. He's managed to make the sum sound like a threat.

My teeth grind against a grimace as the old man shifts his attention beyond me. It's my own damn fault he's dismissing me thusly.

JD's offer didn't invite a negotiation, and the ferry master only waits a shaky breath to agree. He tugs his coat from a hook inside the door and whistles for the hound. "Come on, Turnip. One more passage today."

We follow them to the raft and wait for him to haul it onto the bank. A small sign lists prices, the scrawl visible now that we're less than a foot from it. Turns out a man and horse only cost thirty-two cents to ferry across. I give JD a sheepish grin. He runs his tongue over his teeth and keeps his gaze on the old man.

"So, what's yer hurry?" the ferry master asks once we've pushed off from shore.

I glance at JD, but he's busy scratching Turnip's ears. "We just want to be home, that's all."

A breeze cuts down the river, wrapping cold fingers around my neck.

"Oh? And where'd you say that was?" He's watching JD now too. For his part, JD doesn't even pause his movements.

"I didn't," I say.

"Hmm." The man nods. He waits until we've reached the middle of the Missouri to take up the conversation again. "It's just that there been a lotta commotion 'round these parts. All kinds of men comin' and goin', all lookin' for one man in particular. And now here you are, in such a rush you'll pay ten times the cost to get away."

"I'm not a man."

He snorts. "But *he* is."

JD, ever the dramatic, sucks in a long breath and rises from his crouch beside Turnip. "I hope we won't have any trouble, friend."

I nearly fling up my hands. What's the point of all this perfunctory subterfuge if he's going to own up to the man's barely veiled threat? Standing there in his duster with a hand on his holster, silhouetted against the purple sunset shining off the river, JD looks every inch the renegade.

To his credit, the old man doesn't back down. "Son, I lived a long life. You cain't threaten me with anything that ain't already coming sooner than I like."

"We could make you a little more comfortable," I offer.

JD cuts me with a glare, but his hand shifts from revolver to back pocket. "Bring us the rest of the way across—and forget you saw us—and there's an even ten dollars in it for you."

If he hoped for more, the man's at least smart enough to accept what we've offered. We cross the remaining distance in silence, nothing but the lap of water and the sonorous calls of bullfrogs and cicadas breaking the chilly twilight. True to his word, JD pulls a ten-dollar banknote from his pocket and passes it to the ferry master. As we watch him bob his way back to his home, my hand finds my gun.

"Should we kill him?" I'm mostly joking.

JD's gaze crawls over my face—I feel it like something physical, but don't tear my eyes from the ferry. "And here I thought I was the outlaw," he says.

"There's no guarantee he won't alert the law as soon as he reaches dry land." I turn to JD with a carefree shrug. "Besides, he was practically asking for it."

"I think the money will tide him over. *Besides.*" He drags the word out, mocking me. "All he knows is we're north of the Missouri now. Not much for anyone to go on, long as we keep moving."

He tightens Sal's cinch, but I'm not ready to move on quite yet.

"There's still the matter of the money," I say.

"What's the matter?" JD's wide eyes are pure innocence.

"How much more is there?"

"Maybe that was the last of it."

"Last of it, my foot. You wouldn't give it up that easy." I cross to his horse. "Where's the rest?" I lift the flap on his saddlebag.

"Don't go poking through my—"

My breath stalls. With shaking hands, I pull out a battered novel. "When did you take this?" For all the tremble of my fingers, my voice is dead steady.

JD crosses his arms. "A while ago. You clearly haven't missed it."

I clutch *The Adventures of Tom Sawyer* to my chest. "You had no right to it."

Under the rising moon, JD has the decency to look bashful. Rather than apologize, though, he climbs into Sal's saddle. "We should keep moving."

Seriously? He clucks her forward, not waiting to see if I'm coming along. Part of me wants to let him go his own way, and good riddance. My thumb strokes the tattered cover of my book. Letting JD go would rather defeat the purpose of this entire journey, so I grit my teeth and join him on the trail.

◇━━◦━━◦━━◇

IT'S FULL DARK BEFORE WE agree to make camp. Even then, we're stilted toward each other, our growing companionship fractured. Just what I needed to remember who he really is—a thief and a killer. Tall-grass whispers in the night breeze under a sky full of wispy clouds and shining stars, too peaceful a setting for the betrayals piling up between us.

"You mind telling me if Injun Joe ever gets his revenge?" JD's question is hesitant across the fire as we clean up after supper.

Against my will, my eyes dart to my bedroll, where I've stowed the book.

"Last I read," he adds, "he'd just climbed out the window."

I should relish the fact he's been left with such uncertainty. Instead, the reader in me recognizes an opportunity to pour over one of my most beloved tales. If only he'd been upfront about wanting to read it. "Oh, you mean right after Tom broke his vow? How apt."

His eyes narrow. "I only vowed to see you home safe."

"I told you not to go through my stuff."

"And did I *promise* not to?" He raises his eyebrows.

No.

"I only started reading it 'cause you wake me up most nights, crying out in your sleep."

"I do not." There's a churning inside that warns me I'm lying. I don't always remember my nightmares upon waking, but the chill of cooled sweat and dried tear tracks are proof enough.

"Whimpering, calling for your pa...." His gaze, black in the firelight, skims over my face. His tone is softer when he asks, "Want to talk about it?"

"Not with *you*." Why hasn't he mentioned it before now? "Why don't you wake me up?"

"My ma always said it was bad luck to wake a person from a nightmare. Soul might get stuck in the bad dream."

"That's ridiculous." Despite my words, I shiver at the prospect of reliving the moment of Pa's death for eternity. That would be the very definition of damnation, something I am hell-bent on avoiding.

JD stretches his arms overhead, unaffected by his ominous declaration. "Maybe so, but I, for one, wouldn't want to risk it."

His eyes haven't left me this whole time, staring like they might be able to burrow past the surface to see the soul in question. Between us, the fire crackles and spits, showering sparks into the night sky. I consider telling him about my nightmares—about Pa's death—if only to make him stop looking at me like that.

We're so close, little more than a couple days left. It's getting harder to think about that finish line, about turning him over to the hangman, but it's the only acceptable way to see justice done. Once he's dead and gone, hopefully, these nightmares will end. There's a sucking sensation in my gut, warning it won't be that easy, but I ignore it, same as always.

In the meantime, it might be nice to have my favorite story to discuss. Better than revisiting past crimes or looking toward a murky future. I rise, wincing at the twinge in my ankle, and cross to my bedroll. The novel feels like a little piece of home, soft and comforting in my hand. My thumb flutters the page edges.

"Does Joe get revenge?" I repeat JD's question, then toss him the book. He catches it one-handed against his chest. "Guess you'll have to read on to find out."

12

CLOUDS ROLLED IN OVERNIGHT, AND WE WAKE to a heaviness thrumming in the air. Wind sets the tallgrass shivering.

"Storm's coming," JD says, staring up at the fast-moving mass of gray overhead.

The little hairs on my arms raise, and the humidity settles over me like a second skin. "We should try to find shelter." This time of year, the weather can get downright ferocious in no time. JD knows it as well as I do—he's already stowing his bedroll behind Sal's saddle. I hurry to finish saddling Huck, eager to be on our way before the sky breaks.

It isn't long before the first rumbles reach us.

◇━◦━━◦━◇

THUNDER RIPS ACROSS THE PRAIRIE, chasing forked lightning. We pursue it, too, hoping to reach some sort of cover before the rain catches us. The hair on the back of my neck prickles as flashes throw grotesque shadows across our path. Behind, rain pelts the ground hard enough to beat out a warning.

"We're not gonna make it," JD yells over the violent wind.

Ahead, the trees bend away from us. Black clouds are tinged

a violent green, rolling faster than our horses' hooves. This is not a normal storm.

"We've got to," I call back, urging Huck faster. With the wind at our backs, it feels like we're flying. My hair tangles in front of my face, and I push it back with an impatient hand as the first drops splatter onto my shoulders. "Shit."

As if simply waiting for my acknowledgment, the skies open over us. Thunder cracks, loud enough to shake my bones, and a bolt of lightning splits an oak in two. Huck shies away from the flames. I struggle against her primal pull.

The sky has gone black, the wind clawing in every direction. We crest a hill and as we descend, JD yells for us to stop. He swings off Sal and scrambles to undo his bedroll. "Cover her with your blanket then let her go," he calls over the roaring storm.

I land hard on my still-healing ankle but ignore the throb as I work at the saddle strings. I've seen a tornado before, the damage it can do with broken tree limbs and snapped weather vanes. I *don't* know how to protect against one, though, so the fact that JD seems assured is the only thing keeping me from spiraling into full-blown panic.

As soon as the horses are covered, JD pulls me down against the valley floor. Hail peppers us, stinging my face, the larger pieces bruising my arm and side. JD takes a few solid hits as well, his grunts loud in my ear.

A railroad howl rips through the trees, stripping leaves and yanking at us. I want to close my eyes, as if that would make the nightmare end, but my eyelids won't budge. My fingers are white around JD's arm. He trembles against me. He's murmuring something, but the wind takes most of his words. I've only got one repeating in my mind. *Shit, shit, shit, shit.*

JD starts talking again—this time, I catch "valley," "death," and "with me."

Is he *praying?* Terrified laughter boils up my throat. A piece of hail the size of my kneecap strikes the ground at my elbow—another few inches, and it likely would have shattered my arm. My eyes squeeze shut. Maybe prayer isn't the worst idea.

Seconds crawl into minutes that feel like days.

Then the tornado is gone nearly as quickly as it came, leaving remnants of wind and a strong downpour before that, too, tapers off. I feel frozen against JD's warmth. His heart gallops beneath my ear—when did we shift so that I'm so curled into him? I'm about to force myself away when his chin rests on the top of my head. For all the terror of the last half hour, calm unfurls through my chest now.

His arms loosen around me, but his hands stay at my back. Holding, rather than clinging. His thumbs draw slow circles and a different feeling unfurls. As if my chest were full of stars.

"You okay?" His voice is soft and a little hoarse, but it sounds loud in the aftermath.

I ease back and meet his gaze. His eyes are a warm brown, like molasses candy. A desire that has nothing to do with brandy or Indian tobacco floods me. There's no denying the refuge his arms have been through this storm. The relief that we're still here, alive and unharmed, is enough to make me want to celebrate. A smile curls the edges of my lips. My gaze drops to his mouth.

Before I can gather the courage to lean forward, JD does, pressing his forehead against mine. "Holy shit, right?"

A laugh squeaks out. "You were praying."

He settles back with a grin. "Can you blame me? It's starting to feel like God himself wants to keep us from Bluff City."

One of the horses whinnies. I untangle myself the rest of the way and JD clears his throat. Maybe I'm imagining it, but he looks disappointed. I feel it, too, dousing the fire inside.

Because he's wrong. *Vengeance is mine, sayeth the Lord.*

And if I am made in God's image, His vengeance is mine too. Vengeance for Pa, justice for my family.

"We should wrangle the horses and get going," I say.

THE TREE LINE CREEPS CLOSER to the Missouri, providing us some blessed shade without having to stray too far from the river's guiding force. When we pass the first vineyard, I know we're getting close to home.

"Can't be more'n a day now," JD says, as if he's read my mind.

I glance over at him. "Don't get twitchy on me. That's still plenty of time to shoot you and collect the bounty."

He gives me an easy grin. "Plenty of time to shoot you and make my escape."

I force myself to smile back, as if it's all a game, but my insides are wilder than a traveling menagerie. What will happen when we reach Bluff City? I'm surprised to realize how much I've come to enjoy JD's company, but that only makes me warier. It's a whole lot harder stabbing a friend in the back than shooting an enemy in the face.

I duck a low-hanging branch, trying to picture my return. The image of handing JD off to Sheriff Kline leaves me feeling hollow. Somewhere along the way, it lost the sense of vindication, of pride. I think I can still do it, but I'm not looking forward to turning JD in. That's a pinch almost as brutal as the guilt over Pa's memory.

Without warning, the trees give way to a simple but well-built cabin and a large clearing beyond it.

"Whoa." JD pulls up short, and I follow suit. There's no telling who might be inside that house, whether they're kindly farmers or hostiles hiding out.

"We should head back to the river," JD murmurs, "give them a wide berth—"

Behind us comes the crackle and snap of footsteps, and the distinctive click of a cocked weapon.

"That's far enough," a man says.

We both raise our hands but stay facing forward. I don't want to give the man cause to startle, and even with the beard obscuring most of his face, I'd bet JD is concerned about being recognized.

"Steady, friend," he calls. "We come in peace."

The man doesn't respond, but he doesn't shoot either. His footsteps crunch again as he circles around to stand between us and his home. He looks to have ten years on us, his dark eyes wary and lines etching around his mouth. He glances between the two of us, his rifle inching down. "Who are you?"

"Travelers passing through to Bluff City," I say. "I'm Maggie and this is... Ebenezer." I say the first name I think of, though only Lord knows why.

JD casts me a sidelong look. "Call me Ben. Only my wife insists on calling me by my Christian name."

I swear his lips twitch, and it's all I can do not to glare at him.

The man shifts his shoulders, but the rifle lowers a bit more. "We don't want no trouble."

"Neither do we," JD says quickly.

"You traveling far?"

"Just from Jefferson City."

We're pretty bedraggled, so he could have picked a farther town. Even after the recent storm, my hair is lank and oily in a limp braid, and bits of dead leaves speckle JD's beard. At least his ear's healed enough he's lost the bandage around his head. "It's been"—I glance at JD—"an adventure."

His lips spread with an indulgent smile. Then that bastard says, "We're just hoping to reach family before the baby makes travel difficult."

Shock freezes me—a lucky thing, too, because the few words tumbling through my mind are all curses.

I have to hand it to JD, though, the fictional babe wins the man over. He sighs and drops the rifle completely. "Best come with me. Mirna'll want to feed you."

JD and I exchange surprised looks, but he's already turning for the house.

"You're inviting us into your home?" JD asks.

The man stops and turns again. "You're not murderers, are you?"

Even though he's clearly joking, my heartbeat slams in my ears.

JD recovers first, giving him an easy smile. "Nope."

"Then come on." He leads the way, speaking over his shoulder. "I'm William. You'll meet the rest soon enough."

The rest? JD and I exchange another look. William seems friendly, but what if we're walking right into a trap? He asked if we were murderers, but that doesn't mean he and his family don't kill passing travelers.

JD's hand rests on the butt of his revolver as we cover the last few paces. He looks casual enough, but tension hums through my shoulders. We can't have made it this far to be killed little less than a day outside Bluff City. My thumb taps against the hammer of my Colt. I will not let this be the end of our story.

13

WE SETTLE THE HORSES UNDER A LEAN-TO in a fenced off area about a dozen paces from the cabin. A friendly mule screeches a greeting as we begin to untack Huck and Sal.

"Samuel is my wife's brother," William says as a man around Jonah's age joins us. He's tall and reedy. "This is Maggie and Ben."

"Not often we get visitors," Samuel says, his wary gaze darting between JD and me.

"Where's Mirna?" William asks. "They'll be hungry."

Samuel stares us down until William smacks the back of his head. "Show some manners. Mirna inside?"

A child's laugh tumbles from the trees beyond the lean-to. Samuel runs the back of his thumb along his ribcage in a lazy scratch before turning to William. "She's around back." He raises his voice. "Wondering where her helpers got to."

Another giggle answers, followed by stomping feet and crushed leaves.

William sighs. "Lend a hand with their horses." He starts toward the cabin, calling, "Isabelle Johnson, you get your brothers out here right now and help your mama."

Seconds later, three small kids stampede out of the woods. A boy shoves a girl on their way around the lean-to, another boy toddling after them. Though they all seem a lot closer in age, for a moment I'm reminded of my brothers, our childhood spent chasing each other around the farm.

The girl—Isabelle, I presume—stumbles to a stop halfway between the lean-to and the house, heading our direction instead.

"Watch out for her," Samuel says, brushing down Sal. "She gets her sass from her mama."

"I'ma tell Mama you said that," she calls. She ducks under the fence. Her brothers hesitate in the yard. The younger one changes course to join her—the older one says something, the warning note in his tone carrying even if his words don't, then he darts around the cabin, out of sight.

Samuel grins as Isabelle slides into the shadow of the lean-to. "She gonna be too busy whooping you for shirking your chores to listen."

She sticks out her tongue, then reaches to pet the mule, her gaze cutting to me. "Hi. I'm Isabelle."

"Maggie," I say, biting back a smile at her polite forwardness.

She tells me she's the oldest at nine, and that her brother Theodore tries to say he's eight when he's really only seven.

This time, I can't help the grin. "I have a brother who does the same thing."

"How 'bout you?" JD asks the youngest, who's hovering behind her now.

"Raymond's five," Isabelle responds as he holds up his hand, chubby fingers splayed. "He's run out of fingers to count on, so he might never turn six."

Samuel barks a laugh. Raymond's lower lip puffs out. JD leans down with a conspiratorial whisper, "Try your other hand."

Raymond spreads those fingers too. His eyes widen, and he smirks at his sister even as she scowls.

"Now I'll have two brothers to set straight." She crosses her arms and looks JD up and down, her nose wrinkling. "When's the last time you bathed?"

"Isabelle!" A woman who can only be the famed Mirna stands at the entrance to the paddock, hands on her wide hips.

Samuel slides Isabelle an "I-told-you-so" smirk before reaching for her brother's hand. "Come on, Raymond, let's go find your papa."

Isabelle is still eyeing JD, the dust coating his clothing, grime clinging to his sandy hair. I'm no better—my face feels heavy with dried sweat, and dirt crusts my fingernails. JD rubs the back of his neck. I can't tell if he's playacting, but he looks bashful enough when he answers, "It's been a minute."

"You stink." Her eyes flick to me. "You too."

"What did I do?" I thought we were bonding over our insufferable brothers.

Isabelle lifts a bony shoulder then skips off after her uncle.

I turn my incredulous gaze on JD. He eyes me then nods. "You are pretty rank."

What's left of my good humor falls away and a blush flames across my cheeks. "Not as rank as you."

As soon as it's out, the childishness makes my flush deepen. JD's lips tug down as he shrugs.

"Sorry about her." Mirna's wide-set gaze flits between us, a smile pulling at the corner of her lips. "William tells me you been travelin' long. There is a lake just down that path, if you wanted to freshen up."

I follow the line of her jutting chin to a gap between the trees on the other side of the lean-to.

"That would be lovely," I say.

Mirna's brown eyes brighten. "I even made fresh soap this week. I'll get you a cake. Maybe a change of clothes, too, if you'd like to wash yours?"

She bustles back to the house, leaving JD and me alone in the shade of the makeshift stables.

"Why don't you head down first," JD says. His eyes flick to the horses.

A prickle starts at the base of my skull. "So you can run off with the horses as soon as I'm out of sight?"

"What?" JD looks genuinely taken aback, but I've seen him lie easy enough. "I was just being polite. Thought you might like a bit of privacy."

Skirts swish through grass. JD's eyes flit over my shoulder. Mirna has returned, a flaky white hunk of soap wrapped in a cloth and a stack of clothing in her hands. She looks curiously between JD and me as I take the bundle.

"After all this time on the road without a moment to yourself," JD adds for her benefit, gaze still on me.

"Isn't that sweet of you." Mirna gives him an approving smile. "I've got a stew on the fire round back—gets too hot cookin' inside. It isn't much, but you're welcome to it once you're cleaned up."

We thank her, and she retreats around the side of the cabin. As soon as she's out of earshot, JD says, "I'll go first, if you're so worried."

I grab his collar before he can make it a step. I pull him down to my level and lower my voice. "If you think I'm dumb enough to let you out of my sight this close to Bluff City, you've got another thing coming."

He searches my eyes, something like hurt pinching his forehead. I'm not falling for it.

That something shifts, hardens, then he's leaning closer, so close I can feel the breath leaving his nostrils. "Then by all means, come keep an eye on me."

He steps around me, leaving no choice but to choke down my pride and follow him to the lake.

⟡━◇──◇━⟡

THE SUN IS JUST STARTING to sink toward the horizon as we break through the trees onto a sandy shoreline littered with boulders. It bathes the red-and-orange trees in purifying light and shines off the surface of a lake that curves away from us. For a moment, I'm caught up, my chest swelling with the beauty of it. A bird sings an invitation from the far side of the lake and a chilled breeze presses into my back.

I pause to slide off my boots and socks before venturing onto the coarse sand. My eyes fall on JD at the water's edge. He's already shucked off his shirt and seems to be taking his time arranging it just so on the shore beneath his hat. He starts working his shoulders free of his union suit.

My breath catches. It's a different sort of beauty, the way his back contours and shifts in the falling light, but just as arresting.

He bends to pull off his boots and catches me looking at him. "You gonna stand there gawkin' or get in?"

My voice sticks on its way out, and I have to clear my throat. "You expect me to bathe with you?"

JD takes his time straightening and turning to face me. My eyes keep getting drawn to his muscular chest. "I *expect* it'll be awfully hard to explain why you'd return from the lake as smelly as you came down."

He undoes his belt buckle and starts to push his trousers over his hips. I spin around as a blush overtakes my entire body. Can't for the life of me understand why—his isn't the first male form I've seen, and I've never been squeamish.

Something about this moment feels different from any childhood trips to the swimming hole, though.

JD laughs. "Calm down, Miss Lady. There's plenty of plant life nearby for your modesty."

I bristle at the challenge in his tone, but he's right—pockets of scrubby bushes lace the lake's edge. They're tall and thick and jut into the water in places, so I can indeed bathe in relative privacy. As I start toward one nearby cluster, JD calls, "Toss me a piece of that soap first!"

I've half a mind to hold on to the whole thing, and serves him right, but given that we have a bit more traveling to do, I figure I'm doing myself a favor letting him get fully clean. So I drop the cake against a boulder to break it and toss him a chunk.

Tucked behind my natural privacy screen, I make sure Mirna's spare dress is within easy reach of the lake, then tug off my mud-streaked trousers. My fingers tremble as I unbutton my shirt. I've still got my underthings keeping me decent, but soon enough those will go, too, and no lake feels big enough to hold us both. A glance at the tangled branch-cover assures me I'm well hidden. I can do this.

Sharp as a bird call, I hear Della in my ear, cackling at my sudden propriety. *It's just skin, Mags. We've all got it.* As if we're tucked behind the schoolhouse the last time she showed up for classes, I can almost feel her fingers crawling a pattern up my bare forearm. *And it can be awful nice when someone else touches it* just right.

My body flushes with indignation—why am I letting Jedidiah Dawson of all men get me so flustered? No one said anything about *touching* today. Before I can reason my way out of it, I've ripped off my union suit and left it in a pile beside the skirts. Frigid droplets splash the shore as I stomp into the shallows.

We're both quiet as we bathe, scattered bird chatter and the slap of water on flesh the only sound. Through gaps in my plant cover, I get the occasional flash of pale skin as he dunks under and resurfaces. The lake floor has a gentle slope, so while private, my area is too shallow to fully submerge. I make do, methodically scrubbing from toes to shins to thighs, cleaning my way up. I work the soap through my hair, working out the tangles with my fingers and massaging my scalp. A breeze off the lake surface lifts gooseflesh across my damp skin.

"I've turned my back," JD calls. "In case you wanted to swim out farther."

I peer through the branches. True to his word, he's facing the opposite shore. My eyes trace across his shoulders and follow the dip in his lower back until it disappears beneath the water.

I should thank him and tell him I'm fine where I'm at. Nothing good can come from buff bathing with the likes of him. After days in the saddle, though, most under the unforgiving sun, a quick swim feels well deserved. With tentative strokes, I make my way deeper into the lake.

I'm a stone's throw from JD, buried up to my neck in greenish water. When he turns and smiles across the lake surface, I feel like I'm standing naked before him. Who we are isn't important—we're just a man and a woman, wearing nothing but lake water and the skin God gave us. My blood pulses hot. A smile curls up my own face, inviting. He swims out to the same depth but stays distant. I wait for him to move closer or to speak, but he never does. White light glimmers across the angles of his face, wavering with the gentle motion of the lake's surface.

A sudden wish seizes me—that we'd met under different circumstances, that our future wasn't so cut and dry. That we really were just two people sharing a private moment.

The water takes on a purple hue as the sky trades in sun for evening. Shadows beckon from the shoreline. Our time in this quiet bubble, separated from reality, is dwindling. I don't know how to prolong it, or if I should even want to. All I know is one wrong move and it will pop.

"We should head back soon," I say, reluctance dragging on my words. Everything inside is yelling at JD. *Seize this moment while we still can.* Maybe he'll be the brave one.

JD sighs and tilts his head back until the water laps at his forehead. "S'pose we should."

He turns his gaze to mine and a clench runs through my lower belly. There's something heavy in his shadowed gaze—something honest and painful and hopeful and certain. I feel it, too, a shining, golden sort of loneliness.

His lips tilt up, but something about this smile fills me with sadness. "I'll wait for you on the shore," he says.

Then he's gone, underwater and cutting back toward land.

14

A SHYNESS SETTLES OVER ME AS I dress in borrowed skirts and wring out my hair. I don't know what happened in the lake, but the vulnerability of that moment makes my heart pound as I rinse my clothes before joining JD.

He's got the sleeves of Samuel's wool shirt rolled to his elbows, and his hair is dark with water and sticking up all over his head, like he just ran a hand through it. His eyes take in my outfit, and he whistles.

"I must say, Miss Lady, I like the look of you in a dress." His voice is light and teasing. So at odds with the gravity of his gaze in the lake. A wicked grin twists his lips. "Bet it'll be harder to catch me, if I decide to run."

All the feelings I haven't even started to grasp a hold of wash away with that reminder. There's no room for softness between us. I cross my arms. "I shoot just as well in skirts as pants."

"We'll see." He turns and leads the way back up the path.

Are we still teasing, or was that an actual threat? My gut tells me he isn't going anywhere, and what's more, I'm not certain I could shoot him, even if he tried to run. Damn it all, I might actually *trust* him. My lungs tighten with the realization.

"Get a wiggle on," he calls. "I'm hungry." He's been swallowed by the darkness between the golden trees.

"Hold your horses," I mutter, following.

We lay our clothes to dry on the grass near the lean-to then venture around to the far side of the cabin. Gamey meat and stewed vegetables fill the night with their savory scents. The others are already gathered on carved logs around the fire pit. At our arrival, Isabelle sighs loudly. "Finally! I'm starving."

Mirna fills a bowl and hands it to her. "Guests first. Pass it on."

With a scowl, Isabelle carries it to me. When I thank her, she grants me a crooked smile. "Can I braid your hair?"

"I'd be honored," I say, and she brightens. The other bowls are dispersed, and William says grace in a steady baritone. Our chorus of amens rises like steam from our bowls.

Wedged against me, Isabelle wolfs down her venison stew, then turns her attention to my damp locks.

After everyone has eaten their fill, William trades his bowl for a fiddle. Across the fire, Samuel holds up his own large, black case.

"You play, Mister Ben?" Samuel asks JD. "I noticed you admiring her earlier."

He gets distracted by a stuck fastener. William tunes his fiddle, and Mirna cleans Raymond's hands while Isabelle chases Theodore around the circle.

"*Admiring* it?" With my hand hidden behind my skirt, I pinch the back of JD's knee. "Don't you dare steal from these kind people," I murmur in his ear.

He wraps his hand around mine and laughs, loud enough to carry. "I do play some," he says, to my surprise. His fingers squeeze mine hard enough to hurt. "But my wife doesn't want me to embarrass myself in front of you fine folks."

"Aw, we're all friends here," William says. "Go on, play us something."

"It'll be a nice change from the same three songs Samuel knows," Mirna adds with a good-natured wink at her brother.

Samuel eagerly hands over his guitar and JD takes it carefully. I flex my hand in my lap, coaxing blood flow back to my fingertips.

Then JD starts to play, and there's nothing embarrassing about it.

He strums a tune I vaguely recognize from church, slow and reverent. The little ones creep closer, Raymond leading the pack. He watches JD with eyes luminous in the moonlight.

JD catches sight of him, peering around his daddy's knee. A grin splits JD's beard as he gives the guitar two strong strums then picks up the pace. Fingers pluck across the strings, playing a song I've never heard. He sings of hills and valleys, black-magic preachers, lost souls and found gold. Fire, brimstone, salvation. Mirna starts clapping, keeping time, and Theodore tugs Isabelle into a dance. Their giggles harmonize with JD's song, their smiles flashing bright in the twilight.

William joins in with the fiddle, following JD's seemingly made-up melody with hardly a misstep. I find myself clapping along. Raymond remains fixated on JD. Samuel leans in toward Mirna, but she waves him away. He turns a glowing grin on me.

"How 'bout you, Missus Maggie? Care to dance?"

"Well, all right." I let him hoist me up and spin me away from the fire.

When JD's finished improvising—ending with a flourishing crescendo to everyone's delight—he starts on another song. This one sounds familiar, and judging from the way William starts singing along, my guess is it's a better-known cattle drive song.

"Miss Maggie, want to dance with *me*?" Teddy tugs my hand. Samuel is already forcing his sister up.

"I would be delighted!" I take the seven-year-old's hands and swing him around. When I catch sight of Isabelle bouncing on her own, I hold out my hand to her too. They're doing more running in and leaping backward, twisting and jumping, than actual dancing, but it's so cute I can't help but laugh.

I glance over at JD to find him watching us, his smile soft under the ragged moon.

The song ends with a little less fanfare this time, and Mirna shoos Samuel. "Go take back your guitar and let the poor man have a dance with his wife."

"Oh, I don't mind," JD says. "I'm sure she's sick of me."

"Nonsense. You get on up there and dance with that pretty lady."

My defenses bristle against Mirna's words, however kindly spoken. But then, dipped in silver moonlight and golden firelight, with the way JD's eyes keep finding mine, I might believe it tonight. JD joins me as Samuel plays a few experimental bars.

"We don't have to," I murmur, that shyness from earlier returning. "My ankle's starting to hurt anyway, so...."

The way he's smiling at me makes me lose my train of thought.

"Well then," he says, wrapping a sturdy arm around my back and taking my hand in his, "I guess I'll just have to hold you real close."

I can feel his heart beating against my chest—or maybe it's mine, racing away like a herd of mustangs—as we start to sway. Samuel's chosen a slow ballad about love and trust, truth and home. It feels like a mockery to be dancing to something so sweet with the likes of Jedidiah Dawson.

What's worse, it doesn't actually feel wrong at all.

Even though the moon washes everything silver, JD's eyes are the warmest brown, like a crackling fire log. Despite memorizing his Wanted poster, I don't think I've ever just *looked* at him the way I am while we dance under the stars. The handsome cut of his cheekbones hints at a strong jaw beneath his beard, fuzzy from the recent wash.

There's a smile in his eyes that leaks across his lips the longer we dance. I feel myself responding, glowing, melting. Like in the lake, we're just a man and a woman and a great, unspeakable feeling fills the shrinking space between us. When he dips his head toward me, a thrill runs out to my fingers. He doesn't kiss me. His lips find my ear instead. "Come with me to Colorado."

Rather than answer right away, my head nestles into his chest, fitting in the hollow along his neck. His arm tightens around me so that we're completely flush together. His heart is galloping beneath my chin. Mine has moved to my throat.

In a flash, I can see it—a cabin on a mountainside overlooking the fog rolling through the valley. JD's hands at my waist, lips on my neck. It burrows into the space between our heartbeats like a piece of buried treasure. I *want* it, this promise of both adventure and home. It's an odd sense of security I haven't felt since—

The image shifts. I'm on my knees in the dirt, watching JD become a speck on the horizon and screaming for help as Pa bleeds in my lap.

I shove free of JD's arms and stumble back.

"Maggie?"

"I can't." I turn on my heel before he can respond, before I start untangling the mess my heart's become.

"Maggie," he calls after me.

"Let her go, son." Mirna's voice reaches me. I realize Samuel and William have stopped playing. "Sometimes us women need a moment by our lonesome."

◇━○━━━○━◇

I DON'T GO VERY FAR. Leaving aside the possibility of bobcats and coyotes, my ankle really does hurt. Not like before, but the gentle throb reprimands me with every step. I sink to the grass and bury my head in my hands.

What is happening? How did I go from desperately awaiting Dawson's hanging to dancing with JD under the stars?

My fingers trail through the tallgrass, weaving pieces together the way Ma and I would when I was little and the chores were done. What would she say if she could see me tonight? Heavens, what is she thinking about my absence? It was supposed to be worth it—turning up with Jedidiah Dawson in tow would erase the days of worry I've put my family through.

Not for the first time, I wish I'd shot him that first day.

I wish I could go back further, talk Pa out of that fateful trip to town.

The music and laughter behind me dies out, calls of good night bouncing between the family and JD. I wait longer, staring unseeingly at the wisps of clouds smearing across the stars, until all is quiet and it's safe to head back. I don't want to try to explain my abrupt departure to anyone. Don't want to face JD at all.

When I return to the smoldering campfire, everyone but Mirna has retreated inside for bed. She smiles as I crouch beside the glowing embers.

"He's over there," she says, nodding at the lean-to. "I bet he's waiting up for you."

"I'm fine here."

She just keeps smiling that knowing smile. "He loves you very much. I could see it each time he looked at you tonight."

My heart does a funny little flip.

"He doesn't even know me." The words tumble out before I consider their implication. "I mean—"

"I know it can feel that way. Men aren't usually the best at communicating."

I stifle a laugh. All JD does is "communicate."

"In time, you'll find they know us better than we give them credit for." She squeezes my arm. "Go to him."

Without any plausible reason not to, I do as she says. JD stirs as I approach. I drop to the ground a few feet from him and clasp my arms around my knees. When he doesn't speak, I slowly unfurl until I'm lying down, close enough to imagine I can feel his body heat, though I know there's still a respectable distance between us. Even though we're more protected than ever before, I rest my revolver across my chest for ease of access.

"There's a certain drawback to pretending we're a married couple," I say.

"Don't know I'd call it that," he says, his voice teasing. "Why don't you come a little closer. Don't want to give them cause to speculate." He rolls onto his side. "I can think of a way to make it *very* convincing—"

"Don't make me shoot you so close to the finish line."

"Just being practical." He rolls onto his back and stretches. Whether intentional or not, his hand brushes down my hair. I cock the revolver. He withdraws with a chuckle.

After a pause, I return the hammer and move the gun to the grass beside me. Katydids flutter and chirp in the woods beyond the lean-to. A soft breeze sends the remnants of campfire smoke curling around us, sharp and salty. We're both silent, but I can tell he's as wide awake as I feel.

"Can I tell you a secret?" he finally says.

"Depends. Will it make me hate you or like you?" I can't decide which I'd prefer.

"Guess you'll have to hear it to find out."

"Suppose you'll tell me whether or not I say yes."

"I'm so tired of being an outlaw. When I first joined up, I was reckless and, if I'm honest, had something of a death wish." His voice has gone hoarse. "I don't want to die. I don't like causing people pain, neither."

I don't care about his good intentions. I *can't*. "Your Wanted poster says differently."

JD laughs, a sharp, frigid sound. "Already told you that's mostly lies. The trains, the other banks… and I never murdered anyone." He holds up a hand. "I know it's on my poster, but I never killed anyone who didn't have it coming."

My stomach flashes hot then frozen. *Pa didn't deserve it.* "I'm sure that's a comfort to your victims' families."

He turns toward me, but I keep my face tilted to the blurring stars. If I move my head a fraction either direction, the tears will start falling.

"I just meant, I've never shot anyone who didn't shoot at me first."

My eyes squeeze shut. Such a paltry excuse, simple and fair enough, and yet, the ramifications never end. Further proof that bullet *shouldn't* have hit Pa. That I should be the one rotting six feet deep. A tear escapes and plunges into my ear, but at least it's on the far side from JD.

He's too damned perceptive, though. There's a rustle of grass as he turns on his side, and I blink my eyes carefully open to find him propped on his arm, looking down at me. There's a divot in the skin between his eyebrows.

He reaches a slow hand and draws his thumb along the outer corner of my eye, still wet.

"You thinking about that man outside Warrensburg?"

That man...? Oh. The one I shot without question. He hardly compares to the weight of Pa's death.

"That was still out of defense," he assures me. "He'd have killed us both."

My swallow sticks in my throat. "I know that."

For a few breaths, all I hear are crickets calling to each other within the whispering grasses.

"You know the problem with your mentality?" I say in a desperate attempt to lighten the mood. "If you're always waiting to shoot second, someday you won't get the chance."

"You might be right. But I never wanted to hurt anyone." He shifts, settles back to the ground. He's a little closer now, close enough I can feel his heat all along my right side. This time when I glance at him, I notice JD has changed back into his clothes, now dry.

"Planning on leaving quick?" I mean it to be teasing, but my emotions make it sound all wrong. Accusatory.

The air shifts between us.

"Here I thought we were starting to trust each other," he says quietly.

"Trusting you would break my heart." The words are out before I can pull them back. My heart stomps around my chest.

"Maybe I'd surprise you."

I shake my head. "We'd be no good together."

"I think we're plenty good."

"You're deluding yourself."

There's a smile in his voice now. "Then so be it."

Against my will, I turn my face to him in the dark.

"Break my heart," he whispers. "I've survived it before, and I will again if needs be."

It's there, hovering between us—the shot that killed Pa. The reason for all of this. Would it break his heart like it's still shredding mine?

When I don't speak, he blows out a heavy breath. "You're such a coward."

"Excuse me?"

"You go on about how unhappy you are, how you want adventure and exploration, but you won't take a chance when the opportunity presents itself."

"That's not true." I pushed my way into the posse to hunt him down, for Pete's sake.

"Your family has their teeth dug so deep in you, you don't even realize it's up to you to pull away. You need permission to live your own life? Leave, Maggie. Follow your heart."

"And you're so sure it would lead me to Colorado? To *you?*"

"I'm not a bad man, Maggie. You have no idea how much I regret the things I've done. You think you're the only one with nightmares? I relive that bank all the time." He shoves his hands through his hair, his elbow blotting out the stars. "What are the odds? I may be a damn fine gunslinger, but I never expected I'd hit a man square in the heart, both of us flying on horseback. I couldn't make that shot again, not in a million years." He swallows, loud in the silence between us. His next words are hushed. "I just wanted him off my tail."

Well, it worked. My secret rears up again. I could do it, could tell him everything. It would put him in his place, would certainly get him to shut up. Would effectively put to bed whatever's stirring up between us.

My lips crack apart, but the confession sticks in my throat. I tell myself sharing it would be as good as admitting there's anything needing to be dampened, and there's not a snowball's chance in hell I'll do that.

In truth, it isn't anger or even unearthed attraction making my heart pound. All this time, I've been doing my damnedest to hate him. What if this revelation makes him hate me back? What if he recoils upon learning how closely our stories have been wound this whole time?

Worse, what if he pleads his case, pokes the final holes in the lace-work I've woven to protect myself from the realities of Pa's death?

That's not a risk I'm willing to take. Not so close to an ending for which I've burned night and day.

"That's the problem with 'what-ifs,'" I say. My throat feels coated with all the words I've swallowed, but my voice is steady. "They'll drive you crazy before ever bringing answers. Better to just accept your life for what it is."

JD scoffs, an exhale heavy enough to cloud the air. "I disagree."

"Disagree, then. Doesn't make you any less wrong." I roll over, away from him. "Now go to sleep. We've got a long day of riding ahead, then this will all be over."

He stays blessedly quiet after that, but it takes a long while for his breathing to slow with sleep. Even then, I'm wide awake, my own words pinching at my heart, leaving an ache I feel all the way in my clenched teeth. *This will all be over.*

It's over.

I'm not sure why it hurts so much. It never really began in the first place.

15

SOME TIME IN THE NIGHT I MUST have rolled over because I wake with my forehead against JD's shoulder and my arm slung over his mid-section. Dew-dampened clothes make me shiver despite his warmth. I start to pull my hand back, but my fingers brush something that is decidedly not muscle or bone. I feel around the object—squared edges, but soft through the fabric—and sit up to investigate. Within the lean-to, Huck nickers.

JD's hand closes around my wrist, tight enough to send a warning down the base of my spine.

"Taking liberties, Miss Margaret?" He's watching me with cold, steady eyes.

"What is th—oh." I remember the greenbacks he keeps pulling from nowhere. In my mind's eye, I watch him carefully arrange his shirt before getting into the lake yesterday. "Have you had money strapped to your chest this whole time?"

"Keep your voice down," he hisses. A lone bird sings in a tree behind the lean-to until a chattering squirrel chases it off. "More or less. It's the safest place."

His grip eases.

"How much—" Without thinking, I reach for the buttons of his shirt, but he takes a hold of my hand again and sits up. His heartbeat thrums against my fingertips.

"Much as I'd love to let you undress me, darlin', we do have an audience." He's sitting close enough that his words are hardly more than a whisper. He looks past my shoulder, and I turn my head to follow his gaze.

The Johnson children freeze in the process of creeping across the yard toward us. Raymond squeaks and runs back to the house, but Teddy and Isabelle stand firm.

"Are you about to kiss?" Isabelle demands with matter-of-fact curiosity.

My lips part in surprise. I glance at JD. His free hand snakes up behind my head and pulls me the last couple inches toward him.

"EW!" Twin squeals split the morning as the children react, but the sound is muted by the fact that JD smells like soap from the lake last night and his lips are soft and warm. My fingers curl into the worn cotton of his shirt, and I swear I feel his mouth grinning against mine.

With my hand already in a fist, it's easy to punch him just below the collarbone. He pulls back with a laugh.

"Taking liberties, Je—Benjamin?"

"It's Ebenezer, remember?"

"Whatever." The cabin door slams, indicating the kids are well out of earshot.

He's still holding my hand. We both seem to notice at the same time. He lets go as I tug free.

"By my reckoning," he says, "there's about a hundred left."

It takes me a moment to remember what we'd been talking about. "A hundred dollars *left?*"

He makes a low sound of assent in his throat and reaches for his boots.

"How much did you start with?" Forget the bounty on his head, having a small fortune on hand makes me feel like a fresh-painted target has just been placed on us. Never mind we've made it this far without *me* even knowing about its existence.

JD pauses his careful inspection of his boots—he's already shaken them out, but I've learned he needs to double-check each for snakes before thrusting his foot inside—and looks at me. His lips twitch. "I *did* rob a bank, Maggie."

A flare of remembered rage surges through me. "You don't need to remind me."

He shrugs and pulls on the first boot. "Took one fifty, hid the rest. Got me pretty far, actually." He grins fully at me as he tugs on the second boot. "Between supplies at Warrensburg, the ferry, and the Osage, you've cost me more than five months combined."

"I didn't ask for any of it."

Finished dressing, he turns back to where I sit. He curls a finger under my chin, and my heart beats a desperate tempo. His eyes are the color of fresh-turned earth on the first warm day of spring. He can't kiss me again. It would shatter me into dust. It would gather me back together.

"I know you didn't." His hand shifts, his thumb tapping the end of my nose, then he rises and joins the others gathering around the fire pit.

<hr />

"THAT WAS SOME MIGHTY FINE playing last night, Mister Ben," Samuel is saying as I join them for breakfast after changing back into my clothes. The Johnson family has gathered once again around the fire pit behind the cabin, where Mirna cooks flapjacks in a skillet of what smells like pork grease. The warm scent reminds me of campfire mornings with Pa and my brothers.

JD scratches the back of his neck, oddly bashful. "It's been a while since I've had the chance to play, so I appreciate you all humoring me."

Isabelle and Theodore argue across the circle, escalating whines of "did not" and "did too." I settle on the log beside JD, and Mirna hands me a plate piled high with glistening salted pork and crispy-gold flapjacks. As I thank her, I miss the question posed to JD.

"Ah, I traded mine a while back," he says.

"Your guitar?" I ask. "Why?"

He's so good, I can tell he once played a lot, and he clearly takes joy in it. Was it too cumbersome to take on the run or—

"For a ring." He glances at me then down at his own plate.

His answer catches me by such surprise, my lips part. "Oh."

His words last night return to me, sharpening. The heartbreak he's already suffered stirs up the embers in my heart, no matter how I try to stamp them down.

Isabelle shrieks, drawing all our attention.

"Theodore, don't you pull your sister's hair!" Mirna's voice cracks like a birch switch. She turns a wide smile on me, encouraging. "Well, let's see it. Show us the ring."

She's expecting some sort of happy ending to a story she doesn't know the half of, and I catch myself before telling them all about the cousin who stole JD's would-be bride. After all, I'm the one meant to be playing the part of wife.

Mirna's request settles over me with new meaning. My eyes go wide, and I bury my hands in my lap.

"Ah." JD grins so easily, I almost can't believe he just hinted at a personal tragedy. "Don't worry, darlin'." He fishes in his pocket then holds out a small gold ring. "Forgot to give it back after the lake last night."

From the corner of my eye, I can practically feel Mirna's satisfied smile growing, but the fact that he still carries the ring is another shot to my heart.

And now he's offering it to me. All for show, but after last night, I know it's salt in this particular wound.

I muster a smile as I take it and slip it on my left ring finger. It catches for a moment on my knuckle, then slides down, a near-perfect fit. Considering I've never expected to wear a ring—even if just for show—the gentle weight of it feels at home. Less like the shackle I always pictured, more like a missing piece finally fitted into place. And JD just *gave* it to me, like it was nothing. Like it really has belonged to me all this time.

That thought is enough to prod me back into the ruse. "I was afraid

I'd lost it," I say for the Johnsons' benefit. My voice sounds brittle. "You shouldn't have traded your guitar."

I don't mean to say the last part. The words are just screaming in my mind. *She didn't deserve you.*

JD's smile is just as brittle as he covers my left hand with his. "Got the girl, though."

Mirna sighs and claps her hands to her heart. JD gives my hand a squeeze then excuses himself from our group. He cuts a determined path through the grass until he disappears around the side of the cabin. I shore up my weakening resolve and force down the pork that only moments ago made my mouth water.

◇━◇──◇━◇

AFTER BREAKFAST, I GATHER OUR supplies. Isabelle sits on JD's shoulders, twisting braids into Sal's mane. Her brothers keep up a steady stream of stories, sharing everything they can think of with JD before he leaves them. I bite back the smile that keeps clawing at my lips. Enjoying their contented scene feels wrong after all that's passed between us.

William calls for the children to do their chores, and they scurry off. JD glances my way, but I turn my head back to the blanket I'm rolling before our gazes tangle.

I'm finishing saddling Huck when Mirna joins me, extra food bundled under her arm.

"This should keep you till you get where you're going."

I thank her, my gaze shifting over her shoulder. *Where's JD gotten to?*

"And you make sure you stop by and visit next time you're passing through here," Mirna continues. "I want to see this baby." She pats my flat stomach—I'd nearly forgotten that was the whole reason William invited us to stay.

As I force a smile, I catch movement in the corner of my eye—JD ducking out of their house, alone. He's got one arm tucked behind his back, but his movements are casual enough as he crosses the yard. He walks with determined steps to his horse and lifts the flap of a saddle-bag, stowing something inside.

Everything inside me tightens then unspools in furious ribbons. After all the kindness this family has done us, he has the nerve to steal from them? And here I was, second-guessing everything, ready to see him in the light of the redemptions he's painted over his past deeds.

It won't do to call him out here, though. Whatever injustice he's done to the Johnsons pales compared to my loss. Once we've left the clearing for woods again, and we're well out of range of the house, I turn to JD.

"What were you doing inside their house this morning?" If he truly did steal from those people... well, it'll make things a little easier.

He glances at me. "Thanking them."

He reaches into his saddlebag and pulls out a sweat-stained bundle, which he tosses to me. "Thought about making you strip me for it, but...." He shrugs as I work at the knot. "Only about eighty left now."

My head pulls up as I realize this is his loot. "You gave them twenty dollars?"

He tugs at the shiny new skin of his left earlobe. "They're good people."

Damnation, it's getting harder to ignore that he is too. "How did you explain that much money?"

"No one was inside. Figure we'll be far enough on our way before they discover it."

We leave the shade of the forest for searing sunlight. The heat makes my skin prickle and itch beneath my shirt. Inside, I'm worse off—like I've swallowed a bundle of worms, my gut writhes with uncertainty. At every turn, JD has proven himself a decent sort. *Better than me.* He doesn't deserve what's waiting for him. *I* don't deserve this triumph.

But how can I just let it go? If only I could just open my fingers, let this desire for vengeance fly away like a butterfly from a chrysalis. My fists have been clenched too tight for too long.

Vineyards dot the bluffs now, the river carving its way toward Bluff City.

"You ever seen an old stump in the creek behind the schoolhouse, kinda looks like a bear's head?" JD asks, startling me from my thoughts.

"Old Honey Elm?" I laugh. "We used to hide candy there, until the older kids took it over for stashing whiskey bottles. Then Herman nearly lost his hand to a timber rattler, and I don't know that anyone's used it since."

It occurs to me he shouldn't know this secret from my childhood as he grins. "It *is* a good hiding spot." Then he adds with a frown, "Good to know about the snakes, though."

My neck tightens. "Why are you telling me?" *Why now, when we're so close?*

"Well." JD stretches, rolling his shoulders. "In case this becomes a shootout. I think we both know how that'll end, and someone oughta enjoy the money."

"Wha—"

"I can't let you bring me in, Maggie. I know you want justice, our deal be damned, but I won't hang."

I shake my head, fully intent on denying it, however futile the endeavor. A swallow sticks in my throat. My mouth opens and a single word falls out. "Go."

JD sits there, blinking at me.

My heart feels wrung out and ripping in two directions. Despite the warmth of the day, I rub my arms. It's my fault for losing sight of what matters.

That's the rub, though, isn't it? Hollow justice doesn't matter quite as much as the man sitting next to me. Letting JD go is letting go of hope for closure, but it's the right thing to do.

Still, I can't look at him, turning instead toward the open prairie. "We might as well go our separate ways now—we'll reach Bluff City by nightfall. I can take care of myself the rest of the way. So you should dig up your cash and go."

We stopped moving at some point. The only sounds are the wind rustling the prairie flowers, and my heart drumming in my ears. Fingernails leave deep crescents in my clenched palm.

JD nudges his horse away. My heart pounds a falling echo, but I'm not sure what I expected. There's no world where this ends any differently.

They only make it a handful of steps before he turns back. "I meant what I said last night. Come with me."

"I can't."

"Maggie." My name leaves him on a breath, but he shakes his head at whatever else he wants to say and looks over his shoulder, as if he could see all the way across the prairie to the mountains of Colorado. "We'll leave your family half the money." When I don't respond, he clucks Sal closer again. "All of it, then."

I search his face, disbelieving. He'd really give it all up to have me join him?

My chest rises and falls, each breath searing. I could do it, could leave everything behind, start a new life with JD, knowing my family, the farm, it's all taken care of.

But the money, *that* money.... It's the source of all our strife. As if Pa's life is worth nothing but the three grand he was shot over. Might as well be thirty silver pieces.

JD waits, his gaze roving my face. I wonder what he sees there. I hardly know what I'm feeling myself.

What happens in a month or six or twelve, when we've had time to sit with our decision and uncover all the awful little truths about each other?

"Why me?" It shouldn't matter—*doesn't* matter—but the question hangs in the air between us, and I don't know how to take it back.

"Why *not* you? Damnation, Margaret, you're... maddening. Stunning."

JD is the first man other than Pa to call me anything of the kind, and for some reason, it stings worse than an insult. "I thought pretty was for paintings."

"Never said you were pretty." His nostrils flare—he's moved even closer without my noticing, so I can see all the details of his shaded features beneath his hat. The crease between his eyebrows, the scowl warping his lips. His face is all hard edges, but his eyes are achingly soft.

My chin dips, my gaze fastening on my white-knuckle grip around the saddle horn, on the scant space between our knees. His fingers brush my cheek, coax a wild strand of hair behind my ear. When he speaks, his voice is hushed.

"You've got the beauty of a prairie fire. All that rage and power. You're mesmerizing and terrifying, brilliant as a sky full of sparks."

As if that grassfire has engulfed me, a heat starts at my toes and crawls up to flush across my face. *I'm none of those things.*

Or maybe I'm all of them. Maybe pretty paintings are fine for walls, but I've always known I'm something wild and free.

"So you're a poet now?" I say because I can't put words to all the things he makes me feel.

A grin starts to lift one side of his beard. "You think you're the only person west of the Mississippi with culture and education?"

My chest cracks open. If I look down again, I'm sure I'll see my guts sliding out. Curse this man and all the ways he makes me then breaks me. For one glorious moment, one tender heartbeat, we were all that existed.

But that reminder of my background is all it takes. My mother and brothers are waiting on me—depending on me—and I can't let my family down again.

"Doesn't matter." I turn my face so he won't see the tears building in my eyes. Still, my voice is thick with them. I gather every remnant of anger and pain, scraping the edges of my cracked soul, until there's enough to shield me again. "Just go. Before I change my mind."

"*Why?*" His voice wavers over the simple word, his gaze heavy on the back of my head. "I know you feel this too. Why keep fighting it? They'll understand—"

"They won't." I pull my revolver and aim it at his heart. "My father was killed during the Bluff City Bank robbery."

His eyes close. "Maggie...."

"Shot in the chest by one Jedidiah Dawson."

When he reopens his eyes, they've gone liquid. "It wasn't what you think—"

"So go now." My voice rises, strengthens. As if I might drown out the confessions screaming in my head. I cock the revolver. "Before I repay the favor."

He only waits a heartbeat to do as I say, but it's long enough for a tear to escape. Thank the Lord he's kicking up dust before the rest join it.

I can't remember the last time I cried like this. I give Huckleberry her head and let the tears flow freely as we mosey along the Missouri.

When they finally seem to be slowing, I reach up to wipe my face and the sun catches on the circle of gold around my finger.

"Oh, no!" I start sobbing all over again as I pull off the ring. I should probably hurl it into the river. I'll never see JD again to return it, and it was never meant for me. But I know what this bit of gold cost him, so I can't. I slide it into my pocket beside Pa's watch instead.

16

MY HEART IS A RAGGED MESS. SOMEHOW, the idea of home only fills me with dread. Last time I'd seen everyone, I was full of grand dreams, ready to finally be the hero my family needed. I can't say when those dreams changed—last night, sure, but part of me is starting to realize vengeance stopped being a priority long before yesterday. Seeing JD at the end of a noose wouldn't have brought the closure I've sought—not for me, at least. If anything, it would have only made the weight on my shoulders even heavier.

But this doesn't feel right either. There's a nagging feeling tapping at the back of my skull, like I've forgotten something important, left something crucial behind. But I don't deserve happiness at my family's expense. There's no happily ever after for JD and me. Even if I had run off with him, it could only be a matter of time before cracks formed. Putting whatever might have grown between us to rest now is far better than watching our love die a slow death, like my parents'.

Lord, but my heart won't let go of the idea now that it's been planted.

Bluff City comes into sight, quiet and unassuming in the late afternoon light. How it can look so welcoming is beyond me. As if I'm some prodigal daughter rather than a failure.

It's still early, the sun not quite setting, so I tie off Huckleberry behind the Bell and Iron and slip through the saloon's entrance. The spacious room is fairly empty—a few girls clustered around the piano, a pair of men with their heads close together near the back.

Sidney isn't behind the bar, but I'm not here for a drink. The redhead wiping out the glasses stops me as I pass. "Hang on a second. You can't just walk in here like you own the place."

If I'd agreed to marry Sidney those months ago, I could do just that. "Della around?"

Her eyes flick from my dust-coated boots to my grimy face. She jerks her chin toward the stairs. "You gotta pay like anyone else," she calls. One of the girls glances my way, but I'm not sure I care much about gossip right now.

Della's laugh, sharp like crystal, tinkles from the first room to the right of the landing. The door is cracked open, so I invite myself inside. Two women sit on the bed, their heads bent toward each other—I recognize Della's sleek black curtain of hair, even if her face is hidden by it. The other woman catches sight of me first and leans away from Della.

"Well, look who the dust blew in," she says.

"Hey, Ruby." She's never much liked me, not that it matters.

Della springs from the bed with a shriek that sounds almost like my name and throws her arms around me. "Where the hell have you been? Your poor brother's been worried sick."

"He finding a lot of comfort here, then?"

"Not hardly. The posse's been back three days, and he hasn't stepped foot in here yet. If he had, I'd have reminded him you're the toughest Bennett."

With her warm hands on my arms and her bright eyes beaming at me, there's nothing for it. Fresh tears roll down my cheeks. I don't think I've cried this much in my life.

"Oh, Mags." Della doesn't ask questions, just folds me into an embrace.

There's a shush of skirts and softly closing door as Ruby slips from the room, leaving us to our reunion.

"I couldn't go home without seeing you first," I whisper into her hair. It smells faintly of honeysuckles, her favorite scent. Mine too, truth be told, but only because it reminds me of her. Now that I'm here, though, I don't know what I was thinking. Somewhere between leaving and returning, fear crept in, and now I'm not even sure my best friend can handle the burden I carry.

She knows me better than anyone, but even she doesn't know everything. How could she? My mouth opens, but confessions catch in my throat. The idea of spilling every last sin is too exhausting.

She leans back from our embrace, offers me a wildflower smile. She's always taken anything I have to share and has never asked for more than I can give.

I extract myself from her arms and my gaze drops to my lap. "I let him go."

Because she's my best friend, she knows who I mean. "Dawson? Why? Wait, you *caught* him?"

My lips press together, my heart a hummingbird caught in my throat. I want to lace my fingers through hers, but I keep them twisted in my own lap.

And I tell her everything. As my own personal punishment, I force myself to look at her, watch her face twist through confusion, hurt, anger. When I've poured all I can at her feet, I fall silent. This must be akin to how a criminal feels with a noose around his neck, waiting for the hangman's drop.

Della opens her mouth. Snaps it closed. Her eyes slide shut, and she shakes her head. A heavy breath lifts her chest, drops her shoulders. When she next looks at me, her features are calm.

"Thank you for trusting me."

A strangled sound escapes me. I don't know if I meant to sigh or laugh or sob. Della places her hand over mine.

"Your heart is the same one I've known forever. It's worth following now."

Lord, does her acceptance soothe me. I throw my arms around her, pull her close. "I don't deserve you, Della Mihoni."

"Oh, hush." She squeezes me tight before leaning back. "Love isn't about deserving anything. And I love you always, Maggie, you know that."

I palm the tears from my cheeks. "Love you too," I manage to murmur without falling apart again.

"I suppose I'd better get to work, soon." Della sighs. She knows me well enough to shift away from sentimentality now. "I'm so glad you're home, Maggie. The rest will work itself out."

I can't fathom how, but knowing I'll always have Della on my side helps make the yawning unknown a little less intimidating.

◇━○━○━◇

IT'S FULL DARK BY THE time I leave the main road for the dirt path that leads home. My spirit is lighter than it's been in months, finally unburdened, but confessing to Della drained my physical body. Huckleberry finds some reserve of energy, sensing home is close. As soon as we reach the little yard in front of the house, I dismount. Knowing my bed and supper are just beyond the door makes my legs tremble with exhaustion, but Huck comes first.

Before I can lead her to the stables, the front door swings wide. Silhouetted against the soft light within, a man lifts a rifle.

"State your business, friend," Jonah calls, more threat than hospitality.

"Well, I'm awful hungry and plumb worn-out, so—"

"Maggie?"

Then Jonah is shoved aside as Cole barrels into me. I manage to keep my footing, but barely. My younger brother laugh-cries into my hair.

"I knew you'd be all right," he gulps.

"Oh yeah?" I pull back to look at him. "Why are you crying then?"

Cole scrubs his arm under his nose. "Banged my shin on the way out the door, is all."

Jonah's here now, too, Ma and Camila behind him. I'm engulfed in arms and steered to the house.

"Cole, see to Huckleberry," Jonah says. "She's earned a good long rest."

It's a true sign of his relief that Cole doesn't talk back.

"I'll draw you a bath," Camila offers, grabbing the bucket for the pump. In just a couple weeks, she's grown, her stomach stretching the waistline of her skirt.

"That's not necess—" I try, but she's already gone.

Ma gives a delicate sniff. "It most certainly is necessary."

Should have seen me yesterday. Has it only been a day? The Johnson farm and all that transpired there feels like a lifetime ago.

Familiar scents of woodsmoke and spices greet me as I step into the kitchen's homey warmth. Jonah follows me inside, dropping a litany of questions on my shoulders until Ma tells him to hush.

"There will be time for that later," she says, shooing him. She unties my braid. "You're home now, that's what matters. Let's get you cleaned and fed."

Jonah makes an impatient sort of grunt but goes to stir up the fire in the woodstove without another word. I'm thankful for the reprieve—Della might be understanding, but back within my family's embrace, my burden feels just as heavy as when I first sank onto the edge of Della's bed. Ma pulls open the privacy screen around the tub and Camila adds water to the pot on the stovetop. While we wait for it to heat, Ma sits me down at the table and ladles hearty scoops of roasted beef and root vegetables onto a plate. The beef gravy leaks into steaming mashed potatoes, mixing with the golden, melting butter. Between bites, I put Jonah out of his misery, giving them the scantest details—getting separated from the posse, the storm that turned me around, the days of journeying back. I leave out any mention of JD—Ma doesn't need to know how close we came to avenging Pa.

"You must have been so scared, poor thing," she purrs. She combs her fingers through the length of my hair, pulling out a few strands of grass.

My fork pauses on its way to my mouth. "Not really."

There were terrifying moments, sure, but that's not what I hear in Ma's words. She'd have been frozen from the first moment, would never have had the strength or fortitude to get herself home in one piece. Her hand drops to her side, and she steps back.

"Maggie's the toughest of us all," Jonah says, sounding somehow both proud and chastising. The hand he rests on my shoulder squeezes a little too tightly, and I glance up to see Ma swiping away a tear as she turns to the stove. My lungs shrivel.

"I'm real happy to be home, Ma. I'm sorry to have worried you so." I look up at Jonah. "All of you."

He pats my same shoulder then resumes his seat. "All that matters is you're back safe."

His gaze holds mine, and despite his words, I know he'll want more details later.

Cole slinks in as I'm finishing my meal. He sidles up to me and leans close. "Where'd you get it all?"

"All what?"

"The money in your pack," he mutters with a furtive glance at Ma's back. "I hid it in the barn."

Ah, the remaining loot JD had on him. Never gave that back either. How to explain that without unfolding the entire story?

Since it's Cole asking, I rest my elbow on the back of my chair and muster all the casual bravado I can. "Took it off an outlaw."

Cole's eyes go round as Ma's painted tea saucers, and he forgets to keep his voice down. "You met a real live outlaw? What was he like?"

Ma whirls from the stove. "Don't go filling his head with nonsense!"

I wink at him, thankful for Ma's intervention. Lord, how could I begin to describe Jedidiah Dawson and all he became?

Jonah stands, his hands around the rifle he used to welcome me home. "Speaking of protecting ourselves against outlaws...." He hangs it back in its place over the door then musses Cole's hair. "When's the last time you cleaned that thing?"

Cole scratches his ribs. "I'll get to it."

"Before tomorrow's supper, or you won't get any."

My gaze rests on Jonah. He's only been home without me a few days, but I sense a change. Perhaps my absence managed to scare some responsibility into him.

◇━◦━◦━◇

EVEN MORE THAN MA'S COOKING, I missed the luxury of feeling truly *clean*. The boys go out to do the final chores of the night while I step into the steaming tin tub. My healing ankle throbs in the heat, the rest of my coiled muscles loosening. The swish and clink of Ma washing dishes accents the crackling fire. I stay in the bath until my fingers and toes are prunes and the water is distinctly brown. Every swipe of lavender-studded soap across my body seems to remove another layer of filth.

An even greater luxury—Camila offers to wash my hair. Her slender fingers work the soap into a lather, massaging it into my scalp.

"I think I've died and gone to Heaven," I murmur, my eyes sliding closed.

Camila hums a melodic giggle. "We were so worried when Jonah returned without you. But...."

But what? The fire warms my face as I turn over my shoulder, waiting.

She leans forward, a wicked grin showing off her teeth. In the flickering light, she looks like one of Lucifer's fallen angels—perfectly devious. "It was exciting, no?"

I can't help my answering smile. "It was that."

She holds the side of her hand to my forehead and pours warm water down my hair. "I told Jonah you would be fine. You like adventure."

"This might have been a little more adventure than even I hoped for. Don't tell him I said that!" I turn so fast, a dollop of soap suds rolls into my eye. "Ah, shit!"

"I don't care where you've been, Margaret Bennett," Ma's voice darts around the partition, "*ladies* do not speak that way."

"Sorry, Ma."

Camila's quiet laugh whispers over my shoulders. My scalp tingles and tugs as she wrings out my hair. "I will brush your hair."

"Oh, good." I hold up my fingers, shriveled messes that they are after soaking so long. "'Cause my hands are useless."

She laughs again, then slips her hand around one of mine. "We have a saying. *Perro que no camina, no encuentra hueso.* You had to leave to find what you are looking for." Her fingers squeeze my palm before returning to my hair.

Camila's words float in my mind. What if I only found sorrow? I might've found exactly what I'd never considered hoping for, but it doesn't matter now.

When she's done, I exit the tub to find Ma's laid out a soft, wool shirt and navy cotton skirt.

She peers around the partition as I'm dressing. "Your trousers were so filthy I almost fed them to the stove."

I smile at her. "After so long in them, it actually feels like my legs can breathe more under this skirt."

Ma clasps her hands in front of her chest. "The Lord's blessings just keep coming!" A twinkle in her eye offsets the mocking tone before she returns to tidying up the kitchen.

"This doesn't mean I'll never wear pants again, mind you," I call after her. That's an argument for another day. It feels good to have that normalcy to look forward to again.

◇━◦━━━◦━◇

AFTER THE EXCITEMENT DIES DOWN, Ma and Camila retreat to bed. The fire snaps and hisses in the woodstove, wrapping us Bennett kids in its violent glow through the open hatch. Cole's fallen asleep, sprawled on the woven rug, every so often a soft snore making me nudge his foot until he stops.

"So what happened, Maggie?" Jonah says. "We had the camp surrounded, then all of a sudden the horses were spooked, and you were gone."

"He got past you somehow. Maybe he'd already made us and was trying to sneak away. He took one of the horses, and I gave chase."

Jonah sucks in his breath and shakes his head. "You coulda been killed. Then what happened? The storm really got you that turned around, and you've been wandering your way home all this time?"

I bristle. "You could give me more credit than that. I *caught* him."

"Come now, Mags. It's just me—"

"I did! The storm disoriented me, sure, but once I got my bearings, I was on my way home—Dawson in tow—but then... he got away."

Jonah's gone stock-still, his face tight with rage. I force my lips apart, dredging up an apology, but he finds his voice first. "Did he... hurt you?"

I blink. I'd been so certain he would berate me for being careless. That his first thought is for my well-being.... "Of course not."

"Of course—?" He shakes his head. "He's an outlaw, Maggie. He murdered Pa and who knows how many others. I think it's fair to assume he'd have no issue harming you too."

"And yet, here I am, unscathed. It wasn't—*he* wasn't...." Words fail as I try to explain all that transpired. "Do you want the full story or not?" Maybe if I start at the beginning, he'll understand.

Jonah's jaw is still clenched, but he nods for me to continue. So I tell him about our chase, about tying him to the horse, realizing we were going the wrong way. When I get to the part where I shot a man, he sucks in a breath.

"Jesus, Maggie." He shoves his fingers through his hair, and I once again fight the urge to apologize. "You never should have been with us."

My mouth falls open. Here I am telling how well I handled myself, and he's already dismissing me. Then he shocks me.

"I'm so sorry." His voice trembles, and when he finally looks at me, all I see is pain in his eyes.

"You have nothing to be sorry for."

"I'm the oldest," he bursts out. "Bad enough you had to cradle Pa while I was halfway across the state, and now? My little sister *killed a man* and where was I?" His fist slams into the floor, and he mutters something that sounds like a curse.

"Jonah...." What is there to say, though? It's not something I can brush off, not when I know the exact weight he carries.

He shakes his head, drags his hand down his face. "So then what?" His voice has gone hollow.

I'm not sure I want to tell him about the men in the woods, not when he's already feeling so guilty. "The situation changed not long after that. We formed a shaky sort of truce, Dawson and I. He promised to come willingly and help me on the way home in exchange for his freedom."

His dark eyes snap to mine. "That wasn't yours to give him."

"I know that, Jonah. You think I've got corncobs for brains? I planned to turn on him as soon as we got close."

"And you're telling me he managed to escape without hurting you at all?"

Saying I'm not hurting is a bit of a stretch, but—throbbing ankle notwithstanding—it's just my fickle heart.

Something changes in Jonah's voice when he next speaks, as if he's reading my heartbreak on my face. "Or did you let him go?"

It's not accusing, exactly, but there's a hard edge to the neutrality. My fingers find a pull in the rug, and I focus on that rather than the tornado of thoughts whipping around my head.

"We needed that reward money, Margaret. Not to mention *justice*— what could he have possibly said to convince you none of that mattered anymore?" There it is, the unspoken charge behind his words. *How could you choose him over our family?*

And isn't that the rub that's been chafing me since this morning.

My lips part, but the truth sticks in my throat. The cold ground seeps through the floorboards, past the rug and my skirts to run trembling fingers along my spine. I meet Jonah's searching gaze, trying to find the right words to explain what's shifted in my heart.

"Oh, good Lord," he says in response to whatever he's read in my eyes. "He murdered Pa!"

"It was self-defense."

"You believed that? Tell me, when he gave you his side of the story, just how long had he had you on your back—"

I slap my brother, hard enough to burn my hand and leave a bright red handprint across his face.

Cole gasps and chokes on a snore.

"How dare you," I hiss as our younger brother falls back into his dreams. "I thought you, at least, saw me as an equal, not some simpering fool who'd give myself over so easily. He never touched me."

Except, of course, the night of the Indian tobacco and brandy, and again our last morning, but even then, it was only sloppy kisses and keeping up a facade.

"I was *there* that day," I remind Jonah. "He didn't kill Pa in cold blood. He didn't even know for sure he'd killed anyone until his poster went up."

A log pops in the stove. Glowing crumbs scatter the stone slab beneath it. Jonah crushes them with his bootheel.

My chest stretches with a careful inhale. "It doesn't change the fact that Pa is dead, and by his bullet, of course it doesn't. But"—I shrug—"I don't have the same hate in my heart that used to be there. Letting him hang for a misunderstanding… it doesn't feel like justice."

Jonah rubs his cheek. "Of all the men, Maggie…."

He sounds resigned, though, not angry. I lean my shoulder into his. "You're the one who told me to be less judgmental."

"So this is my fault?" His gaze roves my face, reading me the way I've always been able to read him. A snort of a laugh huffs through his nostrils. "Did you fall for him?"

There's a lurching in my gut at his words, but what else can it be? I always said love turns people into fools, and that's what I've been.

"I'll get over it," I say, but as the full impact settles over me, I'm not sure my heart will ever beat the same.

Right now, it kind of feels like it can't beat at all. As if I haven't cried enough already, a sob charges up my throat.

"Aw, Maggie." My brother's arm comes around me, holding me close.

17

TODAY MARKS THE BEGINNING, A LINE IN the dirt between all that's transpired and what little life has left in store for me. Ma and Jonah let me sleep in, so I'm still in the kitchen sopping up the last of my gravy with one of Ma's buttery biscuits when I hear someone ride up.

Of course Wyatt's managed to hear I've returned....

I shove the last of the biscuit into my mouth and rise. I've half a mind to try sneaking out the back, but the knocking's already started, and Ma is halfway to the door.

The biscuit sticks in my throat at the sight of Mr. Skinner standing where I expected Wyatt. It's been six months since the robbery, and I've avoided him—and the bank he represents—every chance I got. Now he's in our kitchen, wearing a fancy hat and an insincere smile.

"Ah, Miss Bennett," he says after greeting Ma, "I'd heard you'd returned but couldn't believe the good news."

"So you came all this way to see for yourself?"

He chuckles and waves away the seat Ma offers. "I'm sorry to dampen the celebratory mood, truly I am"—he doesn't look sorry at all, with his smirk following the curl of his silver mustache—"but this family's loan is well past due, and I'm afraid I'm here to collect."

My face goes numb. I'd forgotten—with both Jonah and me leaving, no one saw to extending our time. Standing near the head of the table, Ma twists her fingers together in her skirts and looks helplessly at me.

I throw back my shoulders, reaching for bravado I don't feel. "You can't repossess the twine binder. Without it, it'll take twice as long to harvest the hay—if we hire help." *Which we can't afford to do.*

Mr. Skinner's tongue, fat and white-laced, runs along his smirk. "You think I'm here over an old piece of equipment?" His eyes crinkle with patronizing light as he looks from me to Ma. "Is the man of the house available to discuss these matters further?"

Ma narrows her eyes, giving him a look to cut straight through the feigned politeness. "My husband gave his *life* trying to recover the bank's money."

Mr. Skinner's voice cools. "We appreciate your family's sacrifice, Missus Bennett, and we've repeatedly extended your grace period out of respect, but it's been six months now of little more than measly payments. At your request, I've waited for your son to return, but even my patience has its limits. Let Jonah know that if you don't pay by the end of the day, it will be some very unkind men who come knocking next." He plops his hat firmly on his head and turns on his heel before we can protest further.

Ma sinks into a chair and buries her face in her hands. "Why did I let that man talk me into leaving everything for this wasteland?"

"Don't go blaming Missouri for the likes of Mister Skinner," I say as Camila enters through the back.

She stops short, her eyes on Ma. "*Señor* Skinner?" At Ma's nod, Camila sets her basket of gooseberries and cabbage on the table. She sinks to her knees before my mother, taking Ma's trembling hands in hers. "Do not let that bad man upset you."

"Bad man?" I say. I'm well aware Mr. Skinner is a slimy bottom-feeder, but Camila is usually more generous and Ma too genteel to pass judgment on powerful men.

Camila's dark gaze finds mine over Ma's shoulder. "We spoke to him after you left and asked for more time. He agreed, but we still see him often in town. He... *siempre la acosa.*"

I'm impressed Ma took it on herself to speak with the bank, which makes me burn even hotter hearing this. "He's been harassing Ma?"

"It's why she does not go to town often."

Ma's shoulders shake. "Even before your father died, his attentions were... unseemly."

My hand clenches.

"Perhaps you should get Jonah?" Camila's gentle voice is prodding.

I nod, unsure what else to do with the impotent rage crushing my chest.

<hr />

JONAH AND COLE HAVE TAKEN Ace and Marigold to finish fencing the farthest portion of our land. Normally, I'd gladly walk the distance and give poor Huck a day off. With Mr. Skinner's words ringing in my ears, though, I coax the horse from her stall and nudge her to a tired trot. I'm not going to Jonah, though—not yet.

We're headed to the schoolhouse.

It's pointless, I know that, even as we plod along. JD had half the day and all night to clear out the hidden cash and take off. But if there's a chance, however infinitesimal, I'll never forgive myself for not checking.

We pull up well away from the schoolhouse, so Huck can rest, and I can approach on foot. I give the building a wide berth—with harvest time wrapping up, there's no telling whether the teacher is inside preparing school lessons.

With each step, I quiet the naysaying voice in my head until I've nearly convinced myself I'll find the whole stash. JD *told* me where he'd hid it, after all. He practically wanted me to have it. He even offered to leave it behind for my family. Maybe he left it behind for me. After all, he gave me what he'd been carrying on him. Damned if he isn't the generous sort.

It doesn't take long to locate Old Honey Elm, about a hundred paces along the creek.

The hole in his face is rotted around the edges, a gaping maw. I shove my arm inside, impressed JD would be brave enough to risk a snakebite doing the same. He must have, though, because it's empty—my fingers feel nothing but slimy, molding leaves. The air squeezes from my lungs.

I sit back on my legs and wipe my hands on my skirt, fighting despair. I knew it was a long shot, hoping he might have left something for me after all. Doesn't quite lessen the sting of it, though.

With a sigh, I climb back in the saddle and turn Huck for home. Maybe Jonah will have a plan. It doesn't take me too long to find Jonah and Cole, following the ever-lengthening fence line around our property.

When I tell Jonah about Mr. Skinner's threat, he swears. "We need more time."

"He was rather explicit that we won't get it."

"Ah, he's just full of hot air," Cole says with a shrug of one scrawny shoulder.

"Not this time." I pace between fence posts, ruminating. The twine binder is worth nearly two hundred, whatever Skinner said about the equipment not mattering. It's a lot of money, but along with the eighty dollars from JD, I can think of a few items worth near that much. "We've got the watch." Just saying the words makes my tongue go chalky. JD's ring sits heavy beside it in my pocket, and while selling that feels as much a betrayal as Pa's watch, I mentally add it to my tally. We're still short, though. "And the candlesticks."

Ma's gold filigree candlesticks were a wedding gift, the only thing of value she's managed to hold on to from her old life. Pa wasn't the sentimental type most of the time, but he would have died thrice over before he made her part with the last vestiges of her home. Jonah's shaking his head, matching the cadence of my heart. Even Cole is staring at me like I've spilled my marbles.

"I know," I say, "but what choice do we have?"

Jonah turns away, raking a hand through his hair. "If only you hadn't let two-large ride into the sunset...."

I thought he'd understood me last night. That he'd throw it in my face today adds to the weight on my chest.

Jonah pinches the bridge of his nose. "I've got some money saved. I'd hoped a few more wins might get us where we need to be, but maybe with the watch and the candlesticks...."

"You've been saving money?"

"Almost a hundred fifty dollars," Cole says, proud. At Jonah's glare, he shrinks back. "I didn't touch it while you were gone, like you said."

Suddenly, I can't breathe. My hearing's gone fuzzy. I look between the two of them, waiting for the punch line.

"Jonah Bennett." I barely get his name out past the raging thump of my heart in my throat. "Where in God's green earth did you get one fif—" I can't even finish the amount.

"Where do you think? It ain't easy winning just enough to avoid suspicion."

"Why haven't you repaid the binder loan?" My screech sets the horses shuffling and makes Cole take a step back.

"I *did*. But we owe a lot more than that, Maggie." Jonah's voice is hard and low, making my outburst echo with childishness. "You think Pa's debts died with him? I had to take out *eight hundred* to pay off his gambling. Along with the interest, not to mention our overdue credit at Hoffsteder's, even with semi-regular payments we're still about five hundred in the hole and.... Well, you're not the only one heartsick over Dawson."

My fist sinks into his stomach, the soft part between ribcage and belt buckle. He doubles over, and I'm about to admit it was an undeserved blow when his hand closes around the back of my knee and yanks. I go down, the air leaving me in a rush, and my fight along with it.

"All right," I say, staring up at the harsh blue sky. Jonah's right. I could have had more than enough to cover our debts, if only my heart hadn't gotten in the way. "I've brought this on our family, so it's up to me to fix it."

And I know what I've got to do. The sun heats my face as I reconsider the offer made almost three months ago. Rather than the writhing in my gut thoughts of marriage usually bring, today I just feel hollow.

Sidney Ritter can't protect me from a broken heart, but he can still save our farm.

⟡—◦——◦—⟡

SIDNEY'S ALONE WHEN I ENTER the saloon, taking chairs down from tables to prepare for the day.

"Maggie!" He breaks into a genuine smile, and even though I know it's just because I've returned from the seeming dead, it gives me courage.

"All right, I'll marry you."

Maybe I should have built to that, said something sweet and coy, and waited for him to broach the subject of marriage again. But we don't have time, and I don't have the energy.

He carefully sets down the chair in his hands. "Beg pardon?"

"Your proposal? I'll marry you, and take care of your kids, and you help my family with the bank."

Sidney draws a knuckle along his jaw, his lips a wry twist. "Can't do it."

"Why not?" Has he managed to hear about JD? Of all the men in town, he should be the least concerned with trifles like reputation but then, men are men.

He gives a humorless chuckle. "Tell me true, do you even like children?"

I can if I have to. "Sure."

"What are my kids' names?"

My mouth opens, but I have no idea. "We have plenty of time to get acquainted."

Sid's gray-green eyes fairly glow in the weak sunlight streaming through the windows as he studies me. The corner of his lips twitches up. "Now try saying that again like it ain't a death sentence."

Heat flushes up my neck. "Fine, playing mother's never been high on my to-do list, but I'll get over it. I can take care of...." Still nothing on the name front. "...them," I finish lamely.

He sighs and crosses behind the bar. "Thing is, I've seen you dedicated to something. There was a fire in you on the trail that's all but burnt out now. I'm not sure you'll ever actually like spending time with *Libby and Joseph.*" A quicksilver grin accompanies his kids' names.

"But—"

Sid holds up a hand. "Look, I don't need a wife interested in me, but I certainly want her invested in my children. You're not that woman, Maggie, and we both know it."

I drop onto a stool, my legs no longer reliable. "So that's it?" I lay my head down. The polished bar is cool against my cheek. "We're going to lose everything."

Sidney sets a small glass down with a *thunk* that echoes beneath me. "What's your poison?"

"It's barely noon," I mumble into the wood.

"In here, it's whatever time you need it to be, pet." There's a small pop of a stopper, then a hearty glug as amber liquid fills the glass in front of my eyes. Then he pours a second tot and taps his glass against mine. *"Prost."*

He drinks. I don't. He sets his glass upside down beside mine. My head remains on the bar. It smells faintly of alcohol and apple cider vinegar.

"Sit tight," he says.

I can't see him without lifting my head, but I hear him rummaging around. My curiosity has fled. I'm too busy worrying about Mr. Skinner. We've already given back sixty acres of our original homestead. Too much more, and we might as well move Ma to a little house in town, give up the farm altogether. Just the thought sucks the air from my lungs, as if Pa is bleeding out in front of me again. He gave up everything—including his life—for that farm, and we've squandered it away in half a year without him.

Sidney returns. He tilts his head to meet my eyes, then taps the bar by my head. "Come on, sit up. Ain't over yet."

Reluctantly, I push myself up. "Unless you know where I can get three hund—" My gaze snags on a stack of banknotes in his hand and everything skids to a halt inside me. I don't breathe. I don't even think my heart beats.

"Three hundred?" He counts out a handful of bills and slides it across the bar. "Go on, take it."

I'm already shaking my head, even as my hands twitch with the desire to grab the money and run.

Sidney purses his lips. "I tried giving it to Jonah, but he wouldn't hear of it."

"You think I'm any less proud?" Hopeful relief strangles the words.

"Course not, but you're a lot smarter. What other option you got?"

Still, I don't move. Dust motes catch in a shaft of light cutting through heavy velvet curtains.

"Look," Sidney says, running a hand over the gleaming bar, "Hank Bennett was always kind to me. Skinner on the other hand…." He doesn't need to say it. The entire town knows their history, the bad blood between them in the form of Skinner's disowned daughter, Sid's dead wife. He clears his throat, as if brushing aside his pain is that easy. "Besides, Jonah's good for business. Keeps people here longer, drinking more than they might otherwise." He shrugs. "He makes it a more reliable habit, and we'll call it square soon enough."

He reaches across and takes my hand with self-assured fingers, turning it palm up. The greenbacks are warm against my clammy skin as he closes my fingers around them. My hands shake so badly I almost drop the money. He makes it seem like such a simple kindness, one friend looking after another.

"Go on," he says, nodding at the entrance. "Let me do something good."

"I don't know what to say."

"Don't make it a thing." His teeth flash in the dim light, a rogue grin. "Always happy to take the wind outta Skinner's sails."

At the door, I turn. "You've still got a capacity for romance, Sidney

Ritter." I hope his next wife will get to see that side of him, whoever that ends up being.

He blinks, then lifts my untouched glass with a sad smile.

◇━━○━━○━━◇

I STAND ON THE PLANKED walkway outside the bank, turning Pa's watch over and over in my trembling fingers. Sweat sticks my shirt to my arms and down my back. I didn't even set foot in there that day, but my heart is skittering in my throat as if I'd looked down the barrels of the Blue Devils' guns myself. I may have been little more than an outside observer to the bank robbery, but this building is forever linked with Pa's demise in my mind. That same guilt I've carried since rears up, and in this moment, I might as well have been the one to storm in there, holding open a sack and waving my gun at my neighbors.

I can't do it. I can't walk across that rough-plank floor and speak to Mr. Skinner as if the robbery that occurred within these walls didn't lead to my father's death. I turn, ready to race back to Huckleberry and the safety of home.

But there won't be a home to run to much longer if I don't pay off the remainder of Pa's debts.

I could make Jonah do it—he'd offered to come along—but then, he's more likely to end up returning Sidney's gift, the mule. With a deep, jagged breath, I swivel back around and storm through the doors before I can stop myself again.

The main part of the bank's empty, save for the teller at the counter. Mr. Skinner is just visible through the door beyond, poring over a ledger in his office.

"Afternoon, Albert." My voice echoes in the empty space, feeling cavernous without any others waiting in line. "I'm here to see Mister Skinner."

"He asked not to be bothered."

"I'm here about our loan, so go get him." There's no way I'll muster the courage to return. Already, my tension is putting a hard edge to my words.

Albert's ruddy face flushes. "I'm sorry, but—"

"Miss Bennett." Mr. Skinner steps through his office door and tugs the bottom of his vest. "Here with my money so quickly?"

"I am." Without fanfare, I drop the sack of Jonah's poker winnings, the money JD gave me after the Johnson's farm, and the stack of worn bills from Sidney onto the gleaming mahogany counter. "Five hundred. I'll wait while you count it."

Though I'd rather tuck tail and run. Skinner's gunmetal eyes don't leave mine.

"Albert." All he has to say is the man's name, and the teller has our money in hand, sifting through the gold and silver coins. He makes neat, organized stacks. Mr. Skinner just watches me. He might wear velvet brocade suits across his well-fed paunch, but he's as dangerous as any outlaw, a curly wolf through and through.

"You'll leave my ma alone after this." Much as I hate his predatory gaze, the thought of it falling on my mother makes me want to rip his eyes from his pale face.

"I'm not sure I understand your meaning." A smirk invalidates his words.

I lean across the counter and refuse to break eye contact. "You understand perfectly. You have a problem with my family, you speak with Jonah or me. You so much as look at my mother and I'll—"

"What? Keep in mind, I am an upstanding member of this community."

My face twitches with the urge to snarl like some rabid dog. He's right—no matter how I'd like to rip out his throat for the discomfort he's caused my mother, he's protected by his status in Bluff City.

"Five hundred, ten," Albert announces. He slides the extra gold eagle across the counter toward me.

"Our business is now at an end," Mr. Skinner says, taking a step back. It's a tiny victory, and I bite back my grin. "Have a lovely day, Miss Bennett."

"Mister Skinner." I turn on my heel.

Before I can make it through the door, that scoundrel calls one more thing. "Give my regards to your mother."

If I turn around, I'll surely kill him, so I force my feet to carry me outside. I stop on the walkway, sucking at the air to cool the heat in my skin. I'm reminded why Pa hated Mr. Skinner so much. How he'd spit every time we passed this building. I'd love nothing more than to burn it to the ground. I wish that had been part of the plan when the Blue Devils robbed Skinner blind.

As if my thoughts of that day have conjured JD's ghost, my gaze catches on one of three horses tied outside the sheriff's office down the line, a dusty chestnut with three white boots and a limp braid clinging to the middle of her mane. *How is that possible? JD should have been long gone by now.*

Wyatt is just leaving, rushing to his own horse, when he glances up the dusty road and notices me staring.

"Maggie!" he calls, abandoning whatever mission had him hot under the heels to run in my direction.

My feet are stuck, as if the planking was another hollow river tree holding fast to my legs. Then Wyatt's here, elation on his face and a hand at my back.

"Was just coming to tell you," he says between heavy breaths. "We got him! Jedidiah Dawson. He's at the sheriff's now—"

If Wyatt's still talking, I've stopped listening. A haze descends over me. When I come to, I'm standing outside the jail and Sheriff Kline is beaming at me.

"S'pose Wyatt's told you the good news?"

"How?" I'm sure my shock shows on my face, but I can't seem to school my features into anything else. Hopefully they think I'm simply overcome with relief.

"Providence!" Sheriff Kline barks a laugh. "Was on my way to see *you* when I came across him not far from your farm. Turns out the money really was here the whole time."

Near my farm? I storm past him into the jail, but he and Wyatt are right on my heels.

"Hold on now, Maggie," Kline says.

I get a glimpse of JD's bowed head before I turn back to them. "I'd like to speak with him. Alone."

Sheriff Kline chuckles. When I don't budge, he frowns. "You know I can't do that. Hangman'll take care of him soon enough, don't you worry."

"I'm unarmed." I lift my hands to emphasize the lack of a gun belt around my hips. "I just want to talk."

He's still wavering.

I shift my focus to Wyatt. "Don't I deserve that?"

My voice is near breaking from the strain of the situation. I can see it move Wyatt, the softening in his eyes and the line of his shoulders.

"Come on, Gene," he says softly. "We could give her a minute, can't we?"

Sheriff Kline shakes his head, but sighs, defeated. "I've got to send a wire to Jefferson City, letting them know we've caught him." He claps a hand on Wyatt's shoulder. "You can bring the horse to the smith, then you'll see her home?"

"Yes, sir."

"See that neither of them kills the other." With that, he takes his leave.

Wyatt hesitates. "You want me to stay with you?"

I shake my head. "I've got a lot to say to him that don't need an audience."

Wyatt presses his lips together and nods his understanding before ducking outside. When I turn, JD has risen and made his way to the bars. "I do like the look of you in a dress," he says, his gaze running over me as if he were a suitor at a town dance.

"Don't make jokes." I approach, holding my hands out at my sides. "You were free."

JD leans the side of his head into one of the bars, that gaze still heavy on me, curious and wistful. "Spent all night at the schoolhouse thinking it over. I got everything I wanted—all the money, freedom to make my way west.... Except it felt hollow. Turns out, it's not all I want anymore."

"So you let yourself get caught? You'll *hang*."

His tongue wets his lower lip. "Trying not to think about that part, darlin'. Certainly wasn't my intention to get caught, but at least I get to see you one more time."

The reality of the situation sinks beneath my skin. "Why?" I whisper.

"I wanted to give you the money. I know it doesn't change anything, but it felt right. Thought I was pretty well hidden, but"—he coughs a laugh—"Sal gave me away, the damn horse."

My eyes burn, but it seems I'm—finally—out of tears.

"Come on, now, don't cry," he murmurs through a tight smile. In the soft light from the dust-coated window, JD's eyes shine with fear. "Maybe they'll send me to the pen instead, seeing how most of the money was recovered. If not, well...." His throat bobs. "I did take your pa from you."

If he only knew the whole truth.

"There's one thing... I swore I'd tell you if I got the chance." He hesitates. "Though now I'm not so sure it's a good idea after all."

I refuse to hear his deathbed confessions. I shake my head, but my traitorous mouth asks, "What is it?"

"Maggie, I...."

My eyes slide closed. He'll tell me he loves me, and I'll break like the china doll Ma always wished I was.

"The man I shot wasn't trying to stop the robbery, Maggie."

My eyes pop open, my breath caught in my throat.

"Heinous Hank Bennett organized the robbery, carried out half the cash himself. In the aftermath, he must have realized I was making off with more than my share. He shot at me, so I shot back. He missed. I didn't."

"You're wrong."

"I'm so sorry, Maggie, but it's the truth."

"No—"

"I swear to God—"

"He didn't shoot at you." I hold his gaze, forcing myself to watch my next words land. "I did."

18

TRUTH IS, I'VE NEVER BEEN ON A cattle drive despite my claims to convince Jonah I could handle a manhunt.

Truth is, two days into the trip, Pa sent Jonah and Luis with the others to mind the cattle. Me, he took along on darker pursuits.

See, I knew his secret. I'd found him, kneeling along the bluffs overlooking the Missouri, two weeks earlier. At first, I thought he was praying, but there was something in his clasped hands, held higher than chest level. My body understood before my mind could catch up, throwing myself from the saddle and calling Pa's name.

He startled and turned. The revolver dropped to his lap. "Maggie-bear."

He called me the name he'd use when pulling me from schoolyard scrapes, his voice choked with so much emotion I couldn't be sure whether he was relieved or disappointed.

Tears crowded my eyes. My brain still refused to latch on to what might have happened.

"I'm sorry," he said. He turned to look over the river, the shadowed trees beyond. Night was coming on fast. "I couldn't do it somewhere your ma or Cole might find me."

I wanted to lunge forward, rip the gun from his loose grasp and fling it over the cliff. Instead, I took one small step toward him. "But this is *our* spot."

Pa nodded. His shoulders slumped, neck bent. I'd never seen my father look so small. "You're the strongest. My Maggie-bear." He turned a smile on me, so sharp and sudden my chest cracked at the impact. "You'd think of something to say that would spare your mother the God-awful truth."

"That you're a coward?" I had never spoken to my father so. Never even thought the words before that day.

I'm still not sure if I believed them—I only wanted to anger some life back into him.

He started crying instead. "Skinner's going to take everything. The land. The animals. Adelaide."

"He can't take Ma."

"He's had his eye on her since before his own wife passed. He'll find a way."

"You don't think it'll be even easier if you're dead?"

Pa lifted bloodshot eyes to my face. "I can't go on like this."

Now that made me angry. Blood had been thumping in my ears from the moment I realized he'd come to our sacred place to off himself, but this? My hands clenched. "You gotta do what you gotta do, whether you want to or not."

"Mags—"

"Maybe this D really can help." I pulled out the telegram Widow Maude gave me earlier. Waved it at him.

Pa was off his knees, snatching at it, faster than I'd expected. Almost as if he didn't want me to see what it said. It was too late for that—the message was so short, I memorized it without even meaning to. *Love to help STOP New Moon STOP D*

"He actually answered...." Pa muttered.

"Who?" I asked.

"No one you need concern yourself with." He folded the slip and tucked it in his breast pocket. "Go on home, Maggie. I'll take care of everything."

But I was in it, now. If he thought my shoulders sturdy enough to bear the weight of his self-killing, he damn well could trust me with whatever scheme brought him back from despair.

The new moon was the following night. I followed him to our hunting shack where he met someone he called Devil. Together, they planned to rob Bluff City's bank. Devil—Ansel Dawes—he was making a name for himself as an outlaw. Pa knew about Sheriff Kline's upcoming trip to his sister's place two towns over, knew that Wyatt always spent Saturday lunch with his ma on the outskirts of Bluff City. It should have been perfect.

When I confronted Pa after that meeting, he tried to warn me off. Didn't matter. I told him to trust me with his life as much as he'd planned to with his death.

What a joke that turned out to be.

◇━◦━━◦━◦◇

"NOT A WORD ABOUT THIS to your mother or your brothers," Pa said for the umpteenth time as we drew near the gathered gang lurking in the shadows behind the Bell and Iron. His war friend, Ansel, sat tall on his steed, commanding the ragtag band of outlaws sure as he must have led armies in his younger years. In Jonah's hand-me-downs and with my bandana already covering my face, no one batted an eyelash at Pa's "boy." Ansel divvied up the jobs and there were no questions asked—and truth be told, I was so nervous, I was happy to be left in charge of the horses.

Before he followed the others to the bank, Pa slipped his watch into my hand. "If we're not back in fifteen minutes, you know what to do."

I nodded my agreement, knowing he wanted me to leave without him, save myself. Sitting there, though, I wondered which loyalty mattered more? Pa or the family? Our family or the town?

Of all his kids, he'd trusted me to see to Ma and the farm should the worst happen. I was determined that it wouldn't. Of course, I'd felt a lot more bravado insisting he bring me along than I did now, watching Defiance Row for any sign of Pa's return. Fat lot of good I could do him from here.

Beneath my loose-fitting shirt, sweat dripped down my midsection. I told myself it was the sun, watery and spring-fresh though it was. Seconds ticked into minutes on that silver pocket watch. My fingernail traced the groove of Pa's name, *Henry Bennett*, emblazoned on the back. Time crept toward the ten-minute mark, then fifteen. I had a decision to make. I couldn't leave Pa to rot in jail until the hangman came. Wouldn't run, either, so the only option was to charge after the Blue Devils and lend my support. Damnation, why couldn't Jonah have been there? Why did this choice have to fall to me?

I was saved from action when Pa appeared on JD's heels, saddlebags full of cash slung over their shoulders. Gunshots cracked from the direction of the bank. Ansel wasn't far behind, but my attention was on Pa alone, on seeing him safe.

"Here," JD called, reaching for Pa's bags to load them on his horse. Behind them, the others kept firing. One of the Devils fell. Guess the citizens got brave once the outlaws' backs were turned.

Pa climbed onto a clay-painted Marigold as I held her steady. Then a burst of dust as we took off down the main road out of town, Ansel leading the way past hay meadows and fresh-planted cornfields.

The hunting shack on the edge of our property was the meetup spot. We were all headed that way when Wyatt's first bullet caught up. *He wasn't supposed to be here.* Another Devil dropped. Our numbers down to four, Ansel went one way, JD the other. Maybe it was part of the plan—scatter then regroup.

Or maybe the son of a bitch was making off with our score. I couldn't let him. We *needed* that money. Knowing Pa would follow, I turned my horse after JD.

In a moment of blinding clarity, it occurred to me this might be providence—two of us against one man with all the money.

I'm the one who shot at him just before he reached the woods. Might've hit him, too, but I didn't account for his speed. He returned fire, twisting in the saddle and aiming true.

Or near enough.

Pa dropped faster than a sack of coins. Blood unfurled across his chest, a crimson sunset promising darkness.

"No!" I slid from the saddle and fell to my knees beside him. The damned bandana kept flying into my eyes—I ripped it off along with my hat, and the wind took them both. It tore vicious fingers through my hair, spilling free from the pins to tangle down my back.

Lingering dust caught in the tear tracks on my face as blood bubbled over Pa's lips. With shaking fingers, I untied his bandana and pressed it to the hole leaking blood across his jacket.

"Help us!" I screamed. Ansel was long gone, swallowed by dust clouds and tallgrass. No sign of pursuing townsfolk either.

Wyatt found us not long after, but far too late. One of the Devils had winged him—his shooting arm was bloodied and curled tight into his chest—but it didn't seem to matter to him once he caught sight of us. Fool took one look at the scene and made his assumptions. What would I've had to gain from correcting him?

My father was buried as a hero, and I never told anyone any different.

Until now.

◇━○━━○━◇

I TELL JD ALL OF it—the dying farm, the desperate plan, the fateful shot.

In the silence that follows, I wet my lips and await his judgment.

JD's fingers curl around the iron bars. His forearms twitch and tense. "That was you? Then you *know* I was only reacting in self-defense."

I step closer and lower my voice. "You were making off with all the money."

"Money that *you* helped steal." His face is pressed against the bars now, his eyes cold on mine. There's the anger I feared, heavy as the regret I already carry. "You're as guilty as I am."

The small jail feels even more cramped with his words ringing in the air. I grab the bars. "I didn't murder anyone."

"Oh, you've never killed a man?"

My lips part, but he's right. "None that mattered." My voice breaks over the last word.

"Everyone's someone to somebody. How many pas did we leave in the woods near Warrensburg?"

Ice shards stab through my chest. "Stop it."

His voice only roughens. "This whole time, you've been going on about justice, but you're no better than me."

I start to pull back, but he covers my hands on the bars with his.

"You're no better than me," he says again, softer.

Tears fill my eyes. "You shot my father."

His eyes close, chest lifts with a slow inhale. "I just shot *back*."

"Then why didn't you hit *me*?" It comes out like a sob, mortifying and freeing all at once. For all the rage I've been carrying against Jedidiah Dawson, I'm just as angry with myself. I rest my forehead against the cool bar. "I got him killed."

JD's thumbs run across the backs of mine.

"It's my fault," I whisper through the tears.

"For whatever it's worth," he says after a moment, "I'm glad I didn't hit you. I'm so sorry about your pa—truly, I am—but I wouldn't trade him for you. And I doubt he would either."

"Doesn't make it hurt any less."

"Nothing can." He says it with such gravity I look up. His eyes are soft again.

"Miss Maggie, are you—BACK AWAY FROM HER RIGHT NOW." Wyatt fumbles his revolver free in the doorway and levels it at JD, who's already backing to the far wall of his cell, hands in the air. "Maggie." Wyatt holds out his left hand to me, right still training the gun on JD. His gaze never wavers until I'm at his side. He takes in my tear-streaked face, his face morphing from rage to concern. "What's wrong? Did he hurt you?"

I shake my head quickly, scrambling for some explanation. "I—he... he apologized. For Pa."

"Oh." Wyatt blinks at JD in confusion. "Why?"

"It was an accident." JD's quiet voice rumbles over me, and my eyes close against the way it feels like a caress.

"You still did it." Wyatt's voice is hard.

"Wyatt," I say. My voice is barely a whisper. I clear my throat. "I'd like to go home now."

"Of course. Gene should be back in a sec, and I can bring you—"

"Thank you, but no. I'll make my own way home."

Wyatt glances at JD, then steps closer and lowers his voice. "Can I call on you later? Make sure you're all right?" His ears have gone red. The hope in his eyes is enough to break my heart.

This is my life now. My own, private penance. A merciful sentence. With that reminder, I nod. "I'd like that."

Suddenly the sun shines out of Wyatt's face. It's enough to force a small smile from me. I don't look back at JD before making my way from the jailhouse. I'm too afraid it might break me all over again.

19

"WELL?" COLE MEETS ME IN THE YARD, Jonah trailing him from the barn.

I blink, unsure how I got here. "Well, what?"

"What did Mister Skinner say?"

Jonah takes one look at my face and says, "Shoulda let me go down there. I know you hate the bank."

My gaze bounces from Cole's hopeful expression to Jonah's resigned one. My mind scrambles to break free of the cloud Jedidiah Dawson has caught it in.

"Oh," I say, then wet my bottom lip. "It's taken care of. For now, at least. We've got Sidney Ritter to thank."

"Sid?" Jonah's gaze snaps to mine.

"Don't worry, you'll pay him back." I'm in no mood to argue, and thankfully, Jonah doesn't push the issue. "Given that was all our savings, who knows how we'll deal with the next problem."

Jonah nods, stoic in the face of ruin, but I catch sight of his throat bobbing with a heavy swallow. "Worse comes to worst, we can sell some more acreage, cut back. We'll still have the homestead and the pigs, and at least enough hay for us, even if we won't have extra to sell. It'll mean at least another couple lean years, but we'll make do."

I feel so full of tears, I'm fit to burst. I've clung to the idea of saving the farm, as if by keeping it intact, it keeps Pa with us. JD's words linger. *"You're just as guilty as I am."* I've been a fool to think I can force things to stay the same.

Cole takes my hand in his—when did it become so big?—and gives me a crooked grin. "It'll be all right, Maggie."

"What are you all doing, dawdling outside?" Ma calls from the doorway. "Camila needs help bringing in the laundry, and that woodpile's not going to split itself."

Cole drops my hand and rushes around the side of the house, where a recently felled tree waits to be chopped and left to season.

"That rifle is still dirty as all get-out too," Jonah says after him. To me, "I imagine you'd prefer to help him stack the wood?"

"Don't matter to me," I mumble. I start after Cole, but Jonah takes my elbow.

"Hey, Cole's right. We'll figure it out. I'm sorry for what I said earlier."

When I meet his gaze over my shoulder, the truth wells with the tears. "They've got him in a cell."

His forehead furrows then clears. "Dawson?"

"Fool got caught trying to bring us the stolen money."

Half a dozen emotions cross my brother's face—surprise, confusion, relief, understanding, pity. I watch them all, grasping for some sort of feeling myself. I've been drenched in numbness.

"I'm sorry, Maggie," Jonah says.

"Me too."

◇━━◇──◇━━◇

AN AFTERNOON FILLED WITH MUNDANE chores is surprisingly soothing for my raw nerves. The fog is lifting, tentative hope crawling in. There's got to be a way to set JD free, a careful dance to plead his case while preserving my family's reputation. I just have to figure out how.

Maybe I won't get everything I wanted, but maybe we'll be okay. Maybe that's punishment in itself. No one else needs to know about the bank robbery, and the farm *is* secure for now. Maybe that's enough.

Jonah and I are cleaning out the horse stalls when hoofbeats call us into the yard. It's been dry the past few days, evidenced by the dust clouds kicked up by a band of horses coming to a halt. Even through the haze, I think I recognize the blue jacket on the man astride the lead horse. I've gone cold down to my toes, but Jonah takes a step forward.

"You lost, friend?" he calls across the handful of paces separating us. "Bluff City is another few miles down the main road."

As if wandering strangers are common in our neck of the woods. The dust has settled enough for the sun to wink off nearly a dozen weapons, and I'm sure my brother's noticed too.

"You Hank Bennett's boy?"

"I am," Jonah replies, voice steady. I want to drag him into the house and bolt the door.

I only make it one step toward him when the man in blue heaves himself down and crosses the distance between them. His gaze barely skirts me in my dress, focused instead on sizing up my brother, but I know this devil, sure as I know it's me he's after. Everything inside is screaming to get this man away from my family, but I'm frozen where I stand.

"Lot bigger than I recall," Ansel Dawes says, coming to a stop in front of us.

"I don't believe we've met." There's a certain grimness to Jonah's voice that sounds like he knows who he's dealing with regardless, but how can he? More likely he thinks this concerns Pa's history with cards.

Ansel gives a sharp laugh. "Then perhaps you and I can get acquainted in private?"

His eyes slide to me, a knowing smirk on his lips. Must be some crusted sense of fraternity, a misguided desire to spare the fairer sex the details of their unsavory connection. If I wasn't so petrified I might roll my eyes. These two men, incorrectly taking stock of the situation.

"Come on in." Without taking his eyes off Ansel, Jonah tilts his head toward me. "Go see to the chickens."

"But—"

"Now." He turns and leads that Blue Devil right through our door.

Left standing in the waning daylight, I'm seared with indecision. Whatever Ansel's after, Jonah doesn't know anything to help. Whether Ansel will believe that is a different story entirely.

The horses shift behind me, a couple Blue Devils exchanging murmured conversation too quiet to make out. That decides me—I do as my brother asked and go see to the chickens.

Of course, the animals don't need tending, seeing as how Ma and Camila are already in the coop. Jonah just wants to know the other ladies are out of harm's way. No telling where Cole's got to, now I think about it. For once, I hope he's shirking his chores, fishing or playing or anything else far from here.

Out of sight of the gang, I grab the splitting maul where it's propped against the back of the house and follow the short dirt path to the chicken pen, meeting Ma at the gate. Camila peers over her shoulder.

"Everything all right?" Ma asks.

"Nothing to worry about, just some unsavory visitors. You both need to stay out here until one of us comes for you."

Camila's eyes widen. "Jonah—"

"He'll be fine. I'll take care of it. Just promise to hide here until they're gone." To emphasize my point, I lean the maul against the fence. I don't need to wait for their agreement—they're both more apt to follow someone else's commands than I am—but race back to the front of the house. The gang hasn't moved, waiting diligently on their horses for their leader to emerge and give the next command. Even as I run past, no one tries to waylay me beyond one mildly curious, "Where you headed, little lady?" which I ignore.

My chest is heaving as I peer through the seeded glass window in our front door. Could've tried sneaking in through the back door, but that one is solid wood and reason—sounding a lot like Ma's voice—tells me to play it cautious, assess what I'm walking into before barreling in.

Ansel sits in my father's seat at the head of the table, business end of his revolver drifting lazily from Jonah to Cole and back again. Scattered across the tabletop are pieces of our disassembled rifle. *Shit.* Caution be damned, I shove my way through the door.

"Well, isn't this a treat?" Ansel says, shifting the weapon toward me.

"Goddammit, Maggie," Jonah mutters.

"I was just telling these fine young men how their daddy was a bad, bad man. Stole a lot of money from me."

Cole sucks in a breath. "He did no such thing—"

"Cole!" Jonah spits the reprimand through a clenched jaw as Ansel turns back to our younger brother. My heartbeat pulses in my teeth.

My gun belt is up in the loft, and a darted glance to Jonah's hips confirms he's unarmed as well. *Shit and damnation.*

"Well, someone took my money," Ansel says softly. "Who else but dear old Hank? The law's been a little too hot on my trail until now, but my boy's done a fine job of distracting everyone so I could finally come claim what's mine."

Your boy? I run through the Blue Devils as Pa told them to me— Ansel Dawes, Rufus Gordon, Jasper Champlain, and Jedidiah Daws–

Son of a wart-covered toad. "JD's father died in the war." The words slip out, my mind too busy trying to catch up to tell my mouth to keep quiet.

Ansel shifts his full body toward me this time, along with his gun. His head falls to the side, his pale gaze crawling over my face. "Far as his mama knew, I did. But just how would *you* know that, little lady?"

My lips press together. I wish Jonah had lit a lantern. The space is filling with shadows.

Ansel starts to nod. I feel the weight of his entire focus as it settles on my shoulders. Jonah and Cole could likely slip out the door unnoticed—Lord, I pray they try. Behind my skirt, I flick my fingers at Jonah, but with my gaze square on Ansel, I don't see if Jonah notices, much less understands.

"Did *he* steal the take?" Ansel's voice is hardly a whisper now. "He disappeared right around the same time, and I know he was headed back here too. What happened? Your pa introduce you, use you to seduce Jed into betraying us?"

"She only just met him while trying to bring him to justice," Jonah says. My fool brother, trying to shield me.

"Maybe it was you," Ansel says to him. "Maybe Hank had no idea what snakes he unleashed on my gang. Maybe *his* boy saw an opportunity to set us up and threw his sister at my son. Jed's always been a sucker for a skirt."

Despite the tension, his words sting, too close to JD's teasing comments about my dress. Doesn't matter, not with my family in danger.

"Neither of my brothers had anything to do with this." My voice expands into the big room as I try to take control of the conversation. It rings with an authority I sure as hell do not feel. "Let them walk out that door, and I'll tell you what you really want to know. I'll tell you where the money is."

My brothers whip toward me—I catch the movement in my peripheral vision, but my gaze never wavers.

Ansel's eyes brighten like moons in the darkening room. A wolf-smile peels his lips apart. Even still, my heart settles to a more even pace. With this promise, Ansel will let my brothers go, and this will all be over in a matter of minutes. JD may have turned over the cash, but by the time Ansel figures that out, we'll have raised the alarm.

Instead, he gestures to Cole with the gun. "Come here, boy."

I step forward. "Don't—"

Ansel's shooting arm steadies, pointed right between my little brother's eyes. Mind-numbing panic floods me. "Come, or I'll shoot you where you stand."

With a reluctant glance my direction, Cole moves to Ansel's side. Ansel grabs his left wrist and slams Cole's hand to the table. Cole's frozen but trembling, a tear leaking down his cheek. Ansel holsters his gun, but before any relief can filter through my terror, he's pulled a knife.

"Place that foot one step closer," he says as Jonah starts to move, "and I'll gut him like a squealing piglet."

There's no way Jonah could reach them before Ansel acts on his threat. Jonah eases back, widening the distance between them.

"Now, the next words out of your mouth better be exactly where the money is," Ansel says, "or I'll take every one of his fingers, knuckle by knuckle."

"Let him g—" I start.

Ansel brings the sharp edge of the blade down hard on Cole's pinky. The tip bounces across Ma's clean table and my baby brother screams, a sound I feel clear to my bones.

20

"STOP!" I THROW MY HANDS UP—JONAH'S TAKEN a lunging step toward Ansel, which will only make things worse. "Behind the school. It's behind the schoolhouse, in a hollow log shaped like a bear's head." My face is wet, my eyes on my whimpering brother. "Please."

"That wasn't so hard, was it?" He shoves Cole from him. My brother has gone gray-white, and he stumbles over a chair toward me.

"Well, I best be off." Ansel drops his hat onto his head and stands, as if he's a guest leaving a fine tea.

If he were closer, I'd have charged him the second Cole was free. Instead, I cradle Cole against me as Jonah rushes Ansel.

"Jonah!" I say because Ansel still has the knife in hand. Too late— Ansel slashes. I bend my head over Cole, as if I can protect him further, but there's nothing to block the tearing sound of rending flesh from reaching my ears.

When I look up, Jonah is still on his feet. Ansel drops the knife and pulls his gun. "Stand down, boy." He backs the rest of the way out the door. Beyond him, his men have drawn their weapons. The door swings shut, blocking them from view.

Jonah wraps his right hand around his left bicep as he turns back to us. Blood drips through his fingers, but it doesn't seem much more than a flesh wound, God be praised. Ma bursts through the back door, eyes wild, holding our splitting maul overhead. Behind her, Camila cradles a split log. "We heard a scream."

Cole starts sobbing. Ma drops the makeshift weapon and rushes over. I pass Cole to her. "I need to get to town," I say.

Jonah's already hoisting himself one-handed up to the loft and our gun belts. I follow him.

"Is it true?" Jonah asks, his voice low, as he passes me my revolver. "About Pa?"

I meet my brother's gaze. "Don't tell Ma."

"He wasn't trying to stop them?" Then, when I don't deny it, "It wasn't just a card game."

"I'm sorry." For the robbery, for Pa, for leaving them now. "I have to go."

"I'm coming with you," Jonah says.

Relief, pure as a new spring day, spirals through me as I descend the ladder. Ma's already binding Cole's wound, singing softly to him like she would when he'd have a nightmare.

"Get the rest of them somewhere safe," I say to Jonah. I want to tell him to let Ma patch him up, too, but he's a grown man, and our family's safety matters more than a scratch. "No telling if Ansel will be back, and we can't leave them unprotected." I nod to the table. "And fix the rifle. We'll need it."

"I was cleaning it like you said...." Cole mumbles.

"It's okay." Jonah rests a bloodied hand on our brother's back. Over Cole's head, he nods at me.

Whatever I've done, he's telling me with his eyes he'll stick by my side. I nod back and race to Huckleberry, and then down the road to Bluff City.

◇━◦━◦━◦━◇

WYATT IS ALONE AT THE desk in the jail when I burst in.

"Where's Sheriff Kline?" I'm too aware of JD's presence in the cell off to my left, despite my refusal to look at him.

"What's wrong?" Wyatt stands, his chair scraping the worn wooden floor.

"Ansel Dawes and the Blue Devils, just outside town."

JD shoots to his feet. "Ansel's here?"

I start to turn toward him but catch myself. We need the law right now, not scrabbled-together explanations. To Wyatt, I say, "He threatened my family." My voice catches as it all sinks in. "He hurt Cole." Jonah's wound, I could forgive, but I'll never forget the sight of my little brother losing a fingertip.

JD swears.

Wyatt's face hardens from concern to fury. "Cole all right?"

"He'll live." Doesn't change the fact my brother suffered because of me.

"Is Ansel here for the money?" JD asks. "He doesn't know I'm here, does he?"

"Where's he now?" Wyatt pulls down one of the rifles hanging behind the desk.

It's taking all my energy to stay focused on Wyatt. "Cole?"

"Dawes."

Obviously. I shake my head. "He was headed to the schoolhouse."

"Schoolhouse?" Wyatt looks up from loading the rifle, a frown between his eyes.

In hindsight, I should have told Ansel that JD was halfway to Colorado with the money by now. All that appeared in my mind through the panic was the truth, or close to it. I glance at JD. He grips the bars, his eyes holding me tight as a lasso.

"You told him where I hid the banknotes?" he asks. When I don't answer right away, he presses his face between the bars. "Maggie. I turned it all in. He won't find nothing."

"It bought us time."

Wyatt stills. "How did you know where he'd hid—"

"He won't take kindly to being sent on a fool's errand," JD says.

There's a strain in his voice. Takes me a second to realize it's terror. His hands fall from the bars, and he takes a step back. "You need to leave right now. Get back to your family."

"There's still time." I turn back to Wyatt, ignoring the confused furrow of his brow. "If we move. Now."

"How many men he gather since the spring?" JD says at my back. The implication sinks chilled fingers into my spine just before he speaks it aloud. "Your home ain't safe."

"Jonah's seeing to them."

Wyatt smacks a hand on the desk. "What in damnation is going on?"

"You—" JD turns to Wyatt. "Let me go, and I might be able to help."

"Like hell I will. Maggie, talk to me, what's—"

JD raises his voice. "Ansel Dawes is going to be livid when he realizes he's been had, and he'll slaughter this whole town for it. Let me out, and I'll lead him away from Bluff City. No one has to get hurt."

"Let him come," Wyatt says. "He can share the cell with you."

JD smacks the bars. "You're not listening. The Blue Devils will turn Bluff City to ashes."

"Wyatt," I say, fighting to keep calm, "please, unlock the door."

Wyatt turns incredulous eyes on me. "You can't be serious."

"There's almost a dozen riders with Ansel. If JD's right, it'll be a bloodbath. Give him a chance to help us avoid a massacre."

"He killed your pa and robbed us all! I can't just let go the most wanted criminal this town has seen. Bullet or noose, what's it matter at this point?"

"He returned the money. And Pa... it wasn't murder."

"Wasn't murder...?" Wyatt mutters, shaking his head. Furrows line his forehead as he stares at me. "Well, it wasn't all the money, neither, so he'll stay right where he is."

"About one fifty short?" Bile claws up my throat, but my hand slips into my pocket. "This should cover the difference." My fingers tighten around the pocket watch. I force myself to lift my fist to the desk, then again to open my hand.

Wyatt just blinks at it, gleaming in the falling light through the front window.

"Maggie, no...." JD says.

"It's actually perfect," I tell him. "This whole time you wanted redemption. Lead Ansel away—save our town—and you've got it, far as I'm concerned. And this?" I hold up the watch. The lengthening shadows catch in Pa's name etched across the back. "Justice."

"I don't understand," Wyatt says.

Whatsoever a man soweth, that shall he also reap. The truth's been hanging around my neck like a noose this whole time. I don't know if confessing to the law will tighten it or free me, but it's time I find out. "I helped rob the bank that day."

Wyatt huffs a laugh. "That's not even a little funny, Maggie."

"I'm not joking, Wyatt—"

A gunshot cracks somewhere in town and JD mutters another oath.

"There's no time." I cross to the desk, searching for the keys.

Wyatt steps toward me. I know he'd never hurt me, but I pull my revolver to make sure he keeps his distance. "I'm sorry, Wyatt. I'm letting him go. You don't have to help, but I won't let you stop me."

Another shot responds, then another.

"Don't do this, Maggie." Wyatt's voice has gone quiet. Suddenly the jailhouse feels larger than the two cells and the entryway, the desk separating Wyatt and me enormous. He doesn't move, just watches on as I find the key and cross to the first cell.

As soon as I get the door open, I thrust my revolver handle first into JD's chest and nod down the short hall. "There's a back exit down there."

JD checks the chamber. Finding it fully loaded, he gives it a spin, snaps it closed, then winks before stepping around me, toward the door.

"What are you—"

"Christ Almighty." Jonah ducks through the front door, Winchester rifle across his chest. "Blue Devils are tearing up the town. Kline's at the general store holding them off. Could use more firepower."

JD uses the distraction to slip into the street.

"JD!"

Jonah catches me around the upper arm before I can follow. He shoves the rifle into my hands and jerks his chin at the stairs leading up to Wyatt's quarters, and the roof access. With JD gone, Wyatt's in action mode, pulling down extra guns.

"What about the others?" I ask my brother. He knows I don't mean the gang outside.

Jonah frowns. "Cole will be fine. Ma's tending him, and Sid's got them holed up at the Bell. Now, go on. I'll slip out the back and get these to Sheriff Kline," he says to Wyatt as I start up the stairs. At least the fact that the gang is here means no one is hassling my family.

In the street, the gunshots have paused, an echoing silence in their wake. I stumble over the last step, cursing the skirts I put on this morning, and hoist myself onto the roof. A searing sunset momentarily blinds me. The front facade curls into a peak in the center of the roof, providing cover to duck behind and a nice rest for the rifle muzzle.

A voice filters up to me. "Hey, fellas."

Below, JD stands before a line of horses. I can't rip my eyes from the sight of him, small and alone in a sharp cut of sunlight shafting between the buildings. My gun is loose at JD's side, but I've seen his quick draw. I just pray he isn't foolish enough to wait for them to shoot first. At that range, even my ma could hit JD.

There's a thud behind me—Wyatt joining me on the roof. He kneels and sets a revolver down near my foot, then settles his rifle into his shoulder and sights a target below.

"Dawson's not getting away that easy," Wyatt murmurs and cocks the rifle.

"Wyatt!" I hiss before he can squeeze the trigger. "You shoot him, and they'll kill us all."

"There's only nine of them—"

"You couldn't handle six when two of them were Pa and me." I bite my lip as soon as the words escape. I never intended to admit Pa's part in things. Only my own.

Wyatt gapes at me, stricken, but I don't have time for his disappointment. I turn back to the scene below in time to see a tenth Devil hauling Ma into the street. Sweat pools under my arms. *Damn you, Jonah, she's supposed to be safe.*

"No need to drag a lady into this," JD drawls as I adjust my aim. His shoulders have tensed, but he still hasn't raised his weapon. Maybe he's hoping to banter his way out of this. I'm not willing to take that risk. Whoever takes the first shot, it will end up a shootout no matter what.

So I shoot first.

The man holding Ma's arm drops. Horses startle as more gunshots ring out, from the outlaws and from the buildings on either side of the street. A bullet splinters the wood trim near my head, sending me ducking for cover. When I next peer over the parapet, JD has disappeared in the chaos. I catch a flash of Ma's skirts as she crawls back toward the saloon—hopefully it's good sense keeping her low to the ground and not an injury.

Chalky smoke hangs in the air, quiet and calm. Below it, horses scream, people stagger, blood slicks across the dirt road in shiny black pools. It looks like most of the outlaws have taken cover across from the jail, at the Bluff City Gazette building.

Farther down, leaning against the general store's hitching post, Sheriff Kline's been hit—his left arm is close to his chest, a splotch of red staining his forearm. He's still engaging with those hiding in the Gazette. Sidney peers around the corner of the Bell and Iron, fires a shot, but retreats without hitting anyone when they fire in his direction. Black powder mixes with the tang of sweat, thick and hot under a heavy, sinking sun.

I don't know what's happened to Jonah. I fire, pump, fire every time I spot movement across the street. Beside me, Wyatt does the same. In the dust-shrouded street below us, a woman shrieks. Wyatt stows his rifle over his shoulder and slips through the trapdoor. The memory of his responding to my screams threatens to overpower me, especially with the dust in my nose and gunshots ringing in my ears.

Something else rises to the forefront of my mind, sudden and sharp.

Wyatt said there were only ten outlaws. I should have counted for myself.

There'd been eleven at my house.

What's more, there wasn't a telltale blue coat among the riders JD confronted.

Where is Ansel Dawes?

Shots crack and echo. Then, running through the smoke toward the blacksmith, my brother chases one of the bandits. I take aim. They're darting too quick—I won't risk hitting Jonah instead. They disappear around a corner.

The Gazette is quiet across the street, the melee moving farther into town. Now's my chance to check on my family. I slip back inside and cross the small bedroom for the stairs.

A bullet shatters the window behind me. Glass slices through my skirt and bites into the back of my arm. I drop to the floor and crawl toward the window, taking cover behind the solid wall. Must still be someone in the Gazette after all. I peer through the jagged window-pane, then pull back when I catch eyes with one of the Blue Devils, aiming another shot my way. The bullet eats into the far side of the window frame.

I'm almost out of ammunition, and I still need to make it across the street. Rather than waste anymore time or bullets trading potshots with the gazette, I crawl past the window to the stairs. At the bottom, though, I pull up short.

Wyatt is framed in the doorway, gun drawn and pointed. Slowly, I raise my hands. They still hold the rifle and revolver, but Wyatt drops his weapon anyway.

"Fighting's moved toward the church," he says, crossing to the desk. He reaches into a drawer and pulls out a box of ammunition.

I join him as he starts to reload his weapons. "Can I get a few of those?"

He stills. His shoulders move with a heavy breath, then he shakes his head and resumes loading the Peacemaker.

"Wyatt?"

"What am I supposed to do, Maggie? Arm a criminal?"

I pull back as if he slapped me.

"Let you run out there with my bullets? For all I know, you'll join your friends and turn those bullets on us townsfolk."

"They're not my friends."

"*Accomplices*, then." He meets my eyes for the first time since learning the truth. I wish he didn't. His eyes are full of betrayal.

We were desperate. The why doesn't matter, though. Dust and gun smoke curl through the broken windows. The haze clings to my nostrils, forcing me to relive that day.

Pa did betray him, betrayed this whole town, and I helped.

Wyatt rubs at his arm where he'd been shot the last time the Blue Devils came to Bluff City. "You...." His lips press together, heartbreak in the lines on his forehead, the shine of his eyes. "You played the victim real well."

"It wasn't an act. I'd just lost Pa."

"You let us mourn him as a hero. He was anything but."

I step closer. "He was *my* hero."

Wyatt doesn't say anything to that. His gaze flicks to the door before he finishes reloading and stands, weapons and ammo in hand.

"You lied," he says. "You're a liar, and it's in everything now. Every thought, every memory I have of you. And not just the past few months. How far back does it go, that you'd be able to do something like this?" He gives a little humorless laugh. "I used to think you had such honest eyes. It's one of the things I loved most about you. Now?" He shrugs. "I don't even know you."

"That's not fair," I say, even though I know he's right. "I'm the same person I've always been."

"That's the problem." He looks past me. I follow his gaze to the door, to the quiet street beyond. "You should go while they're distracted."

Wyatt's words bring my head around.

"You're not arresting me?"

"What, throw you in a cell where any stray bullet could hit you?"

Wyatt shakes his head. "Jonah said your family's at Sid's—they need you more than I need another dead body on my conscience."

His gaze tangles in mine for a heartbeat. My chest feels dry and hollow. Without another word, he shoves his revolver into its holster and steps past me, out the door.

21

THE BELL AND IRON SITS BACK FAR enough from the main thoroughfare that it's avoided too much damage. A few tables are overturned, the barroom abandoned. My boots echo through the room as I climb to the second floor.

Upstairs is almost as quiet, except for the low murmur of soft whimpers and insistent shushing sounds. "Ma?" I call, to let everyone hiding know I'm not a threat and to find my family. "Cole?"

Della's door cracks open, then Camila throws it wide. "Maggie! We're in here." She clings to me, practically dragging me into the room. Ma is sitting on the floor, legs splayed in front of her in the least ladylike position I've ever seen her take. Cole nestles against one side of her. Camila drops to the other side. Ma's face is purpled and swollen, but she gives me a faint smile as I kneel in front of her.

"I'm okay," she says, a hoarse scrape of a voice.

My gaze finds hers. Bile charges up my throat, catches, chokes. Her left eye is bloodshot. I swallow hard. "Ma." It comes out like a whimper, like I'm a little girl seeing monsters between the trees.

Cole's beside me. "I'm sorry, Mags. Della went to help the wounded and Ma went after her, and one of *them* grabbed her, knocked her around. I should've been the one—" A cracked sob cuts off his words.

Ma tugs us both into her, holds my head to the jut of her collarbone. "It's okay. I'm alive. We're okay."

"You're bleeding," Camila says, her fingers stroking my elbow. The glass from that shot-out window must have sliced my arm deeper than I realized.

Below us, footsteps clatter up the stairs. I pull the revolver, my finger taut against the trigger. Blood sticks my tattered sleeve to my elbow as I wait. *Please be Jonah or Wyatt.*

It isn't, but JD's dirt-streaked face is just as welcome. He's got a bruise across his left cheek and a split lip, but he's alive. His eyes meet mine as I lower the weapon, a sad smirk flickering across his pale face. "'Lo, Margaret. We need to go."

"We're as safe here as anywhere. Everyone else is moving toward the church."

Cole seems to notice JD for the first time. He stiffens. "Wait—"

"It's all right," I say quickly. "He's helping me."

Cole just stares, his arm tightening around Ma, good hand reaching for Camila.

I detach myself from my family and join JD at the top of the stairs. He takes my shooting arm, gently turning me to inspect the cuts above my elbow. I resist the urge to do the same, test the swelling on his cheek.

"I'm fine," I say.

JD shakes his head and looks at me, that terror back in his dark eyes. "I meant Ansel isn't—"

"I know." Ansel and me, we're not all that different. Self-righteous shits who can't let go of a grudge. And if I felt betrayed, I'd go back to the source. I'd make it *hurt.*

"If he's set fire to the farm, there isn't much we can do to stop him now." At least Jonah got the others to safety before Ansel returned.

JD's lips purse, some urgency leaking out of his tense shoulders. "He wouldn't stick around long after, anyway."

"Where else would he go?" I'm only half asking JD. I doubt he has any more insight than I do, but maybe between his knowledge of his father and mine of the area—I see it in his eyes as the thought occurs to me. "The hunting shack."

"Back where it started." He nods.

No rush for action fills my blood, no desire for a foggy shade of justice. If anything, it's as if I'm hearing Pa's words from that fateful day for the first time. *"Let him go, Mags. It's not worth it."*

If I'd listened to him then, none of this would have happened. And he was right. Recovering the money wasn't worth Pa's life, tracking down JD wasn't worth the noose he'd have hung from, and now this. Nothing is worth risking my family again, not even the chance at saving our home.

JD is watching me, waiting for something I can't give him. I shake my head. "He's not worth it."

I shift toward Ma, but JD is everywhere. I can't lose sight of him, even in my peripheral. He shoves a hand through his hair, scowls at the hallway. Nods like he's decided something.

"Stay here," he says, as if I wasn't planning to do just that. "I'm ending this."

The finality in JD's voice is enough to force me away from the huddle of my family. "Don't—"

He's already striding out the door. And, God as my witness, I could let Ansel Dawes go. I *would*. But not JD. I let him go once, and everything inside me is screaming not to do that again.

"JD, wait!" I turn back to Cole, cup his face in my hands. "You need to try to find Jonah." Lord Almighty, please let Jonah be alive.

"I will go," Camila says, more a croak than a statement.

"No. You need to stay here with Ma." I can't in good conscience encourage my brother's pregnant wife to go traipsing off in a town full of outlaws. Good God in Heaven, let their baby survive all this. To Cole, I say, "Be very careful. There's still plenty of them out there, but you're smart, and you're quiet, and you can get in and find help. Whoever you can find, send them to the hunting shack. We're gonna go get Dawes."

Cole hasn't looked away from JD, suspicion twisting his features. "But what—"

"There's no time to explain. Just trust me."

Not that I've given anyone a reason to lately, between betraying the town, getting Pa killed, and now bringing this vengeance down on my entire family. I probably shouldn't be the one giving orders, and Lord knows how I wish this responsibility didn't settle so firmly on my shoulders.

But Cole nods, like trusting me is more natural than breathing. He scrubs his good arm across his face and squares his shoulders. His determined jaw cuts a sharp silhouette against the gaslight on the end table behind him. It occurs to me we're all responsible for our own decisions. Whether we bend or break or keep charging onward, that's on each of us. I've made a mess of things trying to shoulder the burden all on my own, but together, we might be able to end this for good.

After a quick check confirming that Camila isn't about to descend into full-blown shock, I follow JD back through the saloon. He's right beside me when I reach Huck, blessedly unharmed, still hitched outside the sheriff's.

I climb into Huck's saddle, JD behind me.

"How many bullets you got left?" JD asks in my ear as we ride. "Do we have a plan, or are we just charging in there, guns blazing?" There's a hitch in his chest—I can't tell if it's a laugh or a fearful inhalation. "You know how I feel about shooting first."

"It's a small space, so I'm really hoping you'll make an exception if it comes down to it." Otherwise, we could all be dead. He has got me thinking, though. "How forgiving a man is your pa?"

This time the breath is definitely a quiet laugh. "You've met him. Though he's always seemed to have a soft spot for me."

It's not much, but I've got the start of an idea that just might work.

◇━◦━━◦━◇

LANTERN LIGHT SEEPS THROUGH THE cracks between the

boards of the hunting shack. A palomino horse is hitched outside, a smudge of brightness against the dark woods.

We slip off Huckleberry and creep up to the door. There aren't any windows, which means Ansel can't see us sneaking through the dark. Also means we can't catch a glimpse of where inside the small space he is, or what he might be up to in there. As it is, we're pressed up beside each other along the doorframe, so close my body moves with each of JD's inhalations.

He looks down at me, something painful or hopeful or both in his eyes. His lips part, but no whispered words come out. Instead, he nods once, then opens the door.

JD's hands are out in plain view, his gun held high and loose. "Hey, Pa."

I'm able to see Ansel now, standing beside the dead fireplace at the back of the room—he lifted his own revolver to the door, but the tension goes out of his shoulders at JD's words. "Thought I'd lost you."

"You haven't been easy to find yourself."

"Well, you're here now—"

I step in and put my gun to JD's head. "Drop your weapon, or I'll splatter his brains on the wall," I say to Ansel, counting on that hope for a family reunion I'd heard in his voice.

Ansel doesn't move. "Shoot her, son."

"He can't," I say. "His gun's empty."

"Sure about that, darlin'?" JD asks. Even in the grimy half light pouring through the lantern's open hatch, his crooked grin flashes bright.

"I can count to six." To Ansel, I say, "I'll give you half that to put your gun on the ground. One"—I cock the revolver—"two...."

Ansel buys it, bending at the knees to surrender his gun. I smirk at JD.

There's a sudden movement from the corner of my eye, Ansel taking aim, then a gunshot splits the shack.

Ansel crumples all the way to the floor as smoke curls from the end of JD's revolver.

"Never take your eye off the quarry, Margaret," JD says. His face is grim, his eyes still on his father.

"You two-timing sack of shit." Ansel sputters and writhes, clutching at the bloody mass that was his knee. "Shoulda known a woman can't count worth shit."

"No," I say, crossing to him. "You *should've* known that an outlaw is only as good as her bluff." I point my revolver at his head and squeeze the trigger. His eyes clench shut even as the gun gives a metallic click.

Slowly, his eyes reopen. Then Ansel starts laughing. I leave him hooting himself silly and return to JD's side.

"I'll take Huck back to town to get the sheriff—"

The laughter cuts off. "Dumb bitch."

JD's hand closes around my elbow and shoves me behind and away from him. Two shots sound, near simultaneously, and Ansel's gun clatters to the ground—this time well out of reach.

Foolish. How could I not think to fully disarm him? Even after JD's admonishment, I got cocky, and it nearly got me killed.

For good measure, I retrieve Ansel's revolver. His shooting arm is hanging funny below the elbow, the bullet having shattered his forearm. He's breathing too heavy to do much more than shriek every so often, curling in on himself. He cuts a pathetic figure, but I can't find any pity inside for him.

"Maggie." JD's voice is low in the growing silence between Ansel's moans. When I turn, he's sliding down the wall to sit on the floor. It's only once he's turned fully toward me that I see the growing stain across his chest.

No. I'm not sure if I say it aloud. I crawl to his side, terror wrapping around my throat. It's Pa all over again, and I don't think I'll survive watching a bullet meant for me take the life of another man I—

"Why couldn't you have just come to Colorado with me?" His voice is gruff and strained.

I find the bullet wound—higher than I'd feared, thank heavens, closer to the shoulder—and set about applying pressure. "I wish I had right about now."

"Offer stands."

"Let's make it out of this predicament, then we'll talk," I say.

Twilight is fading fast, darkening the room and throwing JD's face into shadow. I help him up, staggering the few steps so he can slump onto the low cot. His chest rises and falls too quickly for my comfort. Behind me, Ansel's cries have dwindled to whimpers that are still too loud in the close space. They bounce between my ears, drowning out any rational thinking.

My teeth grind. I take JD's revolver and return to Ansel's side. Part of me wants to put JD's last bullet between Ansel's eyes and silence him forever. Instead, I tug his belt free from his hips and cinch it tight around his bloodied arm. His knee is ruined, face pale. I wrap my hands under his arms and drag him outside.

The motion sets him howling again, in jagged, choppy bursts of half curses, and once the wall is between us, I'll have some blessed quiet.

Not so just yet. Hoofbeats reach me as soon as I've dropped Ansel in the dirt and straightened. I raise the revolver with a tired arm, not even wavering when the light from the open door catches on the metallic star clipped to the rider's chest.

22

WYATT PULLS HIS HORSE UP SHORT. HIS mouth hangs open as he looks dumbly from me to Ansel's near-unconscious form. He leans, his gaze flicking past me to the open shack door.

"What in tarnation have you gotten yourself into, Maggie Bennett?"

My shoulders ache with the effort to keep my gun trained on him. After everything, he still doesn't believe me capable of anything bad?

He dismounts and comes to stand over Ansel. "He dead?"

"Not yet."

Wyatt's face is still turned toward the ground. "You can put that away."

Somewhere in the trees beyond the shack, a whippoorwill calls its name. I return the hammer and lower the weapon. "Did Cole find you?"

Wyatt seems lost in thought. He hasn't moved from his stance. Finally, his head bobs, the movement a streak against twilit shadows. "Surgeon's patching up his hand best he can."

My chest expands at that, as if one of the many stones crushing my chest has been carried away. "Thank—"

"He's a good kid. He don't deserve any of this." Wyatt turns to me, sharp and sudden. In the cut of light from the door behind me, Wyatt is sliced gold. His lips press together, heartbreak lines his forehead, his eyes shine.

"I'll make it right, somehow." I'm not sure I even know what *right* is, but I don't want my brothers carrying this weight for me.

"Help me get him on the horse," is all Wyatt says in return.

Together, we drape Ansel over Wyatt's saddle. I can't help noticing he's leaving Ansel's horse here. I don't know what that means, and I don't know how to ask him.

Silence stretches as Wyatt makes sure Ansel's situated, feels for a weak-beating pulse, turns back to me. Then he looks past me. I follow his gaze to where JD lies, bleeding, on the cot. "If I send the sawbones, I'll have to take him in."

I nod. I can hardly ask Wyatt alone to keep this a secret. The more who know, the harder it will be. And Wyatt's always had more integrity than any one man should.

My gaze lingers on JD, the shallow rise and fall of his chest, his dark eyes steady on me. I can't read his expression—I know he doesn't want to hang, but would he rather bleed out? At least with Ansel in custody, he could plead his case for the state penitentiary. He could *live*. I don't want to make that decision for him, though.

In fact, I *shouldn't*. We all make our choices—it's not on me to decide for everyone how things should go. I can only say what's right for me. And just in case JD's only hesitation over the surgeon is what I've confessed to Wyatt, I can clear that obstacle.

"I suppose you'll be needing to arrest me as well," I offer to Wyatt. He's already shaking his head before I've finished.

"Dammit, Maggie. I can't—" He breaks off and stares at the wall. "I can't watch you hang. But I can't walk around with you in this town, knowing what you done, seeing you at the store or in *church*." His gaze skirts me to land on JD. "The best I can do for you right now is nothing." He lets out a pained laugh. "Guess that's always been true, huh?"

"Wyatt...."

He shakes his head again, blinking against the shine coating his eyes. "I won't say nothing. Your family will be looked after. Just don't ever show your face in Bluff City again. Either of you."

"Thank—"

"Don't."

I see it there in his eyes, more clearly than ever before, just how much Wyatt Murray loves me. He turns and walks out of my life for good.

⟡━•━◦━━◦━•━⟡

THE RED STAIN HAS SPREAD down JD's chest.

"Why didn't you say anything?" There's a shrill ripping as I slice through the bottom of my skirt, then replace the blood-soaked bandana.

"You knew I been shot." He licks his cracked lips. "Didn't want to interrupt your truce with the law, dampen the victory."

"What victory? You keeling over kind of puts a damper on the whole riding off into the sunset thing." Plus, the sun has long since set. The twilight beyond the cracks in the walls deepens steadily toward blackness.

"You go on without me. Have that adventure you always wanted."

I lean back on my haunches so I can look him in the eyes. "Don't you dare start talking like that."

Once I get another lantern lit, it chases away the worst of the creeping shadows. Then—reminiscent of our first meeting—I start taking inventory of what our horses carry.

I hadn't completely emptied my saddlebags, so there's a pouch of jerky, a box of cartridges for my Colt, a few withered tobacco leaves, and the roll of bandages. Gathering these in one arm, I do a quick sweep of Ansel's horse in case there's anything immediately helpful.

What I find is a heavy sack of twenty-dollar double eagles. A shocked laugh passes my lips.

I drop everything on the table inside. "There isn't any whiskey, though Jonah might've stashed a bottle in here somewhere."

"Don't matter," JD says. He's markedly paler than he'd been even minutes ago. My lungs squeeze.

I kneel on the cot beside him and unbutton his shirt.

"Not the way I pictured you undressing me for the first time," he says, voice hoarse.

"Picture it a lot?"

His eyes slide closed, a smile at the corners of his lips. "All the time."

Warmth gathers inside me, but I force my fingers to continue their work until I can push aside the fabric and see the wound. Dried blood smears across his chest and shoulder—fresh, dark blood still leaking from a hole about three fingers in from the top of his armpit. I press a clean bandage to the wound, and JD groans low in his throat. Carefully as I can, I pull him forward to check if the bullet went through.

He nestles against me, his nose in my hair and his lips brushing my neck.

"Stop that," I say, settling him back again. "Bullet's still in there, and I need a clear head if I'm gonna pull it out."

His blinks are slowing, like Cole's used to as Ma read him bedtime stories. A terror twists through my gut, warning this won't be a normal sleep.

"JD? I need you to hold this bandage in place, all right?"

He smiles and nods with his eyes closed but doesn't move his hand. "JD!"

His eyes pop open. "Yessum?"

I place his hand over the bandage covering his wound. "Press tightly and don't fall asleep. Talk to me."

Taking the lantern, I do a sweep of the shack.

"Why'd you tell me your father died when you were born?" I ask to distract him and keep him conscious.

Between shaggy breaths, he answers. "He did, far as we knew. Wasn't till about two… three years ago Ansel showed up in Abilene, offering adventure. Claimed he'd near given up ever finding me, that we were the ones who disappeared after the war. Ma was already gone, and it was timely enough, what with the whole Lucy situation, so I joined his gang." He shifts and grunts. "Still, never really thought of him as a pa."

"Keep holding pressure." There is indeed an uncorked bottle of whiskey, as well as a small sewing kit and a threadbare blanket. JD has started to tremble by the time I return to his side. I tuck the blanket around his good shoulder and push a wayward lock of hair from my face. "Why didn't you tell me?"

He gives me a sidelong look. "All but did."

My brow pulls down.

"Dawson? Dawes's son? Not the most original outlaw name, but it's what they all called me."

I feel as stupid as the first time I made the connection. I give him two good swigs of whiskey then splash some over the wound. "Think of Colorado. Those mountains of silver, your dream woman in a house—"

His good hand comes up, taking that lock of my hair that keeps falling loose between his fingers. "Bunch of brown-haired kids?"

I glance from his wound to his face. "Sure."

He grins. "Hear Montana's nice too."

"Only if you like the cold." A ghost of a smile touches my lips. "Changing plans?"

"I might, if I had a reason."

His blood coats my hands. Please God, give us both reason.

The tang of whiskey and iron coat the air. I try not to gag as I take a steadying breath. Della has pulled bullets from men a time or two, and she's never been shy about sharing details. Claims it's more exciting than any other part of her job.

Staring down at JD's wound, *exciting* is not a word I'd choose for the situation.

Sometimes you've gotta slice the wound, widen it enough to get your fingers around the bullet. Then you just grab it and pull. It's a cinch.

Her lighthearted voice in my head is at odds with the tremble in my veins, but I get to work. More whiskey fills the air as I pour some on my pocketknife. I meet JD's gaze. "I'm so sorry."

Then I cut.

He yells.

Slick fingers probe and find metal.

I try to block out his cries. My thumb digs. Pinches the bullet.

It falls to the floor with a barely audible *thunk*. I shove a clean bandage over the wound, reach the knife into the lantern flame until the metal glows orange.

"I'm so sorry," I murmur again.

Skin sizzles as I press the blade to his wound. The sharp stench of roasting meat makes me want to vomit. JD has gone limp under my hands. I wrap his shoulder in another fresh bandage and try to clean the worst of the blood from my hands with a used one.

The quiet settles heavy on me, draining the last of my energy.

When the silence is more than I can stand, I give him a gentle shake. Tears slip down my cheeks. I press my ear to his chest, but my heart is pounding so hard in my ears, I can't tell if I'm hearing a sluggish, determined thump, or if it's simply an echo of mine. "JD?"

He stirs. "Am I dead?"

A shaky laugh presses past my lips. "Not yet."

His breaths are little more than huffs. "Say, you still got that ring?"

I reach into my pocket where his ring is nestled in the hollow left by Pa's watch. "Guess you'd like it back, seeing how you won't be hanged after all?"

He shakes his head. "Still want you to have it."

"It wasn't meant for me."

"Sure it was. Just gave it to the wrong girl first."

"JD...." My heart is doing funny things inside, battling with a growing unease. His words are a promise, but they sound more like farewell.

Despite the lantern, the shack grows darker, colder.

"Take it." He folds my fingers over the ring in my palm. "Sell it, trade it. Get yourself to Montana."

His eyes close. I wait for them to reopen, but a breath passes, then another. Could be he's just sleeping, same as any night.

Could be my attempts at repair only butchered him, and those eyes will never open again.

I slip the ring on my finger—for safekeeping, I tell myself, nothing more—and move from the cot to the floor. My head comes to rest in line with his ribcage. I watch his chest, the jagged rise and fall. All that's left to do is wait and pray.

Not sure God'll want much to do with my pleas, but I'll send them on up anyway, just like Pa taught me.

Outside the shack, pounding hoofbeats skid to a stop. I swipe the tears from my face and lift the Colt, but it's only Jonah. At the sight of him in the doorway, the gun clatters to the floor, and I crumple into a sob. My brother's arms come around me, kneeling together beside the cot.

At least for now, everyone else I love is still alive. For now, that's enough.

23

One Month Later

I STILL DON'T KNOW HOW WE ENDED up here. A chill breeze stirs the dead leaves that cling stubbornly to the trees overhead. The campfire flames dip and stretch. My hands rub warmth into my fingers, my thumb twisting the gold band. A pointless bit of metal, but too meaningful to remove.

Across the fire, Cole shifts. Ma probably isn't happy he's out here with me rather than home resting his damaged hand, but I think the fresh air does him good. Keeps his mind off the pain, at least.

"Is Jonah coming soon?" he asks.

"Who knows?" I expected him before sundown. He'll find us, though. I couldn't take another evening inside that stifling shack, but we haven't gone far. The worn planks stand out, pale in the starlight, every time I glance over my shoulder. I'll turn in eventually—doesn't make sense to spurn what'll likely be my last night sleeping under shelter for a long while—but for now, I soak in the frostbitten night air. My lungs fill with decay and woodsmoke, and my ears tingle against the numbness settling in. "You can head home, though."

Cole sucks his teeth and waves his good hand. "I ain't leaving you—"

"You *aren't*."

"It's settled then," he says, smug as the proverbial cat with a saucer of cream.

I sigh and tilt my head to the stars. Ma'll have someone's hide over this, but at least it won't be mine.

An approaching horse stirs the stillness of the night. My hand drifts to the revolver at my hip, but then comes Jonah's whistle, long and low. The tension eases from my shoulders—not all of it, of course, but some. There's still no telling what news he brings.

Cole and I are quiet as Jonah dismounts. Cole picks at the new skin growing over the tip of his shortened pinky until I kick his foot. He scowls at me. Jonah settles to the cold earth between us and holds his hands out to the flame.

"Spoke to Old Man Mueller," Jonah says in greeting. "He'll give a fair price for the land along the bluffs, and I've convinced Luis to stay on with us. Should be able to manage the smaller farm without too much trouble."

He doesn't look at Cole, but I do. Our younger brother stabs at the fire with a long stick. His freckled face twists with something strong and burning—rage or sorrow, maybe both—then tightens into a smirk. "Never much liked farming anyhow," he mutters.

"There's still plenty you can do." Jonah's voice is hard against the self-pity in Cole's. "Could use help with the numbers."

Cole perks up a bit at that. Jonah's getting better at hiding his patronizing tone—he was always the star pupil, good at all three R's. Me, I preferred reading, but Cole loves arithmetic.

Besides, we all know it's me he's talking of replacing. There isn't much holding me to Bluff City anymore—not since I confessed my sins. Wyatt seems to have kept that revelation to himself, seeing as no angry mob has marched onto our land demanding justice. Still, it's only a matter of time before word gets out, and the longer I stay, the harder it will be for my family to separate themselves from my sordid past.

A log shifts and smolders, sending a burst of sparks skyward. It reminds me of JD, that day he compared me to a prairie fire. I touch my ring—cold again—and force my attention to stay on Jonah.

"What else?" I ask, impatient. I'm glad the farm's taken care of, but the news I really care about is—

"It's done." Jonah nods once.

Cole sits straighter. "He's gone?"

Though the firelight emphasizes the sharpening of his cheekbones, in this moment all I see is my baby brother, the fearful child still lurking in his eyes.

Jonah nods again. "Ansel Dawes was hanged by the neck until dead this afternoon."

I hug my knees into my chest. I'd thought the news would bring me relief or vindication, but I just feel hollow. Cole takes a shuddering breath.

"It's good you weren't there," Jonah tells him. "Wouldn't have helped to see him like that, at the end."

"But he *is* dead?"

"Without a doubt."

The grass rustles. I glance back at the hunting shack, but the night appears still apart from the breeze.

"Guess that means you're really leaving?" Jonah asks me.

"Just wanted to make sure Ansel can't hurt us any longer." Now I know he's dead, I can strike out on that adventure without looking over my shoulder every few steps.

Jonah stretches his legs out, the soles of his boots glowing orange only a handbreadth away from the flames. "Far as Bluff City's concerned, justice has been done, but Dawson was wanted for more than just the bank. Everyone knows he was here during the shootout—only a matter of time before people start wondering why the reward's never been collected."

I don't want to think about the shootout—my gut charges up my throat each time I do—but there's no helping it tonight. It's been there at the edges as we waited for confirmation of Ansel's hanging. That same sense of uselessness threatens to choke me. Instead of campfire smoke, the charred stench of cauterized flesh fills my nose. Instead of the night breeze, it's the soft wisps of breath across my knuckles as I watched JD fade in and out.

"Hope you're not having second thoughts." JD's voice makes me jump.

When I turn, he's standing on his own two feet—swaying slightly, but his walking stick isn't in sight. Further proof he can handle sitting in a saddle, as long as we take it slow.

"Don't tempt me," Jonah says, but his voice is carefully light as JD eases to the ground beside me.

"Does it still hurt?" Cole asks, picking at his finger again.

The wince that creases JD's face is answer enough, his eyes hollowed out from his slow recovery. He jerks his chin at Cole. "How 'bout you?"

Cole shrugs. If JD won't admit to being in pain, I know Cole will follow suit. Mules, the pair of them.

"You should go back to bed," I tell JD. "We've got a long road of hard riding ahead of us, especially tomorrow." I want to clear Missouri's state line as soon as possible.

"I want to come with you," Cole says. His gaze sticks to JD, but I glance at our older brother.

Jonah's face is caught somewhere between annoyance and hurt. "You don't want to join a couple criminals like them."

"Maybe I'll find a real gang to join," Cole shoots back.

"So you can fall in with someone the likes of Ansel Dawes?" JD's voice is calm in the face of a brewing storm.

Cole pales at the thought.

"Already told you, you're needed here," Jonah says. I expect him to mention the farm again, but instead, he blows out a heavy breath. "Gonna be a pa soon, and I don't wanna raise the kid without his aunt *or* uncle."

My lungs squeeze as if I've been kicked in the chest. *Stupid.* I've known this'll be a one-way trip, no turning back. Still, everything I'm leaving starts crowding behind my eyes until there's nothing for it. Tears break free.

"Shit, Mags, I didn't mean nothin' by it," Jonah says. "You don't even like kids."

"Bet I'd like yours." My jaw clenches tight, and I focus on my breathing. I don't want to lose a second of this moment with my brothers to crying.

JD's cold finger brushes over my cheek. "It's me they want," he murmurs. "You can stay."

I shake my head, press the moisture from my face. The trail will be long enough to catch my tears. "You wouldn't make it a day without me."

A tired grin flirts with his lips. "True enough."

From the other side of the fire comes a hesitant sniffle. "What are *we* gonna do without you?"

"Dammit, Cole," I say, my voice brittle.

"Go home if you're gonna talk like that," Jonah adds, stern.

I lean my shoulder into his. "See, y'all will be all right."

Jonah gives an over exaggerated scoff to hide a sniffle of his own. "Maggie's got me sitting at Sid's tables every week for the foreseeable future, but sure, we'll be just dandy."

"Least we won't worry about money," Cole says.

"Just quit cheating," JD adds. He and Jonah have played enough hands over the past few weeks that JD's picked up on Jonah's tells. "A kid would rather have a poor dad than a dead one." He says this last bit directly to the fire. The air shifts, tightens. Grows heavy with ghosts.

"Sorry about your pa," Cole says.

JD's head snaps up, his gaze fastening on Cole's. "I'm sorry for yours."

Cole's throat bobs with a swallow. He nods.

Fire paints my brothers gold, while beside me, JD is washed silver by the moon. The trilling call of a screech owl mixes with the buzz and click of cicadas in the grasses. I'm not sure how long we sit, listening to the sounds of a Missouri autumn evening. Long enough for the tip of my nose to go numb with cold.

"Come on, Cole." Jonah climbs to his feet. "They need their rest before tomorrow."

I rise, too, then Jonah surprises me by offering a hand to JD. When they're eye level, Jonah doesn't release him right away. "Take care of her, you hear?"

My lips part, but before I can get a word out, Jonah wraps his arms around me.

"I know, you don't need looking after." His chin rests on my head as I curl against him one last time. "Still, you're the only sister I got. Try to stay outta trouble."

"Don't think we won't hear otherwise," Cole says, coming around behind me.

Sandwiched between my brothers, I commit this night, this moment to memory. The tobacco smoke in Jonah's shirt mingling with the odd, mud-and-sugar scent that's always been Cole. Their warmth chasing away the frigid fingers of a November night. The sigh of grass and creak of dead leaves. And there, just outside our tiny circle, my future waiting on unsteady legs.

ACKNOWLEDGMENTS

Thank you to the entire team at Roan & Weatherford and the Radiance imprint, especially my amazing editor, Lindsay Flanagan. I feel like you plucked me from obscurity not once or twice but three times, and I couldn't ask for a better champion of my stories.

Thank you to Jacqui Lipton for taking a chance on an extremely nauseated mom-to-be, and offering encouragement and advice to sharpen this story.

To my writing community, critique partners, and friends at Scribophile: the Fledgling Society, the Thumb and Finger Pool, Austrian Spencer, JP Stewart, James Anthony, Eliot Masterson, Sean Tibbitts... I could not have done this without your input and enthusiasm for my stories. To JJ Hoover, thank you for countless discussions and brainstorming sessions, and for trusting me with your work as well; your stories have made me a better writer.

I have such supportive friends in the Wildcards and the WashU "Fellow Alumni." I love you all.

Mom and Dad, thanks for always encouraging my (often overactive) imagination. Dad, I think your "prairie" mindset influenced this story as much as the romcoms Mom and I binge.

Joshua: Stay out of my room! (But also, thanks for sending me pictures of bookshelves in stores, saying someday my book will be there.)

Nina, Lisa, and Richard: a girl couldn't ask for better in-laws. I love being a part of your family.

Charlie, thank you for moving me to St. Louis in the first place, so I could fall in love with Missouri scenery. Thank you for filling my life with love, and for shouldering the bulk of the dog walks and belly rubs while I wrote. To Madison, thank you for warming my feet, forcing me to get outside every now and then, and for demanding Maddie-Daddy snuggles so I could focus on writing.

Naomi: You are the love of my life and the best thing I've ever created.

And to my Creator, thanks for making me one, too.

ABOUT THE AUTHOR

ANNIE ATKIN'S LOVE OF A GOOD STORY and engaging characters has always been a defining characteristic, and something she brings to her writing across genres. When not writing, Annie spends most of her time reading, wrangling her goldendoodle, and raising her own little bookworm with her husband. You can find her on Instagram @ annie.atkin and at her website annieatkin.com.

.